# SLAVERY IN THE ARAB WORLD

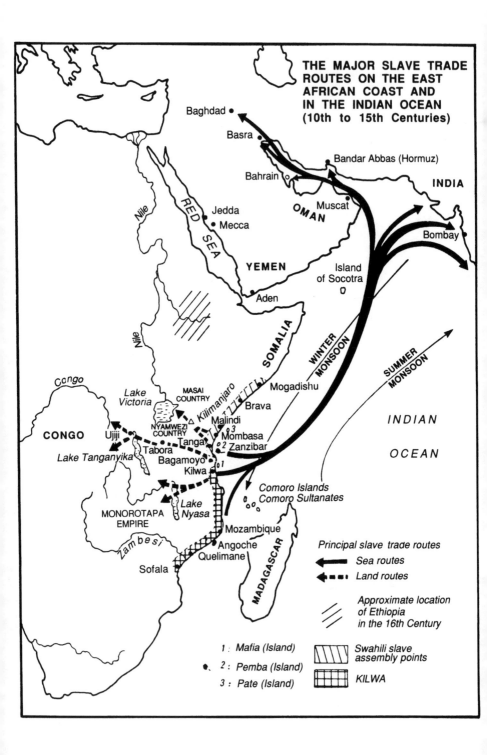

THE MAJOR SLAVE TRADE
ROUTES ON THE EAST
AFRICAN COAST AND
IN THE INDIAN OCEAN
(10th to 15th Centuries)

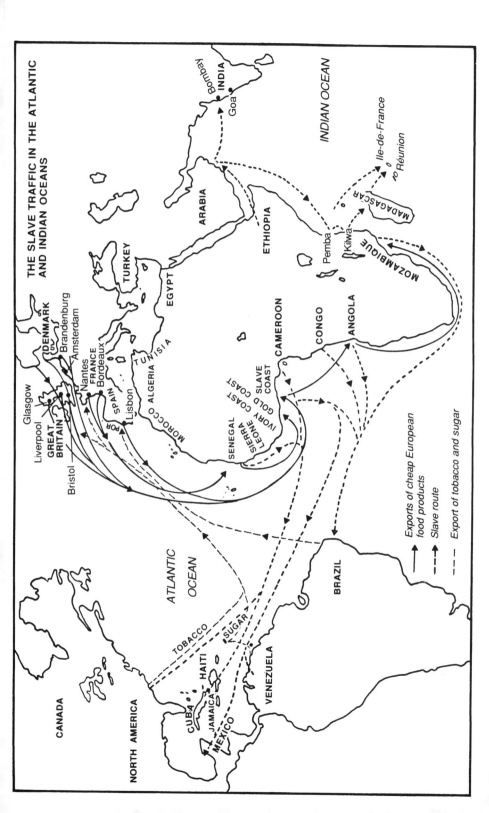

THE SLAVE TRAFFIC IN THE ATLANTIC AND INDIAN OCEANS

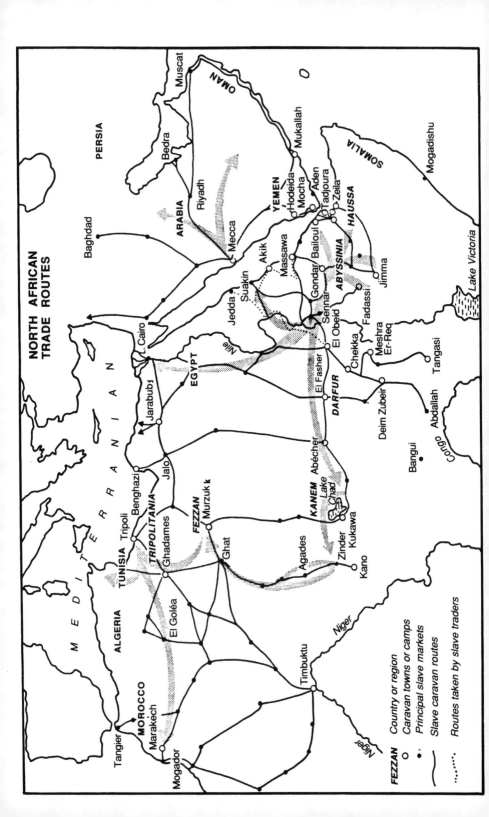

# NORTH AFRICAN TRADE ROUTES

MEDITERRANEAN

MOROCCO
Tangier
Marrakech
Mogador

ALGERIA
El Goléa

TUNISIA
Tripoli

TRIPOLITANIA
Ghadames
Ghat

FEZZAN
Murzuk

Benghazi
Jalo

Agades
Zinder
Kukawa
Kano

KANEM
Lake Chad
Abécher

Timbuktu

Niger

EGYPT
L. Cairo
Jarabub
Nile

DARFUR
El Fasher
Deim Zubeir
Bangui
Abdallah

Jedda
Suakin
Akik
Massawa
El Obeid
Chekka
Meshra Er-Req
Tangasi

ABYSSINIA
Gondar
Bailoul
Sennar
Fadassi
Jimma

HAUSSA

YEMEN
Hodeida
Mocha
Aden
Tadjoura
Zeila

SOMALIA
Mogadishu

ARABIA
Mecca
Riyadh
Bedra

PERSIA
Baghdad

OMAN
Muscat
Mukallah

Lake Victoria

Congo

Niger

FEZZAN  Country or region
○  Caravan towns or camps
•  Principal slave markets
——  Slave caravan routes
······  Routes taken by slave traders

# SLAVERY IN THE ARAB WORLD

by
Murray Gordon

NEW AMSTERDAM

First published in the United States of America in 1989 by
NEW AMSTERDAM BOOKS

First paperback edition published in 1992.

Originally published in France as
*L'Esclavage dans le monde arabe*

**Library of Congress Cataloging-in-Publication Data**

Gordon, Murray.
  Slavery in the Arab world.
  1. Slavery—Arab countries—History. 2. Slave-
trade—Arab countries—History. 3. Slavery and
Islam—History. I. Title.
HT1317.G6713'   1989
306'.362'09174927                           88-34493
                                                CIP

ISBN 0-941533-30-1(cloth)
ISBN 1-56131-023-9 (paper)

*This book is printed on acid-free paper.*

Manufactured in the United States of America.

*To Cora, Elana, Jonathan, Tamara and David*

# Contents

# Introduction to the American Edition

SLAVERY IN THE ARAB WORLD ANTEDATED BY MORE THAN a millennium the establishment of this appalling institution by Europeans in the New World. It continued to flourish, moreover, for more than a century after the tocsin had sounded for it in the West. As many as eleven million Africans, approximately the same number estimated to have been taken from Africa's West Coast in the European-controlled triangular slave trade, were forcibly removed from their families and communities to do service in Arab households, harems and armies.

Despite the long history of slavery in the Arab world and in other Muslim lands, little has been written about this human tragedy. Except for the few abolitionists, mainly in England, who railed against Arab slavery and put pressure upon Western governments to end the traffic in slaves, the issue has all but been ignored in the West. In contrast to the endless flow of books and articles that have enriched our understanding of slavery and the traffic in slaves from West

Africa to the New World, the slavery that for centuries was an integral feature of Arab society has escaped the attention of Western scholars. Ignorance of Arab history or perhaps a bad conscience about the West's shameful record in this sordid business may help account for these vast gaps in Western historiography.

Something better might have been expected of Arab historians. Yet, here too, a conspiracy of silence has prevailed and has blocked out all light on this sensitive subject. Arab writers and jurists, to the limited extent that they touched upon slavery, have done so with approval. No moral opprobrium has clung to slavery since it was sanctioned by the Koran and enjoyed an undisputed place in Arab society.

The decision by Arab states to abolish slavery during this century was taken for reasons that had little to do with the moral aspects of the issue. Pressure from Western powers, the introduction of a money economy, and the realization that maintaining slavery would forever bar Arab nations from entering the councils of international society provide a much better explanation for their announced policy. That slavery and the slave trade were inherently evil and therefore merited abolition were thoughts alien to Arab heads of state and their followers.

It is this failure to have consigned slavery to moral oblivion that explains why it endured so long in the Arab world. The perennial character of this social institution ultimately rested on religiously inspired values—a point that few Arabs were prepared to challenge. And because slavery was never questioned from a moral standpoint, it should be no surprise that it still persists in Mauritania and in the Sudan. Mauritania officially abolished slavery on July 5, 1980, but, as the government itself acknowledges, the practice is still alive and well. It is estimated that 200,000 men, women and children are subject to being bought and sold like so many cattle in this North African country, toiling as domestics, shepherds and farmhands.

Slavery and slave-raiding, which never fully died out in the Sudan, have reappeared on a large scale in the disaffected southern region of the country which has been fighting off and on for autonomy against the Muslin-dominated North. In 1987, the head of International Catholic Mission confirmed reports of widespread slave-raiding in the southern Sudan that was being carried out by armed Arab militias, notably from the Rizagat tribe, against defenseless members of the Dinkas, a people that from time immemorial have been hunted down by Arab slavers.

According to this source, as well as accounts by journalists and scholars, hundreds if not thousands of people have been carried off by slave traffickers. The great majority of the victims are children between the ages of eight and fourteen who are forced to march from their native lands to the North where they are sold into slavery. These reports have it that boys were being sold for the equivalent of $240 and girls for $160. A Sudanese historian from the University of Khartoum who had the courage to write about the recrudescence of slavery and slave-raiding in his country was arrested by the police. Can it be merely a coincidence that the prime minister of the Sudan, who is committed to a policy of imposing Islamic Shari'a law on the country, is Sadek el Mahdi, whose great-grandfather defeated the British a century ago and revived the slave trade?

To many Arabs, the issue of slavery is a source of discomfort. To speak out against it would be to impugn a tenet of Koranic law; to condone slavery would give offense to Africans whose ancestors and not-too-distant relatives in recent times fell victim to Arab slave traders and their agents. As a result, they instinctively keep silent on the subject, which to this day is a source of pain and humiliation for many Africans.

# CHAPTER ONE

# Slavery Concealed in
# the Mist of Time

## 1.

IT IS A CURIOUS TWIST TO THE STUDY OF THE SLAVE TRADE
that historians have conducted their inquiries into this
nefarious traffic from the perspectives of the Americas and
the sugar islands of the Caribbeans. Almost irresistibly, their
attention has been drawn to the transatlantic trade which,
from the middle of the fifteenth century down to the third
quarter of the 1800s, brought an estimated ten million blacks
across the Atlantic Ocean to work the plantations and mines
of the New World. It was this traffic in blacks from Africa's
West Coast, initiated by the Portugese in 1441, that provided
the labor that fueled the rapid economic development of
Brazil and the old American South; it made possible the
growth of the plantations in Jamaica, Barbados, Hispaniola,
St. Lucia, and the other islands in the Caribbean where sugar

fortunes grew. As the trade in each succeeding year bounded forward and as the economic stakes in the service, manufacturing, and shipping industries which were dependent upon the trade multiplied, competition among the key actors, notably Portugal, England, France, Spain, and the United Provinces, for a share in the business intensified.

Countless volumes have been written about the transatlantic trade that resulted in the greatest forced transfer of people from one continent to another. The routes are all too familiar, so much so that every school child in the West has, at one time or other, learned about the "triangular trade." This followed a course that originated in one of the many ports and inlets along Africa's sinuous West Coast. It was at such places as Comenda, Shama, Elmina, or Lagos on the dreaded Bight of Benin that captains of slave ships would cast anchor and stand off, waiting weeks, sometimes months, for their full complement of Negroes or, as it was commonly referred to, "waiting to be slaved."

Innocent victims of a system they could not begin to comprehend, these misfortunates were either seized in early dawn attacks on villages by raiding parties or sold by avaricious African middlemen and then marched in fetters to the coast where they were bartered for the white man's artifacts. The ships that were waiting offshore for their human cargo had brought an assortment of goods from New England and the West Indies that included cloth, glass beads, knives, brassware, rum, and firearms. African human capital was exchanged for Western consumer goods.

Actually, these were the items in great demand by local chiefs and against which captured blacks were exchanged. The Europeans were eager to ply the black chiefs with rum so as to make them more pliable in bartering slaves for their artifacts. The guns emboldened them to resort to greater violence in searching out unsuspecting victims, thereby increasing the supply of slaves to meet the growing demand.

Usually, the Negroes were then stored, as so much merchandise, in one of the forty or so "factories" or trading posts that Europeans began building in the late fifteenth century for the purpose of promoting trade. The most famous and enduring of these trading posts was Elmina—the Mine—which King John II of Portugal ordered built in 1482 as part of a carefully conceived plan to establish a monopoly of trade along the coast. What King John had in mind was Africa's fabled gold. Elmina, located along Ghana's coast, proved no disappointment and, for a while, yielded the expected bonanza. Trade in gold and ivory, the principal exports from Elmina in the early days, soon gave way to traffic in slaves. During the latter part of the sixteenth century, the transatlantic slave trade rapidly escalated, supplying labor to the Portuguese plantations and mines in Brazil and to the Spanish plantations in the Caribbean.

It was in the dreary dungeon of Elmina and similar factories where the captive Negroes were kept until a slaver from across the ocean appeared on the scene. The great majority resignedly accepted their uncertain fate. Those who refused to submit were placed in a tiny dark cell, without food or drink. Each succeeding day, their defiant shouts which pierced the quiet of the courtyard became weaker until death spared them from a life of ignominy and the overseer's whip. After the terms of sale were negotiated, the purchased slaves were branded and then taken to one of the off-lying ships which would transport them across the Atlantic. Those who survived the approximately twelve-week trip across the often storm-swept Atlantic were again sold to toil forever as slaves in the plantations of the sugar islands that dotted the Caribbean or in the cotton fields of the southern states of the United States where the system of slavery held sway.

The Negroes disposed of, the slave stocks dismantled, and the fetters stowed away, the ship was methodically prepared before starting out on the next leg of its voyage. First, it was cleaned and disinfected with vinegar: clinging to these vessels was the stench of death and disease that afflicted so much of the human cargo who were tightly chained to their places in straitened quarters. This having been done, cargoes of sugar and molasses were taken on board, to be sold in European and New England ports. A part of the profits went for the purchase of the usual assortment of wares, as well as rum and brandy, for the fresh voyage to the African West Coast to acquire a new cargo of Negroes to satisfy the insatiable demand of the New World colonists for slave labor. With this, the third side of the triangle was closed.

## 2.

Yet, centuries before the first ship flying the flag of a European country slipped out from one of the numerous inlets along Africa's West Coast laden with human cargo, the peoples of North Africa, Arabia, and the Persian Gulf were forcibly transferring large numbers of blacks down the Nile to Egypt and across the network of the vast Saharan trade routes from West and Central Africa to the countries of the Maghreb. And decades after the last slave ship sailed westward to the Americas and the West Indies, where slavery had been abolished by the early 1870s, Arab dhows were furtively moving out of Zanzibar, Mombasa, and other East African ports, following the familiar Indian Ocean routes for the consignment of "ebony." The masters of these fast lateen-rigged ships, which were methodically packed in sardine-like fashion with men, women, and children, maneuvered skillfully in evading the small force of British sloops charged with the impossible mission of interdicting this illicit traffic. The blacks caught up in this trade were fated to be sold in the slave marts of Arabia, the Persian Gulf, the Ottoman Empire, and India.

Relatively little has been written about this facet of the

slave trade. Although the number of blacks who fell victim to Muslim slave traders can never be determined, there is little doubt that the figures ran to several millions over the centuries that the traffic was carried on. Between 1770 and the end of the nineteenth century, the period about which most is known about the Indian Ocean traffic, it has been estimated that approximately one and a quarter million blacks were shipped to Africa's East Coast (Kenya and Tanganyka).[1] Slightly less than half this number was exported to destinations outside Africa, with the balance accounted for by the proliferating demand by plantation owners on the Coast. The introduction of the clove culture in Zanzibar by Omani Arabs in the early part of the nineteenth century transformed the island into a major importer of slaves. As this market grew in importance and with demand for slaves from the more traditional markets in the Muslim world continuing undiminished, the East Coast and its vast hinterland took on an even greater importance as a source for slaves. So thoroughly were many parts of the region combed by Arab slavers that whole areas were depopulated. Africa was exporting its human capital through other routes as well. Uncounted thousands were shipped across the Sahara to Barbary, down the Nile to Egypt, and from ports on the Red Sea to Arabia. Many were sold as slaves in these countries, and untold others were resold to traders who transported them to Turkey, Syria, the Persian Gulf region, and as far east as India.

In light of this, it is puzzling indeed that the Muslim-dominated slave trade has been shunted off into an obscure corner of historiography. This dimension of the slave trade, it is worth noting, is not unique in the relative neglect it has suffered from at the hands of Western historians. There has been a similar tendency to gloss over the widespread practice of slavery and the extensive traffic in slaves that were carried on in Africa itself.

It could be argued that the reticence of Western historians

to probe deeply into these two aspects of the slave trade is the result of a bad conscience. To make them the object of close scrutiny might be construed by Africans and Arabs as an artful attempt to draw attention away from the transatlantic trade and the shameful role that Europeans and Americans had in it.

This reasoning is somewhat far-fetched in regard to the slave trade and slavery in Africa. Europeans, to be sure, did not introduce slavery or the slave trade in Africa: these institutions had been an established feature of life long before the arrival of the Europeans. Both slavery and the slave trade were known to have existed in the major states and empires of the West African Sudan from the eleventh to the sixteenth century. Slavery, however, as practiced in much of African society, was far more benign than its Western counterpart. Slaves were, to a great extent, integrated into the family who owned them, and they performed much the same domestic and farm chores as did other members of the family.[2]

By and large, blacks, whether enslaved by pagans or Muslims, enjoyed certain civic and personal rights which the master could not easily ignore. It was, for example, not uncommon for slaves to marry, farm their own plots of land, earn money, and even maintain a limited freedom of action and movement. In parts of Africa, slavery bore strong similarities to the institution of serfdom that was widespread in Europe during the Middle Ages. Some Africans, such as the Kru on the West Coast and the Fang, even boasted of never having known of slavery among their people and, even more, of having nothing to do with the trafficking in slaves.[3]

Inevitably, there was also a harsher aspect to African slavery. It was not uncommon to find in Africa slaves who were considered as mere chattel and treated as such. European travelers who went to Africa in growing numbers in the eighteenth and nineteenth centuries reported witnessing or hearing about cruel and inhuman practices that were commonly inflicted on slaves by the owners. In the non-Muslim parts of Africa, there was a widespread custom of burying alive one or two young slaves with the body of a chief who had died. One of the beneficial aspects resulting from the spread of Islam in Africa was the doing away with such pagan practices.

Blacks, moreover, were not strangers to the slave trade. They were known to have exchanged their fellow human beings for Arab wares long before the Europeans set foot in Africa. "The people of Lemlem," observed one writer, "are being perpetually invaded by their neighbors, who take them as slaves . . . and carry them off to their own lands to sell them by the dozens to the merchants. Every year great numbers of them are sent off to the Western Maghreb."[4]

In early times, such transactions did not involve great numbers of blacks. The victims were often prisoners of wars, common criminals, or troublemakers. This was to change with the coming of the Europeans. There is considerable evidence that the traffic in slaves, notably in large areas of West Africa, was more the consequence of European demand for slaves and less the result of indigenous practice.[5] The commercialization of the West African slave trade on a trans-oceanic basis had the effect of luring African slave traders into the expanding web of the Europeans. These traders thus became the victims of the relentless workings of the European-driven slave machine.

Calling attention to the African slave trade could not have the effect, even if intended, of obscuring from view the transatlantic slave trade. Both were inextricably linked to one another. The African trade implicated the Europeans who benefited from it, no less than the black traders who, in exchange for the white man's artifacts, showed no scruples in enslaving other blacks.

By contrast, focusing on the Muslim-dominated trade could do very little to show up Europeans and Americans in a bad light. Except in certain instances, as when French and Portuguese merchants acquired slaves from Arab traders for their sugar plantations in the Mascarene Islands and Brazil, European slave traders had little to do with their Arabian counterparts. The Arab slave traders operated within fairly well established commercial circuits which were oriented mainly to supplying the demands of Muslim countries. It was this vast market that provided the underpinnings of the slave trade in West, Central, and East Africa.

Beginning in the nineteenth century, the European maritime nations, led by England and gradually joined by others, used their power to curtail and finally end the Muslim traffic in slaves. This laudable objective, which was later merged with narrow colonial ambitions, prompted these powers to suppress slavery itself in Africa. British diplomacy, often backed by naval power, contributed much to getting Muslim leaders in Oman, Persia, Zanzibar, and the Ottoman Empire to put an end to slavery in these lands. As shall be seen, it took England the better part of the nineteenth century to rid the Indian Ocean of the traffic in slaves. The British pursued this anti-slavery campaign in this region only so far and fast as it meshed with its larger diplomatic strategy of assuring their primacy on the East African coast, the Red Sea, and Persian Gulf. Abolishing slavery and the slave trade in these increasingly important regions was subordinated to the political imperative of safeguarding the lines of transportation to India and promoting British economic interests. These self-serving policies have for the most part been glossed over in British textbooks, which depict England as the dauntless foe of the Indian Ocean slave traffic.

In light of this, writing about the Muslim role in the slave trade could scarcely evoke bad memories about a Western tie to this trade. The trade was essentially a Muslim enterprise: Arabs hunted for slaves in the vast spaces of Africa or acquired them from middlemen to sell in the markets of the

Muslim world. The existence of slavery in Muslim society and, by implication, the traffic in slaves, moreover, found sanction in the Koran and in the *shari'a*—the body of Islamic law.

## 3.

The limited interest shown in treating the Muslim connection to the African slave trade has to be explained by reasons other than an uneasy conscience. In part, this lack of interest has to do with the very nature of the subject whose origins are obscured in the mist of a remote past. The time frame of the Muslim-dominated slave trade, unlike that of the transatlantic traffic which lasted from the middle of the fifteenth to the last third of the nineteenth century, stretched back more than a millenium and carried over well into this century. The Indian Ocean and trans-Saharan traffic, moreover, involved many countries, a good number of which sprang from ancient civilizations. The journey back into this distant past is longer and the stops along the way more numerous than anything we know about the Atlantic trade. The latter conjures up the names of such port cities as Liverpool, London, Nantes, and Charleston, to mention but a few, which waxed rich on the ill-gotten gains of the slave trade. These are familiar places whose role in the slave trade is well known to every college student in the West.

The Indian Ocean and trans-Saharan trade, on the other hand, call forth such exotic places as Kilwa, Zanzibar, Fezzan, Sur, Tripoli, and Alexandria, which to most Westerners are storybook names. That slavery and the slave trade existed in these far-off places would scarcely arouse their indignation. Such practices would seem to be of a piece with the tales of *The Thousand and One Nights,* whose myths have pretty much made do for what passes as knowledge for these places and civilizations.

Grasping the reality of the Arab slave becomes far less of a problem for the nineteenth century, when the Muslim traffic in slaves reached its zenith. There are consular reports, official documents, and census reports which provide indications of the nature of the trade and numbers of blacks exported to foreign markets. Explorers and missionaries such as Mungo Park, Henryk Barth, Gustav Nachtigal, and David Livingstone, whose efforts in Africa excited the imagination of Europe, offer detailed accounts of the slave trade and its mournful effects on the countryside. Their writings etched a clearer picture of the workings of this trade and provided indications of its volume.

Other factors of a more practical nature have discouraged historians from inquiring into the slave trade and slavery in the Muslim world. Foremost among these is the lack of documents, personal accounts, and reliable data on the number of blacks who were enslaved. The little that is known about the early history of the Indian Ocean trade, for example, comes from the accounts of explorers, geographers, poets, and writers. Arab geographers and essayists are an important source of information about the traffic in slaves from the East African Coast between the tenth and thirteenth centuries. The accounts of these contemporary sources provide useful information which, however, is not always unbiased and is necessarily limited in its coverage. Even here, one must tread with great caution. What records there are from official and commercial sources are spotty and their reliability uncertain. Reports of consular officials from Zanzibar, Tripoli, and Sur, which provide the basis for some of the estimates of the volume of the trade in the area, are incomplete or have been criticized as reflecting abolitionist tendencies of inflating figures in order to justify the adoption of stronger measure to crack down on slavers.

As for non-Western sources, the problems are no less formidable.[6] Public records on slave trading simply do not exist or are inaccessible. In the Persian Gulf port of Sur, one of the most active in the region, no customs records were kept of slave imports. In India, official records are scattered or are virtually nonexistent.

As for the Arab traders, most were small dealers who, in addition to trafficking in slaves, also traded in spices, ivory, and leathers. The numbers of slaves they packed into their dhows ranged from ten to twenty-five and rarely exceeded seventy-five to one hundred. There were a few established small brokers in the trade, but none was of the order of those who were active in the transatlantic traffic. These *petits commercants* disposed of their merchandise at scattered points along the Red Sea, Arabia, the Persian Gulf, and even beyond. Since their trade was small and conducted on a personal basis, records were seldom kept. Whatever inclination individual traders may have had to maintain records was discouraged by the enactment of anti-slavery ordinances by Western countries which made the traffic an illicit affair and subject to severe penalties. Few and far between were those who left behind a record of this traffic. Among Africans this was even more the case; the written word was scarcely used by them. Thus, records or accounts of African middlemen who supplied Arab traders with slaves are conspicuously lacking.

The lack of information turns up on another front. The victims of this great human tragedy were silent witnesses to what they experienced and observed. Except in rare cases, slaves left no account of the events leading to their capture, the march to the coast or across the hot sands of the Sahara, in which many died along the way, deportation to an utterly foreign land, and, finally, the life they were forced to lead in the service of a master or under the observant eye of the house eunuch.

Denied the testimony of the victims of this inhuman system and burdened by inadequate knowledge of a practice that stretches back to the dawn on recorded history, the historian is confronted with a daunting task of reconstructing a story that conveys an unclouded picture of the slave trade in the Muslim world and how the slave fared in his or her new environment.

Of necessity, the historian must make use of firsthand information which is suspect. These are the accounts of the champions and apologists of a system from which both profited. Arrayed against them were the abolitionists and others whose conscience led them to oppose slavery. Their accounts, notwithstanding the decency of the cause they had given themselves to, were often biased or self-serving.

Writers who allow themselves to borrow excessively from one side or the other in order to justify their own preconceived notions necessarily come up with a caricature of the truth. Others, as a reaction against such distortion of history, proceed by putting their own interpretation on the thoughts of the silent actors. The dearth of reliable information has often led some investigators to treat the subject in an overly technical or dispassionate manner, thereby draining it of its human dimensions, or to engage in polemics. The former ". . . become over-meticulous, counting, standing up and knocking down their Negroes like skittles; others, obsessed by the existence of this forest of fossilized men, of whom only patchy traces remain, launch into bold hypotheses and parade their millions of captives in flamboyant funeral processions."[7]

Because the Indian Ocean slave trade had for so long been obscured in the shadow of history, much about it remains unknown or lies in the fertile field of speculation. Not surprisingly, there are no baseline figures of the actual number of blacks who were transported into a life of slavery in the countries situated along the rim of this vast ocean basin. The British authority on East Africa, Sir Reginald Coupland, has argued that millions of blacks were sent from the region to the slave marts of Asia, resulting in widespread depopulation of the area. This trade, he observed, ran "like a scarlet thread through all the subsequent history of East Africa until our day."[8] According to the calculations of Raymond Mauny, a French authority on Africa, approximately fourteen million blacks were wrenched from their society and brought to the Muslim world from the seventh to the twentieth century.[9]

The Coupland thesis, which has gained widespread acceptance and is repeated in standard European school textbooks, has come under strong criticism in recent years. One historian, G. S. P. Freeman-Grenville, has argued that only after the Omani Arabs began to play a role in East African affairs in the seventeenth century were slaves actually exported from the Somali region.[10] Carrying this revisionist thesis even further is E. A. Alpers, who condemned Coupland's assertion that the slave trade had begun with the first contacts between Africa and Asia and that the Arabs had engaged in the trade for time immemorial. To the extent that such a trade did exist, he contends, it was a mere trickle. In line with this revisionist theory, Alpers categorically states: "It is very clear that the East African slave trade as a factor of continuing historical significance traces its roots back no further than the first half of the eighteenth century. Coupland's argument that it was of continuing importance from the earliest contacts with Asia simply cannot be substantiated."[11] These polar differences stem, in no small measure, from the lacunae in existing information and data.

Another difficulty that has undoubtedly served to discourage research is the uncertainty of what was meant by a slave in the Muslim world. The fairly uniform model of the slave in Greek and Roman times, which was the one adopted in the West, clearly defined the relationship between owner and slave. Basically, the slave had all the attributes of chattel and, within broad limits, could be used or disposed of as his master saw fit.

This distinction between free person and slave, clearly defined in Western civil law, had no counterpart in Muslim society. Under Islamic law, whose precepts commanded wide respect in Muslim lands, a slave was both chattel and person. As chattel, his owner had full title to him, enjoyed the fruits of his economic surplus, and, finally, could sell or dispose of him (or her) as he saw fit. In Muslim society, slavery, which was sanctioned by Islamic law, had human attributes as well. The slave had certain prescriptive rights which the owner was duty bound to maintain. The latter, for example, was not allowed to separate a slave from his children, burden him with excessive work, or mistreat him. In a more positive light, the owner was encouraged to manumit his slaves. These practices were unknown in those Western countries where slavery flourished. If anything, they would have been considered inimical to the very existence of the slave system.

Slaves, moreover, performed different roles in Muslim society than their brothers and sisters were assigned to in the West. With some notable exceptions, slaves were not used in large agricultural undertakings, at least during the early centuries of Islam. They had quite different functions to fulfill. They were much sought after in Muslim society to perform household chores and to serve in harems; government leaders wanted slaves to fill in the ranks of their armies and to serve in the bureaucracy; and both government officialdom and private individuals had a continuing need to acquire eunuchs to watch over their harems and serve in administrative posts.

Within this order of things, slavery and, by implication, the traffic in slaves were seen as an integral part of daily life. The moral issue of slavery was never called into question because it was sanctioned by no less a source than Islam. As a result, it rarely became the object of political or social concern among religious and secular leaders. Given this moral climate, slavery and the slave trade never provoked a serious public outcry or a *crise de conscience*. And unlike slavery in the

West, whose merits were ultimately adjudged by economic criteria, slavery in the Muslim world was not subject to such scrutiny. Slaves were, with few exceptions, not used on large plantations for the production of commercial products such as cotton, sugar, and cloves but were made to perform household tasks or placed in the service of the court. One could scarcely lay open to question the economic utility of these forms of human bondage or compare the return from them to work performed by paid laborers.

The relatively benign nature of slavery undoubtedly made it more acceptable to society and to the slaves themselves. Slaves, who were the property of poor peasants, often lived no worse than their masters. Based on available evidence, slaves often tended to be accepting of their situation. This notwithstanding, there is both indirect and direct evidence that many slaves, over the centuries that slavery was in force in Muslim countries, had attempted to flee. Large-scale revolts, however, were uncommon. Slaves, because of the integrative nature of Islam, whose tenets made it easy for slaves to enter the fold, did not feel like strangers in Muslim society. Social stratification in this society was far less rigid than in the West, with the result that slaves could aspire to roles above their station. Eunuchs who rose to high positions in government and military service are part of this legend of slavery in the Muslim world. Many were gradually absorbed into the local societies.

These aspects of slavery, which were dwelt upon at length by Muslim jurists and essayists in extolling the virtues of slavery, strongly influenced the attitude of not a few Western scholars. Some viewed slavery in the Muslim world as not much different than the position of the nineteenth century industrial worker. The Dutch traveler and writer, C. Snouck Hurgronje, argued that ". . . the condition of the Muslim slave is only formally differentiated from that of the European servant and workman." Consistent with this apologetic view was Hurgronje's belief that slavery was nothing less than "a blessing for most of them that they are made slaves." The notion of the "happy" black slave, not uncommon in the proslavery literature in the West, also finds somewhat of an echo in the writings of other Western scholars whose legalistic approach to the study of slavery in Islam largely ignored this dimension. Also glossed over as well was the slave trade itself, whose barbarities were no less shocking than those associated with the transatlantic trade. These apologetic views have undoubtedly had the effect over the years of obscuring the tragic aspects of slavery and the slave trade in the Muslim world and, as a result, reducing it to merely another form of servitude that was so common in the East.

There is yet another reason that can help shed light on the lack of interest in slavery and slave trade in Muslim society: the absence of a large and racially conscious black diaspora who would have a longing to fathom the depths of this great human-interest story. The great interest that slavery and the slave trade have had to Americans—white and black—is due in large measure to the presence of such a large black diaspora thirsting to learn about its historical and cultural roots.

Large numbers of black people, to be sure, are found in most Arab countries.[12] A traveler to Egypt, Libya, Morocco, Saudi Arabia, or Syria, countries in which slavery had been deeply embedded in society, could not help but notice Arabs whose skin pigmentation ranged from light or dark to deep black. A great many of these people are descendants of slaves, yet they account for a small fraction of the great numbers of slaves who were transported to these once slave-importing societies. Many, as was already noted, were absorbed in the society. Substantial numbers died in slavery. Life expectancy was low considering the climatic and social conditions to which slaves were abruptly exposed. There are indications as well that the slave population shrank because slave women had far lower fertility rates than the population at large. In many instances, demographic growth fell below the replacement level. In Constantinople, the seat of the Ottoman Empire, where it was a commonplace for Turkish gentlemen to have numerous concubines, it was rare to see a mulatto. The offspring of such relationships generally fell victim to infanticide which, according to one report of the *Anti-Slavery Reporter,* the organ of the British Anti-Slavery Society (that appeared on September 1, 1856), was widely practiced in Stamboul "as a matter of course and without the least remorse or dread."[13]

# CHAPTER TWO

# The Attitude of
# Islam Toward Slavery

## 1.

WHEN THE PROPHET MUHAMMED BROUGHT THE MESSAGE of Allah to his followers in the seventh century, slavery was already a deeply rooted and widely accepted institution in that part of the world. Pre-Islamic Arabia and Egypt were terminal points of well traveled slave-trade circuits, some of the most important of which originated in the Sudan and Somalia. The *bilad-as Sudan* (the land of the blacks) had for time immemorial attracted slave raiders who found a ready demand for their captives in nearby Egypt. A brief reference contained in the annals of the eighteenth dynasty in the reign of Thutmose III (1504–1450 B.C.) to "slaves, male and female" pointed to the existence of a continuous flow of slaves into Egypt from the land of Punt (modern-day Somalia).[1] Further northwest along the horn of Africa was

Ethiopia, another rich catchment area for slaves. *Habashas,* the name given to the Ethiopians by the Arabs, filled the slave marts of Mecca, returning great profits to the merchants who put up their capital to trade in them.

It was not surprising that Muhammed, who accepted the existing sociopolitical order, looked upon slavery as part of the natural order of things. His approach to what was already an age-old institution was reformist and not revolutionary. The Prophet had not in mind to bring about the abolition of slavery. Rather, his purpose was to improve the conditions of slaves by correcting abuses and appealing to the conscience of his followers to treat them humanely. "As to your slaves, male and female," he exhorted them at the Farewell Pilgrimage, "feed them with what you eat yourself and clothe them with what you wear. If you cannot keep them or they commit any fault, discharge them. They are God's people like unto you and be kind unto them."[2]

Muhammed also took pains in urging the faithful to free their slaves as a way of expiating their sins. Some Muslim scholars have taken this to mean that his true motive was to bring about a gradual elimination of slavery.[3] Far more persuasive is the argument that by lending the moral authority of Islam to slavery, Muhammed assured its legitimacy. Thus, in lightening the fetter, he riveted it ever more firmly in place.

Actually, there is nothing in the Prophet's prescription regarding slavery that would have us conclude that he even as much favored a gradual abolition of slavery. So radical an approach would have alienated the very people whom he had sought to win over to his teaching. The abolitionist's credo was alien to him for sound pragmatic reasons as well. Slaves were one of the main props of the Arabian pastoral economy and formed an integral part of social life. The end of slavery would have wrought something of a social revolution by obliging Arabs to perform a multitude of household chores and field tasks which they had traditionally eschewed. Viewed from its impact on slaves, abolition would have led to severe hardship by depriving them of the security of work and home that a life of slavery afforded.

Religious reasons as well as established customs offered equally strong grounds in justifying slavery. Both Judaism and Christianity, whose moral authority did not go unrecognized by Muhammed, justified a two-tiered society whose members were part free and part slave. The Old Testament, in sanctioning slavery, treats in considerable detail such matters as the acquisition of slaves and the manner of their treatment. Christianity, as a system of governance, also raised no protest against slavery.

In supporting slavery, Christian moral theologians drew inspiration from a combination of divine, civil, and intellectual sources. Slavery, it was reasoned, was not morally wrong; it existed uncondemned among the ancient Israelites, uncondemned by the Apostles in the Greco-Roman world of apostolic times, and uncondemned by the church in Europe in subsequent centuries. Churchmen were fond of quoting from diverse texts in the Old Testament that allowed for a two-class Israelite society of free men and slaves.[4] The case in favor of slavery gained further support in their eyes by the teachings of the Apostles in the New Testament and the early church fathers who spoke out in support of a dual society of free men and slaves. All of this was elevated into natural law, which was neatly summed up by Aristotle: "It is thus clear that, just as some are by nature free, so others are by nature slaves, and for these latter the condition of slavery is both beneficial and just."

Thus, for those assailed by moral doubts about enslaving "God's people," the Koran provided a ready-made answer. It contained nothing to cast in doubt the essential rightness of owning a slave. And whatever the Prophet's real beliefs may have been regarding slavery, these were lost on the large numbers of Muslim slave holders who had a strong stake in maintaining a system that bestowed inestimable benefits.

The weight of Islamic authority in a society where its writ ran far was sufficient to deaden any impulse to challenge slavery on religious grounds. Unlike Western societies which in their opposition to slavery spawned anti-slavery movements whose numbers and enthusiasm often grew out of church groups, no such grass-roots organizations ever developed in Muslim societies. Muslim countries never knew of dissenting religious groups as the Methodists, Unitarians, and Quakers of eighteenth century England who railed against the Church of England for finding virtue in slavery. In Muslim politics, the state unquestioningly accepted the teachings of Islam and applied them as law. And lest it be lost sight of, Islam, by sanctioning slavery, however mild a form it generally took, also extended legitimacy to the nefarious traffic in slaves.

## 2.

It was only natural that in sanctioning slavery Islam would be influenced by the practice of other religions and civilizations as well as by the customs of pre-Islamic Arabia. Muhammed and the jurists who came after him were familiar with the Mosaic law and what it had to say about slavery. It was scarcely conceivable that they were unknowledgeable about slavery in Greece and Rome. Much of this legacy from the Old Testament and from Greece and Rome found its way into the *shari'a*—the corpus of Islamic law.

That many of these laws and customs were derived from the Old Testament, which was regarded by Muslims as divinely inspired, only added to their legitimacy. What made them even more appealing was that they responded to the day-to-day needs of the emerging Muslim society. These received laws and customs had much to say about such important matters as to which kinds of people should be reduced to slavery, the manner of their enslavement, and, finally, the mutual obligations between owner and slave. Islam borrowed whole certain of these accepted practices while adapting others to meet the social needs of the faithful and the requirements of its rapidly expanding imperium.

## 3.

Securing an uninterrupted and ample supply of slaves was an unending problem that taxed the resources of all slave-owning societies. This was as much a problem for the antebellum American South as it was for the slave owners of ancient Rome. Two methods were commonly used in maintaining a balance between demand and supply. One was by waging war against other countries which were militarily vulnerable and whose people were considered fit subjects for enslavement.[5] The other time-honored approach was by breeding.

In ancient Rome, both methods were used, although warfare, at least in the early years of the empire, yielded far more slaves. Barbarians by the thousands were brought back to Rome following military expeditions to Europe, North Africa, and Asia and made into slaves. Roman militarism was the engine that pumped back home a continuous stream of slaves. As Rome consolidated its political power and foreign military campaigns declined, the number of slaves brought from abroad diminished. As this source of servile labor dried up, the Romans had to turn to domestically generated supplies to satisfy local demand. This phasing-out of one source of slaves and introducing another was noted by Gibbon in his classic history of the Roman empire: "But when the principle nations of Europe, Asia and Africa were united under the laws of one sovereign, the source of foreign supplies flowed with much less abundance, and the Romans were reduced to the milder but more tedious method of propagation. In their numerous families, and particularly in their country estates, they encouraged the marriage of their slaves."[6]

The age-old practice of enslaving outsiders could not be explained for want of suitable numbers of low-status people at home. Ample numbers of them were to be found in Rome as well as in the Muslim world who could be coerced into a life of slavery. Such people, it was intuitively understood, make poor slaves. They become hostile to the class of people that seeks to enslave them. The spirit of rebellion constantly moves them to rise up and throw off their shackles. And because they possess some resources, maintain ties with other elements of the population, and have a knowledge of the foibles as well as strengths of society, there always remained the possibility that their constant plotting to gain freedom just might succeed. In such a constant state of real or threatened restlessness, slave owners would not be able to derive the full benefit of their priviledged positions.

Foreigners uprooted by force from their own society, on the other hand, are more easily transformed into totally submissive subjects. The trauma of enslavement and deracination, often entailing great physical and psychological suffering, produces among its victims a sense of powerlessness and defenselessness. This is reinforced by the real or imagined hostility that these uprooted foreigners experience in their new surroundings in which they have no contact with similarly situated groups with whom they could make common cause. The submission of the newly made slaves is further ensured by the potential or actual use of punishment, which is an inescapable factor conditioning their relationship to their owner. Transformation to servile status is made total by the need to give up their personal identity, often by being forced to adopt a new name, religion and code of behavior.

Slavery, as carried on in Islamic countries, bore the imprint of many of these earlier practices. As in other societies, only foreigners, who in Islam were defined as unbelievers, could be reduced to slavery. Islamic law laid down and, to varying degrees, enforced the rule that no born Muslim could be enslaved. Thus, the important distinction between the insider and outsider was retained in Islamic law which, in regard to enslavement, was based on a confessional criterion. Religious belief and not race, national origin, or territoriality was the determining factor in whether an individual was enslaved.

Under Islamic law, there are two prescribed ways of making people into slaves. One was by way of the *jihad,* or holy war, and the second by birth. Children born to slave parents were themselves slaves. Through these two methods, it was possible to go a long way in ensuring that only non-Muslims would be enslaved.

The *jihad* was a uniquely Islamic practice which may be lawfully carried out solely for the purpose of extending or consolidating Islamic law. All other forms of war *(harb)* pitting Muslim against Muslim were proscribed because they were considered brutal and ungodly and motivated by earthly interests.[7]

For the proselytizing people of Islam, the *jihad* served as a convenient license to wage war against unbelievers. Prisoners taken in such conflicts could, in the view of the Koran, be enslaved. While the jurisconsults of the law differed over the details of enslavement by war, certain principal ways were observed on how this would actually take place. Unbelievers captured in battle were generally offered the choice of embracing Islam, paying a tax and retaining their religion and property or fighting to the death. There were, in addition to these choices, three other options that Muslim conquerors could invoke against a vanquished enemy. Execution of prisoners was one such possibility, although this was carried out only in exceptional circumstances. Enslavement was a step up over the informal "rules of warfare" which, in earlier times, had condemned captives to death. Ransoming, a second choice, was also widely followed, its attraction laying in the substantial sums of money it produced. Capturing Christians and holding them for ransom was widely practiced by the Barbary states. The third option was to exchange prisoners for Muslims held as captives.

Apparently, in most instances, prisoners were enslaved either in default of payment of a tax, the *jizya* and *kharaj,* or to avoid being massacred on the battlefield.[8] Whatever the reason, prisoners by the thousands were brought back to Muslim lands and made into slaves by the conquering armies of Islam that swept through Asia, North Africa, and southern Europe.

Spared from this fate were Christians and Jews, who were considered People of the Book. These people, commonly referred to as *dhimmis,* were free from the threat of enslavement by paying the tax. They forfeited their immunity to enslavement if, after pledging to pay the tax, they broke their word and sought to flee to a non-Muslim land. Muslim authorities were not always anxious to enslave even unbelievers as long as they could extract the *kharaj* from them. 'Umar, the second caliph, was keen on having the population of occupied Syria and Iraq remain free and pay the tax rather than making them into slaves.[9]

The *jihad* was widely pursued in the first century of the Islamic era, which was the period of great religious and imperial expansion. This was the time when the *jihad,* as a religious imperative, inspired many of the faithful to carry the message of the Prophet to the far corners of the earth. The belief that animated this proselytizing spirit was derived from Islamic doctrine that divided the world between two irreconcilable camps—*dar al-Islam* (house of Islam) and *dar al-harb* (house of war). The former is made up of lands where the law of Islam prevails and the latter includes everything else. It was the obligation of the Muslim world to wage an unrelenting struggle against the *dar al-harb* until all unbelievers accepted the will of Allah.

This philosophy animated Muslim thought and action for the better part of a century following the Prophet's death, during which time victorious Muslim armies expanded the domain of Islam. Yet, it remains open to question how many of these military expeditions and those pursued later on in Africa and elsewhere were inspired by the lofty ideal of pushing back the bounds of *dar al-harb* or were motivated by a crass desire to collect the material and human spoils of battle. Although the answer is not likely to be ever fully known, there is evidence enough to assume that the taking of slaves remained an enduring motive in waging war even during the great religious and military campaigns of expansion. The frequent Arab incursions into the Eurasian steppes during the ninth century, for example, were often motivated by the desire to acquire slaves.[10] During the Abbasid rule in Baghdad, there arose, in addition to the regular demand for domestic and agricultural servile labor, the need for military slaves to take the place of what remained of the old free Arab cavalry of Basra and the Khurasanian guards. Turks were supremely favored because of their prowess as archers, skill in horsemanship, and devotion to their masters.

Once the impulse for conquest faded and a relationship of mutual accomodation set in between Islam and the rest of the world, the *jihad* ceased being a primary method for acquiring slaves. This served to reduce the supply of Slavs, a term that was usually applied to all Europeans, and of Turks. Increasingly, slaves were acquired by purchase, a practice not countenanced by Koranic law. This change was introduced by the first Umayyad Caliph Mu'awiya (661–80), a resourceful ruler who showed a special interest in alchemy. He was the first Arab potentate to adopt the Byzantine custom of guarding his women with eunuchs.

Military campaigns, to be sure, were still carried out for

the purpose of taking slaves and were freely consecrated as *jihads*. In truth, the aims of the *jihad* over the centuries were often distorted. The taking of slaves, if proper form were to be observed, was to be a consequent of a holy war and never its purpose. In Africa, the reverse was often true, and the waging of a *jihad* was usually but a pretext for capturing slaves. The Fishers, in their study of slavery and Islam in Africa, noted that slave raiding was ". . . only rarely marked by the procedures proper to a *jihad* . . . but the conclusion of a campaign, whether consecrated as a *jihad* or not, might be much the same, and the subsequent fate of those who were captured on a slave raid had at least to some extent to be determined according to the principles of the Muslim law."[11]

The abuse of the principle of *jihad* was nowhere better seen than in the depredations of the Barbary pirates along the North African coast against ships of Christian nations.[12] This warfare, which lasted until the early nineteenth century, was often carried on in the guise of a *jihad*. This was particularly in evidence in the Mediterranean Christendom from Spain to Byzantium. This thinly disguised privateering or piracy netted large numbers of captives. Many were held for ransom or reduced to slavery. In retaliation, organized raids were carried out by Christians against adjacent Muslim lands, bringing back with them "Moors and Saracens," many of whom finished out their lives as gally slaves on European ships.

Under Islamic law, a Muslim could not reduce a co-religionist to a state of slavery: this was a state reserved only to pagans and nonbelievers. This practice undoubtedly had its origins in Old Testament law by which Israelites were forbidden to enslave fellow Israelites after capture in battle (2 Chron. 28:8–15). Islamic law is quite strict on this point. A nonbeliever, however, who converted to Islam following his (or her) enslavement, remained a slave. As it was common for a slave to adopt the religion of his master, it turned out that Muslims quite frequently owned Muslim slaves. Ironically, had those same slaves converted to Islam prior to their capture, they could not have lawfully been placed in bondage. Islam offered to these unfortunates no passport to freedom.

The prohibition against enslaving fellow Muslims raised a question of the effect that this law had on proselytizing. The more blacks and others who converted to Islam, the smaller the number of people available to be enslaved. A vigorously supported policy of making converts was at odds with the public interest in promoting the slave-owning society to which most Muslims were committed.

In principle, the slave trader had no interest in narrowing the catchment areas where blacks were taken from by fostering conversions. By remaining indifferent to the religious preferences of the black nonbelievers or by discreetly placing obstacles in the path of the proselytizer, the slave trader had a larger reservoir to tap into. Finally, if religious scruples conflicted with his instincts as a trader, he could, in good conscience, set aside his principles and purchase the black, sure in the knowledge that once enslaved, his master would see to it that he converted to Islam. Such a Muslim, as was already observed, could not invoke reasons of religion for gaining freedom.

In practice, traditional propagators of Islam in Africa often revealed a cautious attitude towards proselytizing because of its effect in reducing the potential reservoir of slaves. The famous German African explorer Nachtigal attributed such an attitude to the Muslims of Bagirmi. He noted that they had made no effort to share the blessings of Islam with their pagan neighbors out of fear this would dry up a rich source of slaves that they had tapped for more than three hundred years.[13] A similar attitude influenced Muslim warriors in Adamawa (modern northern Cameroun) in exercising great caution in converting people who could be enslaved or pay taxes.[14] The Songhay masses, it has been argued, were excluded from Islam in the sixteenth century on grounds that once converted they were by nature free men.[15] For much the same reason, Arab traders, who always played a key role in propagating Islam, played an inconsistent role in proselytizing in the East African interior out of concern that conversions would restrict the supply of slaves.

A parallel to these attitudes could be found among Christians toward their Muslim captives during the period of the Crusades. Baptism resulted in limits on the economic exploitation of the converts and in some regions opened the way to manumission.[16] In order to prevent this from happening on a large scale, crusader lords, in defiance of papal edicts, hampered mendicant efforts at converting enslaved Muslims.

What assurances, it may be asked, did Muslims themselves have in not falling afoul the slave traders' net? Although the answer to this question is far from certain, there is ample evidence that Muslims in different parts of Africa could not always count on their religion as a shield against enslavement. Barth, the reknown German explorer, expressed this point of view in 1857 before the Anti-Slavery Society in London.[17] Nevertheless, even if this protection was limited, there is reason to believe that Muslims were many times influenced by scruples about enslaving their coreligionists.

To the extent this was the case, it could be attributed to the nature of Islam and its influence on the behavior of believers. Islamic law is not statute law but is the product of juristic speculation and reasoning. It derives its authority not from legal prescriptions but from ethical considerations. The system, as two western scholars have noted, ". . . arose out of the Kur'anic prescriptions for social conduct, which appeal to the religious duty and conscience of the Believer, and only exceptionally enforce them by specific penalties."[18] Within this state of things, there has always been the presumption that individual Muslims would abide by the law. Although, as in all religions, contradictions always have existed between the principles of the law and personal practice, one would not be wide of the mark in concluding that divergences between principle and practice did not often go beyond established norms. The widespread practice among slaveholders of following the Prophet's advice in treating slaves humanely attests to this.

Consistent with this caring attitude, there are numerous instances showing that Muslim traders or raiders adhered to the letter of the law and refrained from enslaving fellow Muslims who turned up as booty following a raid or released them after their religious identity had been established. In 1823 the sultan of Mandara called off a combined Arab, Bornu, and Mandara slave raid on grounds that the pagan tribes in the area were voluntarily converting to Islam.[19] And there were, to be sure, many instances of Muslims ransoming fellow Muslims from slavery.

This, not withstanding religious scruples, often did not inhibit Muslim traders and slave raiders from enslaving fellow Muslims. There are numerous recorded instances where, in disregard of the law, they made their coreligionists into slaves. In 1077, thousands of women from a Berber tribe who had risen up in arms were publicly sold in the slave marts of Cairo. In 1391–92, a letter was received in Cairo from the ruler of Bornu complaining that Arab tribes from the east were enslaving free Muslims, keeping some, and selling others to Egypt, Syria, and elsewhere. Sonni Ali, a ruler of Songhay in the fifteenth century, though a Muslim himself, sometimes indulged his fancy by taking free Muslims and giving them as slaves and, adding insult to injury, by pretending to bestow them as pious alms. In the seventeenth and eighteenth centuries, raids and counterraids between Timbuktu and the Tuaregs resulted in the enslavement of Muslim prisoners of both sides. This practice of taking Muslim captives as slaves by other Muslims continued in different places in the nineteenth and even into the early part of the twentieth century. As late as 1915 the ruler of Darfur accused the

Muslim Kababish tribe of selling as slaves free Muslims, refugees from the French in Wadai (present-day Chad).

The motives for taking Muslims as slaves varied. In large measure, it undoubtedly sprang from an uncaring attitude toward the law. More commonly, it could be attributed to the greed of slave traders to make money. Undoubtedly, Muslims were also taken because it was not always possible to distinguish between believer and pagan prisoners of battle who did not differ from one another except in religion. The possibility of distinguishing between pagan and believer was not always easy because black Muslims were often not as vigilant in conforming to the letter of the law as Arabs.

Extremely devout Muslims, not uncommonly, refused to acknowledge as true believers those whose practice of Islam fell short of accepted norms. There existed in those parts of Africa which came under the sway of Islam a distinct tendency to adapt Islamic law to local practices, much the same as converts to Christianity have done for as long as missionaries have been spreading the Gospel on the Continent. The temptation to take such people as slaves often proved irresistible, made easier by the absence of a readily accessible higher juridical authority. In actual practice, this made blacks professing Islam particularly vulnerable.

By and large, Muslim jurists held to the view that punishment for erring Muslims should stop short of enslavement. Heresy or apostasy might, under certain circumstances, justify enslavement. Where such a doctrine was accepted, it encouraged would-be raiders to impute apostasy to anyone whom, for quite other reasons, they might wish to attack. Denham, the English explorer who traveled through northern and central Africa in the early 1870s, wrote that people were routinely stigmatized by slavers as being guilty of apostasy kaffering, as it was commonly referred to (Arabic: *kaffera*—deny the existence of God), as a pretext to wage war against them for the purpose of enslavement.[20]

To the extent that Arabs and, to a larger extent, Muslims enslaved their coreligionists, a practice whose full dimensions remain unknown, this usually involved Africans and not whites. Arabs were from time to time enslaved, although they were generally ransomed by members of their tribes. The practice, in any event was not widespread. The Caliph 'Umar opposed the practice and was reported to have said: "No ownership of an Arab is permitted."[21]

Enslaving black Muslims was not uncommonly, discussed within the context of the curse of Ham (Gen. 9:20–27), the Old Testament story in which Ham, the youngest of Noah's three sons, transgressed against his father. Ham's descendants, commonly identified as Negroes, were condemned to slavery as a consequence of his sins. What made such a fate all the more plausible was that the blacks, because of their presumed ancestral background and unusual capacity for work, were eminently suited for a life of slavery. Might not this curse, some were inclined to ask, be reason enough to deny black Muslims the immunity against enslavement that other Muslims had as a right? This question became a matter of growing concern among tribal and religious leaders in Africa who were increasingly alarmed by the tendency among Muslim traders to enslave their black coreligionists.

One celebrated jurist who attempted to answer this and related questions was Ahmed Baba from Timbuktu.[22] Ahmed Baba had himself been taken prisoner in the battle of Tondibi in which the Moroccans defeated the Songhay in 1591 and broke the power of this important state. Invoking the letter of Islamic law, Ahmed Baba had the audacity to speak up to the sultan and to demand an explanation by what right he, a Muslim, could be enslaved. Eventually freed, he was approached in 1611 by his admirers from the region of Tuat about the propriety of enslaving Muslims, as was apparently frequently happening as a result of incessant warfare between the Muslim rulers in the states from the western

Sudan. They were appalled by the amount of "ebony" passing through their oases and spoke to him about their misgivings. They knew that in the Sudan many blacks were taken as slaves; and, it was feared, there might be some "brothers" among those poor wretches who were snatched away from their families. Could one be involved in this kind of traffic without putting his soul in danger?[22]

In reply to this question, Ahmed Baba drew up a treatise entitled *Framework for an Appreciation of the Legal Position of Sudanese Taken as Slaves.* In it, the jurisconsult explained that, even though at times it may be difficult to distinguish between Muslim and pagan prisoners of war, a Negro who voluntarily embraced Islam could not under any circumstances be made a slave. "The reason for enslavement," he stated, "is disbelief. The position of unbelieving Negroes is the same as that of other unbelievers, Christians, Jews, Persians, Turks, etc."[23] Following from that, he unequivocally rejected the notion that the curse of Ham could be regarded as justifying the enslavement of blacks. "On the contrary, any believer, if he persists in his original unbelief, may be made a slave, whether he is descended from Ham or not. In this respect there is no difference between the races."[24]

Invoking the laws of Islam, Ahmed Baba went on to say that slavery was permissable within the context of a *jihad* and if the captives are non-Muslims. First, the nonbelievers must be called upon to embrace Islam. If they refused, they had the option of paying capitation, in exchange for which they could continue to practice their religion. Only if they refused to comply with either of these alternatives could they be taken as slaves.

Ahmed Baba was an erudite jurist and his commitment to the law of the Prophet was beyond any doubt. On the one hand, he demolished the argument that the curse of Ham could be an argument in favor of enslaving Muslim Negroes. On the other hand, he did not avail himself of the opportunity to rule in favor of his fellow blacks who were enslaved because of uncertainty of their religious origins. The claim of many captives that they were believers before being taken prisoner tended to be conveniently ignored by their new masters. In a sense, this was understandable. Self-interest dictated that they turn a deaf ear to the claim of prior belief, a position that sometimes appeared reasonable because of the laxness of many blacks in following the letter of the law. Were the masters to allow themselves to be persuaded of the truth of their captives' plea that they had been a believer prior to being taken prisoner, they would have had to forego their newly acquired property.

Actually, the issue of enslaving a person where there was uncertainty about his prior religious belief had already been resolved in a legal ruling by the fifteenth century Moroccan jurist, Ahmad al-Wansharisi. In deciding whether an Ethiopian professing belief in Islam and observing its laws could be sold, al-Wansharisi came up with the standard interpretation that Ahmed Baba later on upheld. In the key matter of uncertainty whether conversion took place before or after enslavement, the Moroccan jurist ruled that this did not invalidate ownership or sale of the slave.[25] What was significant was that this and subsequent rulings on this crucial point gave the benefit of the doubt to the dealers or the owners and not to the slave. Property rights took precedence over human rights.

That these questions were raised and discussed so seriously within the context of the enslavement of blacks leads one to believe that they were the main victims of the widespread practice of enslavement of Muslims by Muslims. It clearly indicates that slavery in Islam—a religion largely free of racism—struck harshly and unfairly at people with black skin. This suspicion is reinforced by judicial rulings which gave to the owner or dealer the benefit of the doubt when there was uncertainty about the religious origins of a slave.

These rulings, by African jurists, also brought home the harsh reality that conversion to Islam after enslavement carried with it no passport to freedom.

## 4.

In sanctioning slavery, the Koran did not lay the groundwork for a new social institution in Arabia: what it did was to give its blessings to one that had been a way of life for a long time in the region. The existence of slavery implied that there had evolved over the years a normative set of relationships between master and slave that was part of the woof and warp of Muslim society. In decreeing the validity of slavery, the Koran accepted discrimination between human beings as in keeping with the divine order of things. The slave, by his scheme of values, had to resign himself to serve his master. However, the Koran sought to temper the rigors of this institution and strike a proper balance between the rights and obligations of both master and slave. A slave had an obligation to serve his or her master but also had acknowledged rights; these rights could not be ignored by his owner, who, indeed, had a lawful responsibility to live up to them.

At a spiritual level, the slave was possessed of the same value as a freeman in that he could look forward to the same eternal benefits for his soul in the hereafter. In this respect, he was in God's judgment, the equal of his master. In regard to more earthly matters, the Koran was quite solicitous of the human and social needs of the slave as well as his rights under the law. This reflected the values of Islamic law which held that a slave was both a thing, i.e., chattel, and a person. This distinction stood in sharp contrast to public law in the West which posited that a slave was mere chattel over which the owner enjoyed full proprietary rights. Islamic law, as expressed in the Koran and in the *hadiths* and as developed by jurists of the several schools of the law, attempted to strike a balance between these antipodal qualities.

In which manner was the slave reckoned to be a person and, alternatively, considered property? In regard to the latter, this was tied to rights of ownership by which a slave was subject to ordinary legal transactions affecting his status. A slave could be sold, given away as a gift, hired out, or inherited. In matters of these sorts, he was generally indistinguishable from any other forms of property.

The principle of selling a slave in parts of the Arab world and Africa was often tempered by an ancient Semitic practice of distinguishing between two kinds of slaves—purchased slaves *('abd mamluka)* and slaves born in a master's household *('abd kinn)*. The slave born and bred in his master's household was, in the normal course of events, unlikely to be sold or disposed of.[26] Such slaves were often considered as much part of the family as a long-employed maid servant or nanny might be in a Western household, whom no one would ever consider firing. As a child, the slave could well have been the playmate of the master's children. Evidence of preferential treatment given to slaves born into the domestic household could still be observed among the Badawin tribes in Kuwait as recently as sixty years ago.[27]

Reinforcing the notion of a slave as chattel was that in the classification of property the slave was generally ranked with animals and his lot was much like theirs. And like property, a slave could be owned by two or more people. When a runaway slave was found, his fate was to be returned to the lawful owner. The non-Muslim slave who ran way to the enemy was, according to one school of law, killed or crucified at the discretion of the government. Injury to a slave or his loss was merely considered the loss of property. This appears to have been based on the common ancient doctrine which found expression in the legal maxim that "the weregeld of a slave is his value."[28]

While these provisions of the law reveal that a slave was invested with many of the attributes of property, he was, in important respects, considered a person. The effect of this was to temper the principle of absolute ownership. An owner, for example, was expected to adopt a sympathetic attitude toward those among his slaves who sought to buy their way to freedom. Tradition, as was already noted, abounds with statements by the Prophet and his companions calling on owners of slaves to treat them kindly. An owner could not refer to his charge as "my slave" but as "my boy, my servant." He was forbidden to separate a slave woman from her young child by selling them to separate buyers. He was enjoined to share his food with his slaves, clothe them properly, not overwork them, and not punish them excessively for mistakes they had committed; and where the owner and slave did not get along well, the master was encouraged to sell the slave. As some texts remind the master: "Do not forget that they are your brothers," at any rate, when they are Muslims, as some texts specify. Another verse reminding the master of his duties was: "God has given you the right of ownership over them; He could have given them the right of ownership over you."[29]

Because slaves were invested with attributes of a person, Islam safeguarded certain of their human rights. A slave, male or female, could, subject to the master's consent, marry another slave or free person; a slave woman who married a freeman was entitled to receive a "reasonable dowry" from her husband. Such a marriage, however, raised a serious problem for the couple as their children did not belong to them but became the slaves of the mother's master. Islam was also concerned about protecting a slave woman from sexual exploitation by making it illegal to force her into prostitution. This was a reform of no small significance as it was a common practice in the Near East in the pre-Islamic period to prostitute slaves for the benefit of their masters.[30]

In matters of criminal law, the slave, whether a victim or perpetrator of a crime, was always at a disadvantage. He could not serve as a witness in court, even in litigation to which he was an interested party. Thus, a slave could not testify against the master at whose hands he suffered. Because of his servitude, a slave often received half the punishment meted out to a freeman. This was particularly true in regard to sexual offenses. A slave found guilty of a "false charge of fornication" against a free person was liable to forty lashes instead of eighty. Not surprisingly, a slave who was the victim of such a slanderous accusation could not derive similar satisfaction because the law, which did protect the person of the slave, did not go as far as to regard him or her as a man or woman of honor. In keeping with this line of reasoning, fornication committed by a slave did not carry a death penalty because neither a male or female slave met the condition of being a spouse within the meaning of the law.

A free person was not subject to retaliatory action for bodily injury he caused to slaves. Most schools of law, however, objected to putting a freeman to death for murdering a slave, even if it was his own. Generally, the slave has no protection against his owner in criminal matters because retaliation and blood money are private claims that he alone retained. The master, however, was obliged to adhere to accepted standards by seeing to it that his slaves were not overworked, denied adequate rest, and were not physically maltreated. Owners who flouted thse standards were under a moral obligation to sell the abused slave to someone else. A slave who was maltreated could, on his own initiative, go to the qadi (judge) and demand that he be sold.

### 5.

Much to the credit of Islam, it did not permanently freeze a slave's status. Whereas in the West enslavement generally meant a life sentence, Islam law was far more lenient by allowing, if not encouraging, emancipation of slaves by their owners.[31] Whether intended or not, this provided a safety valve for the institution of slavery by keeping alive the hope for freedom. A slave could also gain his freedom by buying his way out of bondage. In theory, at least, these regulations inspired hope among the enslaved, unlike the feeling of hopelessness and despair that gripped blacks who toiled on the plantations and in the mines in the Americas and on the sugar islands and for whom there was no exit except through flight, rebellion, or suicide.

Freeing a slave was considered a praiseworthy act which the Prophet himself urged on his followers, whether for secular or heavenly reward. No less a person than Muhammed set free one hundred of the Banu Mustaliq tribe as a gesture to Juwayriyya, a beautiful woman from this tribe whom he married. Mansa Musa, the famous fourteenth century ruler of Mali, won renown for freeing a slave each day. Manumission was regarded as a proper way for a Muslim to expiate certain sins. It offered one possible way of atonement for the voluntary breaking of the fast of Ramadan or for excessive punishment of a slave. Piety was another reason for freeing a slave. One school of law, the Maliki, cites the tradition: "Whosoever frees a slave who is a Muslim, God will redeem every member of his body, limb for limb, from hellfire." A double reward is held out to the man who educates his slave girl, frees her, and then takes her hand in marriage. Manumission, according to the Koran and tradition, was, however, best reserved for Muslim slaves and not those who remained outside the faith. Most deserving were slaves who accompanied their master on a pilgrimage to Mecca or demonstrated unusual piety or knowledge of the Koran.

The Koran, however, availed the sinner and those wishing to perform pious acts with alternative ways of satisfying their religious obligations. Manumission was only one of several virtuous observances that the pious could avail themselves of and was by no means the most important. Giving alms *(sadaqa)* was preferable to freeing a slave *('itq)*. This latter act was rewarded by absolution from damnation, but so was affirming the unity of God. Reaffirmation of this belief ten times was equivalent to freeing four slaves, or to freeing ten slaves if proclaimed one hundred times. Such an option was likely to make the average slaveholder spend more time invoking Allah, with all the implications it carried for symbolic acts of manumission, than actually freeing one or two slaves.

Another ground for freeing a slave was to expiate a sin or a public offense. Manumission had the double virtue in that the wrongdoer would find favor in the eyes of the Lord and, at the same time, deprive him of property. Here again, the law made emancipation a less desirable option by offering alternative ways of atonement. For intentionally breaking the Ramadan fast, the transgressor could free a slave or fast for two months. Another way out was offering a *mudd,* or peck of grain, to sixty poor persons. Charity, so it seemed, was preferred to manumission. Emancipation, however, was the only way to atone for recanting *tazahara*—an oath that a man made renouncing sexual relations with his wife. As a condition for returning to the connubial bed, the husband had no other choice but to free a slave.

The act of manumission, which was often turned into a festive occasion, was carried out through a prescribed legal procedure. In Sokoto (in the northwest of modern Nigeria), the letter of manumission had to be signed before a *qadi* and attested to by two witnesses. This procedure was not without its problems in African society, where slavery was commonplace, paper rare, and the possibilities of losing a document or having it stolen endless.

Emancipation remained available to slaves through two other channels. One came about through an action of the owner, and the other through the initiative of the slave. In the former instance, the owner informed his slave "when I die you shall be free," a procedure called *tadbir* (liberation). E. W. Lane, in his classic social history of Egypt, observed that the death of the master was the principal occasion for freeing a slave.[32] The *mudabbar*, the slave to whom the owner promised his freedom, became free on his master's death. There is some disagreement among the doctors of the law whether the owner, once having pledged *tadbir*, could recall it. What was not subject to disagreement was that on the death of the owner the pledge took effect and the slave gained his or her freedom.

The other form of manumission allowed the slave to purchase his freedom. In this contractual arrangement between slave and owner, known as *mukataba*, the slave could ask for his freedom and would agree to pay a stipulated price in instalments over a period of time.[33] Although the owner did not have to comply with the request, it was considered praiseworthy to do so. Having given his consent, the owner was not permitted to change his mind, although the slave had such an option. In the event the slave became delinquent in meeting the payments, he was obliged to return to unqualified servitude, with the master keeping the money already paid him.

The *mukataba* pointed up a singularly important right of slaves to earn and retain an income without which such a contract would be devoid of meaning. That such a contract existed suggested that opportunities for gainful employment could be found even in societies where slave labor abounded. Slaves with skills in carpentry, woodwork, tanning, and sailing and who lived in a town or port had far better opportunities to earn a wage than those who had no skills or who lived in rural areas. Since slavery in most of the Arab world remained more an urban than a rural phenomenon, it is reasonable to assume that many male slaves earned their own price and bought their way to freedom.

Not uncommonly, a patron-client relationship supplanted

the former master-slave tie. This frequently occurred in the Islamic northern states of Nigeria after a slave paid redemption money and was given a certificate of manumission. It was often the custom for the owner to give one of his daughters in marriage to the freedman as a way of solidifying the patron-client link.[34] The social consequences of such patronage relationships could be observed in the tendency of descendants of slaves to regard themselves as clients of their one-time masters by addressing them as *baba* (father) and paying them *zakat,* a financial offering, at festivals.

In the absence of meaningful figures of emancipated slaves in the different Arab countries, it is not possible to approximate the number of those who gained their freedom. It would not be farfetched, however, to believe that many slaves did benefit from an act of grace and were set free. In Middle East society, where the pervasive influence of Islam shaped the beliefs and regulated the behavior of the elites and, no less, the common people, many slave owners apparently complied with the provision of the law calling for emancipation. Political leaders, such as Mansa Musa, who often owed large numbers of slaves, freed some of them as a way of demonstrating piety. A liberal attitude was shown by the Arabs in nineteenth century Oman regarding emancipation. William Palgrave, who visited the country in 1862–63, observed that most slaves who did not die young eventually gained their freedom.[35] He noted that about a quarter of the population was made up of freed slaves and their dependents.

Yet, despite the magnanimous attitude of many Muslims, it is to be doubted whether emancipation approached anything of a mass phenomenon. Slavery, as an institution, had deep roots in Muslim society. The law itself, as already noted, did not place a premium on manumission but held it out as one way for atonement of sin. And while freeing a slave was held to be a meritorious act, enslaving a free person was not viewed with opprobrium. Plainly, there was no contradiction between being a devout Muslim and a slave-owning one as well.

Emanicipation did not result only from the procedures that have already been described. It also was provided for in the laws relating to concubinage, which was an inseparable part of slavery. A Muslim was strictly forbidden from marrying his slave. There was absolute incompatability between ownership and marriage. A Muslim, however, was free to acquire as many concubines as his purse allowed. Under Islamic law, it was both legally and morally correct for a man to have sexual relations with his female slaves as with his wives. Children born of such a relationship, assuming the father acknowledged paternity, which was usually the case, assumed his status. They were, in the eyes of the law, free and legitimate and had equal standing with other children in the family born by his free wives. The slave mother acquired the status of *umm walad* (mother of child) and benefited from a privileged relationship with her master. She could no longer be sold or alienated by him and on his death became free.[36]

Concubinage had also far-reaching racial as well as social consequences in Islamic society. Since the fathers were predominantly white and the mothers were usually Negro, their offspring became genetically mulattos. Miscegenation inevitably led to the creation of a racially mixed population which can be observed throughout the Arab world and North Africa. The physical type found among the numerous Arab-Berber populations in Algeria and Morocco, for example, suggests that miscegenation was fairly prevalent among black slaves and Berbers in the urban centers of North Africa.[37] This "whitening" of the population along social and racial lines meant that color by itself was not a definitive indicator of status. The male issue of an African woman by her Arab master could become a man of high status, as much an Arab and fully the equal of his fairer skinned brothers. This is not to say that Arabs were free of racist attitudes towards blacks;

there has been a distinct, albeit muted, feeling of racism which, as we shall later see, was evident in Arab practices and attitudes towards Africans.

Ironically, the liberal provisions of Islamic law regarding emancipation and conferring free status on the children of *umm walad* meant that the slave population had to be replaced more regularly than slaves who retained their status over lifetimes and even generations. The practical effect of this was, coupled with the religious requirement that new slaves had to be pagans, to quicken the demand for slaves from abroad. As the number of white slaves imported from the country of the Slavs and other parts of Europe dwindled, Muslim traders turned to Africa for fresh supplies. Prisoners taken in local wars and *razzias,* the human prey of kidnapers, debtors, and convicted criminals provided the main sources of slaves for visiting merchants who gathered their victims in small lots in boats for shipment down the Nile, across the Red Sea, or up the East African coast or marched them alongside caravans across the vast expanses of the Sahara desert.

**6.**

That slavery persisted as long as it did in the Muslim world—it was only abolished in Saudi Arabia in 1962 and as late as 1981 in Mauritania—owed much to the fact that it was deeply anchored in Islamic law. By legitimizing slavery and, by extension, the sordid traffic in slaves (for which there was no legal sanction), Islam elevated these practices to an unassailable moral plan. As a result, in no part of the Muslim world was an ideological challenge ever mounted against slavery. The political structure and social system in Muslim society would have taken a dim view of such a challenge. The sultan of the Ottoman Empire and the potentates who ruled in other Muslim lands owed their thrones as much as to their being religious as well as secular leaders and were therefore duty bound to uphold the faith. Part of this obligation was to assure the normal functioning of the slave system which was an integral part of Islamic society that is embellished in the Koran. To have done otherwise, a Muslim ruler would have come into conflict with the clergy, men of influence, and a great number of ordinary people who had a stake in the slave system.

Toward the end of the nineteenth century, questions were raised in liberal religions and intellectual circles about slavery. The impact of Western ideology and contact with the realities of the modern world brought about an evolution in the thinking of many educated Muslims. While many of them tended to emphasize the benign conditions under which slaves lived and worked, they increasingly felt uncomfortable about the existence of slavery and its effects on the future development of Muslim society. Slavery, they readily grasped, was incompatible with the modern society they wished to create. Progressive Muslims directed their criticism toward not only slavery but other practices which they felt were out of keeping with the times, notably unregulated polygamy and divorce by repudiation. One of the best known of these reform-minded leaders was the Indian Muslim scholar, Seyyid Ahmed Khan, whose influence extended far beyond the subcontinent.[38] His liberal philosophy and rationalist approach to the study of Islam led him to reassess traditional Muslim ethics toward society. Sounding a similar message was a compatriot, Seyyid Amir Ali, a leading jurist who did much to popularize this liberal approach to Islam. Amir Ali interpreted the teachings of the Prophet in terms of contemporary ideas that stressed social equality and human progress. Slavery, in this order of things, he argued, was antithetical to Koranic precepts which teach the equality of all people. In his book *The Spirit of Islam* he wrote: "The Prophet exhorted his followers repeatedly in the name of God to enfranchise their slaves 'than which there is not an act more acceptable to God.' " Amir Ali held that slavery was one of the pre-Islamic practices that was tolerated out of temporary necessity and which Islam greatly ameliorated. The task of finally abrogating slavery was to be left to man-made laws.

A similar view was propagated by Ahmed Shefiq in a book on Islam and slavery that was published in Cairo in 1891.[39] Shefiq argued that initially Islam wanted to do away with slavery but was fearful of the effects of total abolition on society and contented itself temporarily with laws that ameliorated the conditions of slaves and encouraged their manumission. But Shefiq, who wrote his book as an apologia for attacks by prominent members of the Catholic church against Islam and the Arabs for their part in the African slavery and the slave trade, did not rest his case there. He concluded that the slaves brought to Egypt from Africa were not even lawfully enslaved. Some were Muslims and hence protected against enslavement; all were taken as prisoners in wars that were not waged in conformity with the *shari'a*. In Shefiq's view the Egyptian government was in its right to set free all those considered as slaves in Egypt and to approve the 1877 Convention on slavery and the slave trade.

In the nineteenth century, a number of Muslim leaders who, under pressure from western governments to abolish the slave trade, also expressed the view that slavery was not in keeping with Islamic tradition. The bey of Tunis, who formally set free all slaves in the regency in 1846, justified his actions by saying that although slavery was lawful in principle it was harmful in the way it was carried out. Masters no longer performed the obligations of providing proper care for their slaves nor were they solicitous of their rights. The sultan of Turkey, in justifying the issuance of a *firman* in 1854 banning the traffic in Circassia, far from defending the principle of slavery, condemned it as contrary to Islam. "Man," he stated, "is the most noble of all the creatures God has formed, in making him free; selling people as animals, or articles of furniture, is contrary to the will of the Sovereign Creator." No less a position was taken by the shah of Persia in 1846 in a correspondence with the British government in regard to the abolition of the African slave trade.

In more recent times, the Muslim World Conference held in Mecca in 1926 adopted a resolution condemning slavery. This position was reaffirmed in a resolution adopted at its sixth world conference that met in 1964 in Mogadishu, Somalia. It noted: "Islam condemns enslavement of men by men." It made no mention, however, of women. This action followed by two years the abolition of slavery in Saudi Arabia, which until then had remained unaffected by the League of Nations and United Nations resolutions calling for the end of slavery. From the viewpoint of Islamic law, the action of Saudi Arabia, historically a bastion of Islamic fundamentalism, in abolishing slavery upheld the right of secular power to abrogate by statute law what Saudi society had regarded as an inviolable right under the *shari'a*.[40]

# CHAPTER THREE

# Occupation and Status of Slaves in the Islamic World

## 1.

SLAVES WERE ACQUIRED IN MUSLIM SOCIETIES FOR PUR-
poses that bore only a limited resemblance to the uses their
brethren were put to in the New World. Although social
status was often a factor that prompted many plantation
owners in the Old South to add to their slave holdings, this
was almost subordinated to the calculation of profit and loss.
In a business environment where prices for sugar and cotton
were determined in national and international markets, labor
was another factor of production which directly affected
overall costs of doing business. The profitability of labor-
intensive plantations and mines inescapably depended upon a

continuous supply of cheap, servile labor who could stand up to the rigors of long and arduous work. Black Africans, because of their low purchase price and maintenance costs and adaptability to a regimen of hard physical labor, proved eminently suitable to the requirements of plantation slavery. By contrast, the situation in Arab and Muslim countries revealed a far more complex set of factors which determined the occupational status of slaves. Here, slaves were generally acquired for reasons that were rooted in societal and sexual mores of the people and the requirements of their leaders in managing the affairs of state.

In Islamic societies, different as they were over time and space, slaves were generally not acquired for large-scale agricultural undertakings,[1] which was the *raison d'etre* of this peculiar institution in the New World. The supply of cultivatable land available for plantation agriculture in most of the Middle East and North Africa was severely limited. Exceptions to this are to be found in the ninth century in Mesopotamia and a thousand years later in Zanzibar, where there developed a demand for large numbers of slaves for rural and agriculture, which in most Muslim societies was of the small-holder variety. The people who worked the land were neither serfs nor slaves but freemen. The general absence of slaves from agriculture in Muslim society cannot be sufficiently emphasized in view of the tendency in the Western world to link slavery with the plantation economies of the New World, whose very existence was based on slave labor.

There were, to be sure, important instances where slaves were employed on a continuing and large scale in agriculture or outdoor work. From the seventh century on, blacks were exported in small but steady numbers from the Zanj coast stretching from Ethiopia and Somalia in the north to Mozambique in the south. They were put to work on date plantations in Basra, Bandar Abbas, and Minab and along the

Batinah coast; they also proved adaptable for use on large estates in Hijaz. Slaves were used for the drainage of marginal lands in Ifriqya, the eastern part of the Maghreb, during the ninth century. They were pressed into service for pearl diving in Lingeh and Bahrein and continued to be used in this highly profitable industry well into the twentieth century. Those who developed the ability to dive in deep waters were valued well above normal market values. The lot of the thousands of slaves employed in this thriving industry over the centuries was harsh indeed; and many young boys, newly exposed to the perils of this vocation, died of shock or fright.[2]

Many thousands of blacks, known as Zanj, were taken from the East African coast to Iraq in the ninth century for the removal of salt encrustations from land that was re-claimed for agriculture.[3] It was then that occurred what was undoubtedly the first great slave revolt in the Muslim world.[4] This uprising threatened Baghdad, the seat of the Abbasid empire. Significantly, black troops of the imperial army sent out to put down the uprising defected and joined up with the erstwhile slaves—an indication of racial unrest within Islam. In 894, fourteen years after the revolt first broke out, the Zanj were finally defeated; the head of their leader, Ali, was carried back to Baghdad on the top of a pole.

Agricultural slavery, generally not known in the eastern Arab world in the early centuries of Islam, was practiced in selected parts of the Muslim world where local conditions proved favorable. Thus, despite frequent assertions to the contrary, this form of outdoor slavery was not uncommon in nineteenth century Egypt.[5] The family of Muhammed Ali, whose rule during the better part of the first half of the nineteenth century did much to modernize Egypt, used hun-dreds of slaves on its sugar plantation in upper Egypt. Eyp-tian peasants found it practical to buy slaves to grow cotton. The sharp decline of cotton exports from the Southern states during the American Civil War triggered a boom in cotton production in lower Egypt and, with it, the use of slaves. Reports by British consular agents in Egypt attested to the widespread practice during the 1860s to employ black slave labor for agricultural and other outdoor work. In one memorandum, it was reported: "The peasantry of Egypt, who suddenly gained extraordinary sums of money for their cotton during the American Civil War, spent some of their profits in the purchase of slaves to help them in the cultivation of their lands . . . nearly all the slaves who had applied for emancipation were agricultural, not domestic slaves."[6]

With the coming of growing numbers of Omani Arabs to Zanzibar in the early decades of the nineteenth century, the stage was soon set for the large-scale use of agricultural slave labor. In 1840, the resourceful sultan of Oman and Muscat, Seyyid Said, whose sea power made him a force to be reckoned with in the Persian Gulf, made the fateful decision of moving the seat of his dynasty to Zanzibar, where he was better able to watch over his African possessions and extensive commercial activities. Not the least of these was the well developed Omani traffic in slaves. This transfer of political authority served to consolidate power in the hands of the sultan and put an end to a long period of political instability on the island.

Actually, Omani interest in Zanzibar and along the East Coast had developed some years before the sultan's move. Omani elites had emerged as the dominant commercial element on the island. In large measure, this commerce was tied to the slave trade with the Muslim world and with the closer Mascarene Islands, whose sugar plantations depended upon a continuous influx of slave labor. Starting around 1818, Omani entrepreneurs discovered a new outlet for their investment capital. This was cloves, a cash crop for which there was a strong demand in India and Arabia and, to a lesser extent, in North America and Europe. It is claimed that an Arab brought clove plants from Mauritius to Zanzibar in

1818 as a gift for Seyyid Said.[7] The sultan, who had yet to consolidate his political power on the island, planted the trees and soon realized that a crop of potentially immense value had been brought to Zanzibar.

The success of the clove culture depended upon the availability of land and ample supplies of slaves. Omani entrepreneurs set out to procure both. Between 1835 and 1845, the more successful among them purchased large estates possessing 200–300 slaves per plantation. The sultan and his immediate family became large estate owners, and in some cases the number of their slaves ran in the thousands. Seyyid Said, who purchased 45 estates, had 6,000 slaves on one plantation alone. As clove production and profits increased, so did the demand for slaves. By 1849 it was estimated that the slave population of Zanzibar alone was 100,000. That number doubled by 1860, when it was estimated there were 200,000 slaves out of the total population of 300,000. The great majority of these agricultural slaves were owned by Omani Arabs. A bare 300 in 1776, the Omani Arab population in Zanzibar numbered approximately 5,000 in 1872. In 1877 alone, about 1,000 Omanis settled on the island.

The magnetic appeal of clove farming had a profound effect on the economic and social structure of Zanzibar. More and more land was brought under cultivation by the Omanis, traders increasingly turned away from commerce to become farmers, and many became slaveowners. By 1870 the plantation economy had become important as an investment and as a way of life on the island. Ownership of the means of production—land, slaves, and capital—contributed much to defining the principal social groups on the island.

To meet the demand for slaves, large numbers had to be imported from the mainland. According to one study,[8] between 15,000 and 20,000 were brought to Zanzibar each year. In keeping with the island's character as a trading *entrepot*, many were re-exported to markets in the Persian Gulf, Arabia, and the Mascarene Island. Those who worked on the plantations did not enjoy the generally gentle treatment that household slaves were wont to receive in Muslim society. Gangs of slaves were assigned specific amounts of work to perform in clearing, weeding, and harvesting and were held strictly accountable by the *nakoa,* or headslave. The *nakoas* were widely reputed for their harshness to their fellow slaves.[9]

By taking into account slaves who were exported, those needed for the burgeoning Zanzibar economy, and the volume of slaves originating from the northern section of the East Coast, the number of blacks caught up in the East African slave trade approximated 20,000 to 25,000 a year. The Atlantic slave trade, according to one authoritative study, did not exceed this magnitude until the eighteenth century.[10]

Zanzibar and Pemba were not the only markets on the coast for agricultural slave labor. Other agricultural systems along the coast were in need of such labor as well. A plantation system based on grain and coconut cultivation owed its success to an abundance of slaves. By using labor-intensive methods on large estates in place of traditional farming techniques using a few slaves, Arab and Swahili farmers were able to produce a surplus of grains which they exported to markets in Arabia, Somalia, and Zanzibar. The later, with its heavy dependence on cash crops, had to import substantial amounts of wheat to feed its growing free and slave populations.

Agricultural development in Malindi, one of the many towns along the coast whose origins go back to the first centuries of the millenium, came to exemplify this plantation farming. Around the middle of the nineteenth century, Malindi was an all but abandoned town. Within a decade, it had attracted many Arab farmers who succeeded in growing different grains for export. During the 1870s and the 1880s

Malindi prospered, becoming the words of one writer "the granary of East Africa." Its spectacular success was based on the entrepreneurial skills of the local Arab and Swahili farmers who took advantage of Malindi's ample agricultural lands and bountiful supply of slaves. By 1873 the town's slave population was reported to have grown to 6,000, and to 10,000 by the middle of the 1880s when Malindi's prosperity reached its peak.[11]

Despite these varied uses of slaves for agricultural purposes, these practices were clearly of secondary importance in the overall picture of slavery in the Islamic world. Where agricultural or other forms of large-scale outdoor slavery did exist, as in Mesopotamia, certain West African Islamic states, or in nineteenth century Zanzibar and Egypt, this was in response to economic conditions which favored it. In the latter two countries, the labor-intensive requirements of clove and cotton production made it worthwhile for Arab and Swahili farmers to emulate the practice of American and European plantation owners of acquiring large numbers of slaves. The economics of producing cash crops for worldwide markets differed but little whether it was growing cotton in Louisiana or cloves in Zanzibar.

Slaves were used on a more systematic and regular basis in Muslim society in sub-Saharan Africa. Most of the slaves, as well as the free population, probably worked on the land. This form of agricultural slavery, it should be recalled, occurred in the context of a society where land was abundant and slaves were not without rights in regard to the ownership or use of land.

In the sixteenth century in the West African state of Songhay, the village headman distributed seed to the slave farm workers, who, in return, paid him a certain proportion of their harvest. There were in Futa Jallon slave villages which farmed the valleys while their Fulani overlords lived above on hilltops or plateaus. In the Sokoto empire, slave farming on the estates of the rich reached massive proportions. Very often, the ratio of free people to the slave population was small indeed. The nineteenth century German traveler, Gustav Nachtigal, observed that of the Arabs settled in Wadai, located in the western part of modern Chad, those engaged in agriculture relied almost exclusively on slave labor.

Different systems were used to ensure the smooth running of slave farming. Under one system followed in the Sokoto empire in 1826, a young male slave would be given a wife and sent to a village or farm. There, he and his wife were fed by the owner until the harvest. The slave worked for his master from daybreak until midday, after which he was free to do as he pleased. The slave was compensated with additional amounts of grain at harvest time. During off seasons, he was obliged, if his master so wished, to travel with him or to become part of his military entourage and to do battle on his behalf.

In East Africa, two different arrangements were followed. Under one system, a slave paid his master a monthly or annual rent, known as *ijara,* but kept the harvest. The second approach, which involved no *ijara,* allowed the master to claim the harvest; in return, he gave tracts of land to his slaves, who were permitted to work them on Thursdays and Fridays. On these days, slaves were free to work for wages and often found work in such low-paid jobs as porters, cleaners, washermen, and assistants to carpenters and black-smiths.

As agriculture became more complex or varied, slaves were trained to perform more skilled tasks. On the East Coast, slaves who scaled palm trees were greatly prized. The Trarza Moors who inhabited the western Sahara kept slaves who were skilled in the collection of gum arabic, the principal export of the region. Should a slave not collect his assigned quota, his master would rebuke or even beat him.

The most extensive use of agricultural slave labor occurred in nomadic societies. The colorful, blue-robed Tuaregs, who have lived for centuries in the mountainous regions of the central Sahara, were probably the best known among slave-holding nomads. Their slaves engaged in agriculture at oases and in other places where they cultivated dates, millet, barley, and wheat. In addition, they performed household chores and cared for the cattle, sheep, and camels. This left the Tuaregs free to fight, raid, and govern, as well as to pursue their pastoral ways, which often took them hundreds of miles from their homes. In this respect, the settled work of the slaves complemented the pastoral ways of their owners. This deep-rooted symbiotic relationship from which both master and slave benefited explains the persistence of slavery in the inhospitable climate and harsh terrain of parts of the region to this day. It is the reason why slavery continues to exist in the northwest African country of Mauritan despite a government decree in 1982 abolishing involuntary servitude.

## 2.

The most common and enduring purpose for which slaves were acquired in the Arab world was to work in private households. The wealthier the master of a household, the more slaves he was likely to acquire as domestics and con-cubines. In a society where investment opportunities in agri-culture were limited, acquiring slaves for household use was one of the few available forms of conspicuous consumption. Domestic slavery became more widespread with the arrival of a constant stream of slaves—the human booty of the *jihad*—and the disinclination of Arab women to be tethered to household chores.

Male slaves were used as servants, gardeners, watchmen, and all-around household help. Girl slaves were assigned such tasks as chambermaids, cooks, seamstresses, wet nurses, and confidantes. The more menial and harder work was usually reserved for unattractive, black-skin Negresses. The pretty and fair skinned among them were more often used for assignments involving personal chores for the master and mistress of the household. Slaves who demonstrated trust and responsibility might even be assigned to the task of managing their master's household affairs. The Old Testament story of Joseph sold into slavery by his brothers and who later became the overseer of his master's house could be told many times over for other slaves whose talents were recognized and rewarded. Children of slaves also had a role in the household by often becoming companions to their master's sons and daughters and, where relationship developed, their confidantes as well. As late as the 1870s in Egypt, the wealthier beys and pashas bought white boys to serve as playmates for their sons.

Female slaves were in much greater demand than males because of the numerous household assignments available for them. Young and attractive slaves were much sought after as concubines, about which more will be said later. Not uncommonly, women slaves played an important role in the household, which gained them both respect and status. In Morocco, the wet nurse, or *bada,* was often a slave who commanded much respect. The Fassi (inhabitants of Fez) imputed special healing powers to their dark-skinned bedchamber slaves because their skin was supposed to be warmer than that of white women. For Moroccans, every sickness derived from cold and healing from warmth. In more recent times, female domestic slaves owned by members of the Badawin tribe in Kuwait and Saudi Arabia often held responsible household positions.[13] The female slave looked after her mistress, served as her seamstress and cook, and accompanied her wherever she went. The life of this kind of slave, even if hard, was not much more difficult than her master's and generally less arduous than the one she left behind in Africa.

The greater importance attached to female slaves could generally be found in the higher prices they fetched in slave markets for males of comparable age, health, and origin. Records available from Cairene markets that specialized in trade with black Africa for selected periods in the eighteenth and nineteenth centuries reflect this disparity in prices. Averages for key base periods range from 68 to 74 percent in the former century (1720–29, 1770–79), with an intermittent period (1760–69) when female slaves outpriced males by 174 percent, and from 40 to 80 percent higher in the latter period (base periods 1821–25, 1836–40).[14] Not surprisingly, female slaves, because of the greater demand for their services, tended to outnumber male slaves. Evidence for this comes from a census taken in Cairo sometime in the 1850s which places the ratio between male and female slaves at about one to three. According to this tally, which was a rarity in this part of the world, the number of slaves in Cairo was 11,481, of whom 8,674 were females and 2,807 males.[15]

Household slavery was an indispensable form of labor in Arab society, where the people were ill-disposed to doing menial work. Those who could afford the price of slaves did so because the mass of Arabs were too proud to work as servants or too independent in spirit to serve a master.[16] That Arab women turned their back on household work is not surprising in view of their sheltered status in society and at home decreed by Islam. Under Muhammed's initial social reforms, women fared quite well by winning recognition for their religious, social, and civic rights. Worshiping alongside men was allowed by the Prophet, who also stressed that learning was a "duty incumbent on every Muslim, male and female." Poetesses who sang the praises of society rediscovered their roles as historians and social critics; many of them acted as nurses and warriors who took up arms in self-defense or to avenge a loved one lost in battle. One of the most spirited of these women was Um Umarah, one of the earliest converts to Islam. Such strong-willed and independent women represented an ideal for which they struggled against a conservative society. It was only natural, where circumstances allowed, that such women would fight for their full rights and oppose an age-old practice which gained sanction under Islamic law.

These rights were chipped away while Muhammed was still alive. His wives, whom he proclaimed Mothers of Believers, came under pressure to live up to their title by accepting limits on their freedom of movement. Henceforth, they could no longer mix freely with other men and women as had been their wont. They were now secluded in their homes in the tradition of the aristocratic women of Mecca. Their homes became a true *harim*—quarters reserved exclusively for members of their own sex. Houses were built with central courtyards so that neighboring women could have contact with one another without being exposed to strangers. The separation became even more complete when they were allowed to speak to men unrelated to them only from behind a curtain. When the need arose for them to go out into the street, they had to cover their faces with veils. By the middle of the eighth century, the *harim* and the veil, the status symbols of the subject Byzantine and Persian peoples, were taken over by the Arabs. God's message calling on women to "draw their veils over their bosoms" and "throw around them a part of their mantle" came to be interpreted as an injunction to hide their faces. As so often happens in religion, tradition becomes congealed into law.

Hand in hand with the loss by women of control over their physical and social space came a diminution of their religious and civic rights. Not long after the Prophet died in A.D. 632, women's limited rights to participate in public affairs were further curtailed. They were no longer invited to take part in political and religious matters, notably the selection of the caliph, who, as spiritual and temporal leader, became the supreme guide of the Islamic community. Women's right to worship in the mosque, which was confirmed by Muhammed in his lifetime, was also taken away; and in the same spirit, women were forbidden to go unaccompanied on the annual pilgrimage to Mecca.

The effect of these changes was to deny women the opportunity to intermingle with men on a basis of equality and to express themselves in community and religious matters. Women were tied to the home and allowed out only under conditions that restricted their movements and freedom of action. Significantly, seclusion rarely extended to poor women and peasants who had a need to contribute to household earnings. It fell heaviest on the better educated and potentially more influential women who were denied contact with the outside world. Secluded within the confines of her own home and obliged to veil her face wherever she went in public, the Arab woman was turned into a sex object. As one writer on Arab women observed, the "long era of the 'feminine mystique' was born in the Islamic world."[17]

### 3.

These changes in the status of women took place against a background of a vast transformation in Arab society resulting from military conquest. A great many military captives were brought back to Arabia where they became vassals to their Muslim lords by paying a capitation tax in exchange for protection or converted to Islam to enjoy the full benefits of society. Many also came back as slaves, who were acquired in the thousands by the conquering Muslims. This cheap, servile form of labor was quickly substituted in the place of free women whose interest in work was dulled by the confining dicta of Islamic law. What purpose was there for a wife to take on the daily time-consuming and laborious chores of the household when obedient hands could be directed to do them in her place? The household work ethic could scarcely survive in these circumstances, particularly when free women were forced to while away much of their time in their sexually segregated quarters. This set the stage for use of imported slaves around the house.

Setting aside the harsh conditions attending the transport of slaves, an ordeal that many did not survive, the lot of the majority of household slaves was, in the view of many foreign observers, tolerable. The treatment accorded them tended to measure up to the standard called for by Muhammed and prescribed by Islamic law. Westerners traveling in Arabia, Egypt, and other parts of the far-flung Ottoman Empire who observed household slavery firsthand were generally impressed by its benign nature.[18] The early nineteenth century Swiss traveler Burckhardt thought both in Egypt and Arabia "slavery had little dreadful in it but the name." Henry Dunand, the founder of the Red Cross, who was familiar with Tunisia and its social customs around the middle of the nineteenth century, commented favorably on the mildness of urban slavery in this North African country as compared with the situation in the southern slave states. During the period of the Arab caliphate hundreds of years earlier, slave women, particularly the more talented and attractive, were often instructed in the arts, poetry, and music.

There were exceptions to this standard of treatment where black slaves, usually men, came off badly at the hands of their masters. Usually such slaves were shunted off to perform the meanest work. During the reign of the Moroccan Sultan Muley Archy in the eighteenth century, black slaves suffered greatly. They were kept in irons as punishment for mistakes or breaches of discipline and, not infrequently, were put to death for these infractions.[19] And in contrast to what Dunand observed, another visitor to Tunisia noted that male slaves in Tunis led a harsh existence.[20] Cases of manumission were few, and there was little hope for slaves to gain their freedom.

At best, they might be freed on the death of their master. Once delivered from slavery, they were allowed to take up a rather normal life by mixing with the population and even owning property.

In explaining the reasons for the benign nature of slavery, much has to be attributed to the humane laws of Islam regarding the proper treatment of slaves. In Muslim society, where the writ of Islam ran far, a climate of public opinion was fostered, as was noted in the previous chapter, that made it difficult for owners to evade responsibility towards their slaves. Although the social inferiors of Muslims, slaves, who invariably were converted upon enslavement, were the spiritual equals of their masters. This very law, which obliged a Muslim to share his food and clothing with his slaves, not to overwork them, or to punish them severely in the event of wrongdoing, also urged him to manumit his slaves or to let them buy their way to freedom. In nineteenth century Egypt, Turkey, and Oman, enfranchised slaves were not all uncommon in the city and countryside, where they often carved out a niche for themselves, usually as porters, common workmen, or domestics. The existence of such an escape hatch gave hope to those who aspired to freedom and undoubtedly provided an incentive to keep in line. In Oman, slaves became sailors and were even appointed ships' officers. The sight of some slaves moving up the occupational scale had to provide even the lowliest slave with hope that his own fortunes might, one day, turn in his favor and allow him to reclaim his freedom. It was this feeling of hope which undoubtedly dulled the sharp edge of servitude and which did much to make life as a slave in Muslim society relatively bearable.

In spite of this, it would be farfetched to conclude that the mass of slaves were content with their lot. Slave uprisings, to be sure, were rare, nor is there evidence that slave owners lived in constant fear for their lives. Yet, during certain periods, the number of runaway slaves ran high.[21] This is all the more striking in view of the relatively easy lives that many slaves were able to lead. This just might suggest that conformity or compliance, traits often observed by foreigners among slaves, was an acquired response to dealing with their everyday situation and not an indication of acquiescence in their fate. Where the opportunity to run away presented itself, many slaves used it and made off. Court dockets in Egypt in the nineteenth century often contained cases of masters seeking to reclaim runaway slaves.

The evidence about slave conditions in Muslim countries did not come from the victims themselves. Had they been asked, it is most probable they would have presented another picture than the one depicted by foreign travelers. The latter often expected to run across conditions similar to those that prevailed in the Caribbean and in the Old South. When they encountered this benign form of slavery and drew the inevitable comparisons between slave conditions in the New World, there was a tendency to conclude that life could not be all that bad for the slaves.

How the great mass of slaves felt about their condition of servitude is something that is not known. They would have been less than human, a conviction that many slaveholders undoubtedly shared, if they did not grieve from their parents and brothers and sisters, as well as the life from which they were snatched. Nor is it clear that most slaves, in adjusting to a life of a slave or a concubine in a *harim*, made their peace with this way of life. In the absence of firm evidence that that was indeed the case, it is illusory to conclude, as some Western scholars have done, that because of the reasonably good conditions in which many slaves lived and the opportunities avialable to some of them, slavery "carried with it scarcely any social inferiority."[22] Regardless of the conditions and possible economic advantages derived from it, which, in any event, benefited only small numbers of slaves, an unfree status was always considered a disgrace. Slave ancestry, even only on the mother's side, was taken as a reason for scorn and a source of shame. Not even the lowliest members of the most despised tribes would marry a slave women. For even the poorest bedouin is free *(horr)* while the slave remains subject *('abd)* for ever. Stories showing slaves in a good light generally have to be taken with more than usual grain of caution as they are often meant to show that good qualities or noble deeds might even be found among persons of servile status. Another indication of the attitude towards slave status may be gleaned from birth control practices among Muslims during the Middle Ages. Such practices were followed among medieval Muslims partly to avoid fathering children who would be slaves.[23]

Moving through the Arab-controlled slave circuits in the early centuries of Islam was a wide mix of people taken from different parts of the world. Under the guise of the *jihad,* the Arabs took into captivity peoples of diverse ethnic, racial, and religious stock from such far-flung places as Asia, Persia, North Africa, and the Iberian peninsula. Many others were supplied by those who were attracted to the trade for profit. From the middle of the eighth century, Venetian traders were purveyors of slaves, sometimes Christians, to Islamic countries. Jewish merchants in the ninth and tenth centuries also played a role in the traffic of Slavs (from whence comes the word slaves) across central and western Europe. It was not unknown for fanatical Muslim sects who laid claim to the true belief to enslave their coreligionists whom they regarded as being beyond the pale of the law.

The influx of large numbers of enslaved peoples into the towns and cities of the Muslim world led to the establishment of a marketing system to facilitate trade in this human commodity. The commerce in slaves was a business in which traders, middlemen, and an interested public had an important stake. Although relatively little is known about early trading practices, there is enough information to form a rough idea about how trading in slaves was carried on. Every big town had a "place of display" *(ma'rid)* or slave market, commonly referred to as *suq erraqiq*. Slaves were collectively called "heads" *(ru'us raqiq)*, the term being applied to livestock as well. The slave market in the ninth century Egyptian town of Samarra is described as a vast quadrangle intersected with alleys lined with one-story houses. The slave merchant, often referred to as "importer" *(djallab)* or "cattle dealer" *(nakhkhas)*, brought his slaves to the open market where they were available for inspection by the public. Better class slaves were often sold in private homes or through one of the more prominent dealers. Young attractive females, who were considered desirable as concubines, were, as a rule, available for inspection in private homes. The same was true for eunuchs who fetched a far greater price than regular young males.

Buyers could often expect to find an assortment of slaves to choose from, although the actual supply would depend on the most recent caravan arrivals. A particularly active market drawing on a broad public would be stocked with men, women, and children of different ages taken from Asia, the Balkans, and Africa. Factors such as national origin, age, sex, health, and demonstrated talents determined the price of a slave. Generally, white slaves were worth more than blacks. Popular lore which ascribed to slaves of different origins certain virtues or defects also influenced buyer preferences and, indirectly, prices. Many of these popular attitudes were written up by the eleventh century Eastern Christian physician, Ibn-Butlan, in a slave trader's *vade mecum*.[24] Indian women, in his view, do not make good slaves but "are excellent breeders of children." Their men are reputed to be "good house managers and experts in fine handicrafts" but die at an early age. Ibn-Butlan also praised the virtues of Turkish, Greek, and Bujah (located between Abyssinia and Nubia) women although they, too, are not without their shortcomings. Berber women, in his view, make excellent slaves because of their pliant character and willingness to do every kind of work. By contrast, he had little regard for the Armenian, whom he described "as the worst of the white, as the Negro is of the black." In referring to "Negroes" Ibn-Butlan may well have had East Coast or Zanj Africans in mind. The low esteem in which he held them was not out of keeping with the views of other Arab writers. In contrast, he was attracted to the qualities of Abyssinian and Nubian women. "Of all the blacks," he wrote, "the Nubian woman is the most adaptable and cheerful."

In the eyes of the society he served, the *djallab* inspired at once contempt for his vocation and envy for his wealth. His ill-gotten gains were often fattened by the added profits of pawning off on unsuspecting buyers slaves whose condition was somewhat other than made out in the bill of sale. *Caveat emptor* was a watchword that the buyer had ever to be mindful of. So widespread were such deceptive practices that Ibn-Butlan saw fit to remind his readers of them in his slave trader's guide. "How many brown girls of impure coloring," he plaintively wrote, "have been sold as gold blonde! How many decrepit ones as sound! How many stodgy ones as slim and slender! They paint blue eyes black, yellow cheeks red, make emaciated faces chubby, remove the hair from the cheek, make light hair deep black, convert the straight into curly, thin into well-rounded arms, efface smallpox marks, warts, moles and pimples."

### 4.

One of the more interesting aspects of slavery in Araby was the use of slaves as soldiers and as guards.[25] Slave soldiers were not only acquired on an individual basis but often constituted large separate military units and, in some Muslim countries, actually composed a major element of the army.

At different times in history, slaves—both white and black—were a dominant force in the armies of Egypt, Turkey, and Morocco and in certain Muslim African countries. In the New World, by contrast, it would have been unthinkable to entrust arms to slaves, let along recruit them for service in the military.

The seeming paradox of having lowly slaves serve in the military, as well as in administrative and diplomatic posts, can largely be explained by understanding the nature of society in the non-Western World. Slaves could be relied upon because of their extreme dependence: they lived in a society to which they were strangers and in which they had no family or kin who could provide material support or spiritual succor. Hence, they were dependent upon their master for their every reward and pleasure. The master or ruler, ironically, was also vulnerable inasmuch as he depended on family and kin for protection and political support. This source of strength, a characteristic of societies structured along kinship lines, was not without its weakness. These very kith and kin, because they stood to inherit from the ruler upon his death, were a potential threat. The temptation was never far to cut short his rule by violence. The ruler might seek to bypass kin and family by enlisting outsiders, such as mercenaries, for support; they, too, however, were tied to kinship groups of their own and had divided loyalties. Slaves, because they lacked such ties, were free from such obligations. Properly rewarded and controlled, they could be made into trusted guards and loyal soldiers. This was a point intuitively grasped by many Muslim rulers who made slaves into a prop for their thrones.

Black slaves made their appearance in Muslim military ranks not long after the Abbasid caliphs established their rule in Baghdad in the middle of the eighth century. Initially, they did not represent a strong factor in the military but served in an auxilliary capacity by the following century. The Abbasid army swelled by the recruitment of white as well as black slaves.[26] Most of the white soldiers were taken from a gallery of nations and were notably Mongols, Persians, Slavs, and Turks. The latter were highly regarded by the Iraqis because of their equestrian skills and military prowess. The Abbasid ruler Mu 'tasim (833–842), fearful of the political designs of his own Arab cavalry, replaced them with the Turkish soldier slaves. At the same time, black slaves were enrolled in the army and were incorporated into racially integrated units. With the portals of military service already ajar, it was not long before blacks passed through it in increasing numbers. When the Zanj slave uprising broke out in the middle of the ninth century, threatening Baghdad, black troops of the imperial army were among those used in putting it down.

Despite their loyalty and fighting record, blacks were not allowed to join the cavalry units but were restricted to serving as foot soldiers. The cavalry became the preserve of Turkish and Slavic soldiers. For reasons that are not known, the blacks did not always comport as a disciplined force, showing, at times, an insolent and defiant demeanor. Tension developed between them and white soldiers that led to open conflict. Around 930, mounted Turkish troops decimated the black infantrymen and put their separate living quarters in Bab Oman to the torch. Following this massacre, white soldiers took over the ranks of the infantry and black slaves disappeared from the Abbasid army. The pattern of events that unfolded in Iraq over two centuries of recruiting blacks into the army, using them for rough or menial tasks and ultimately driving them from ranks, was to be repeated in other Arab countries in the following centuries.

It was in Egypt and in the western Arab world that black slaves made their strongest mark as soldiers. The first independent ruler of Muslim Egypt, Ahmad Ibn Tulun (d. 884), relied heavily on black slave soldiers to consolidate his power. Egypt's proximity to Sudan made it a natural market for slaves coming down the Nile. Ibn Tulun, it was reported, recruited 7,000 freeborn fighters—possibly Arabs, 24,000 Turkish slaves, and 40,000 Sudanis. Although the number of blacks, referred to as Nubians, were secured in the form of tribute from Nubian rules, most of them were acquired through purchase. What possibly attracted these Nubians to the Tulunids was their fame as archers; more likely, however, their attraction lay in their being cheaper and easier to acquire than Turkish slaves.[27]

The racially mixed nature of this army was in itself a source of tension, as proved to be the case in other Arab countries. Mindful of this, Ibn Tulun had a separate quarter known as *al-qata'i* built for the black soldiers. This anticipated a pattern in other Arab countries, where black slave soldiers were quartered in racially separate quarters. In Baghdad, black soldiers and their families lived in the Bab Oman district and during the Fatimid period in Egypt also lived in separate sections of Cairo. Their concentration in a single quarter, as has already been noted, served to make them vulnerable to attack in time of tension.

The loyalty given by the black levies to the Tulunids earned them a privileged place in the military hierarchy. When the son and successor of Ibn Tulun, Khumarawayh, rode in procession, he was followed, according to one chronciler, by a guard of a thousand black soldiers decked out in black cloaks and black turbans, armed with swords and shields. With the restoration of caliphal authority, the short-lived Tulunid dynasty came to an abrupt end in 905. The newly appointed governor gave the order to attack the black praetorian guard, who were mercilessly cut down.

The attraction of Egyptian rulers to black soldiers did not end here but continued to develop through the period of Ikhshidid rule and the more famous Fatimid dynasty. Muhammad Ibn Tughj, founder of the Ikhshidid dynasty (935–969), continued to recruit Nubians into his army.

Among his personal guards was a Nubian eunuch, Abu'l Misk Kafur, better known by the nickname "Musky Camphor," who, upon his master's death, became a regent of Egypt for almost twenty years. Kafur, the only black ever to become a ruler over an Arab land, distinguished himself as an able administrator. Probably, as a way of consolidating his own power, he did not hesitate to recruit many of his countrymen into his military service. Whatever his accomplishments, not all Egyptians took kindly to having this one-time slave rule over them. The Arab poet al-Mutanabbi, in a poem brimming with scorn and sarcasm, makes Kafur the object of a biting attack:

> Whenever a wicked slave assassinates his master
> or betrays him, he has to get his training in Egypt.
>
> There, the eunuch has become a chieftain of the runaway
> slaves, the free man is enslaved, and the slave obeyed.
> .   .   .   .   .   .   .   .   .   .   .   .   .   .   .   .   .   .
> or his ear bleeding in the hand of the slave broker?
> or his worth, seeing that for two farthings
> he would be rejected?
> Wretched Kafur is the most deserving of the base
> to be excused in regard to every baseness—
> and sometimes excusing is a reproach—
> and that is because white stallions are incapable
> of gentility, so how about black eunuchs?[28]

A high point of black warrior slaves in Islam was reached during the rule of the Fatimids, who, moving from Ifriqiya, which was basically modern Tunisia, and a section of present-day Algeria, captured Egypt in 969 with the help of Berber tribes. During the time of this Shi'ite dynasty, which rivaled the Abassid caliphs in Baghdad for power and influence, Egypt became the center of a vast kingdom; by the end of the tenth century, it embraced an area of almost all of North Africa, Syria, and Palestine. Although they claimed Arab descent, the Fatimids rested their support on foreign troops—Berbers, Turks, and blacks. The latter, organized into their own regiments known as *'abid al-shira* (the "slaves by purchase"), probably originated in the central Sudan, from whence they came to Ifriqiya via Zawila in the Fezzan.[29]

In an atmosphere where racism, as the poem of al-Mutanabbi so eloquently attested to, was never far removed from the surface, the rulers of Cairo had the uneviable task of keeping what was an uneasy balance between the competing disparate elements of the military, whose behavior was characterized by jealousy and intrigue. In the latter part of the reign of the third Fatimid caliph, al-Hakim (996–1020), the founder of the Druze sect, a series of clashes broke out pitting the Berbers and Turks, on the one hand, against the Sudani. These factional struggles were triggered by a decision taken by al-Hakim to despatch his black troops to attack the inhabitants of Old Cairo. The Berbers and Turks responded by joining forces to protect the Cairoites. In the ensuing struggle, a chronicler of the events described a tale of looting, destruction, and rape. The effect of this internecine fighting was to sap the power of the black military slaves.

The fortunes of the black soldiers revived for a while during the reign of Caliph al-Mustansir (1035–1094). Apparently, the Sudanis owed this turn of the tide to the caliph's mother—herself a former black slave—who took advantage of her position to bestow favors on the black soldiers and recruit large numbers of them into the military. This political support coupled with the growth in their numbers only whetted the Sudanis' appetite for political intrigue. Inevitably, this provoked unrest and racial rivalry which pitted the Berbers and Turks against the blacks.[30] These two groups waged a murderous battle against the blacks levies in 1062 and drove them from Cairo into upper Egypt. They were decisively defeated in 1076 following an unsuccessful attempt to return to Cairo.

Again defeat turned out to be temporary for the Sudanis, who remained a potent military and political force in the country. By the time of the last Fatimid caliph, al-'Adid, they had become a force to reckoned with in the Fatimid state, with their fate closely linked to its ruler. It was only natural that they resisted efforts by Salah 'al-Din to win control of Egypt. The issue was finally joined when this great military leader, born of Kurdesh parents in Mesopotamia, ordered the murder of a leading court eunuch, who was accused of being in league with the Crusaders.

This deed, together with the dismissal of many black eunuchs from the court, prompted the blacks to make a last-ditch effort to save the Fatimids from the rising power of the new dynastic challengers—the Ayyubids. In August 1169, 50,000 black troops were arrayed against the forces of Salah 'al-Din in the area between the palaces of the caliph and the vizier. Outmaneuvered and possibly betrayed by the very caliph whose cause they championed, the blacks were decisively defeated, marking their end as a political factor in Egypt. Following this, the white military elements of the Fatimid forces, notably Turks, Kurds, and Daylamites, were integrated into the Ayyubud establishment while the blacks were not. In the succeeding centuries when the power of the *mamluks* held sway in Egypt, only menial roles in the military were open to black slaves.

During this period that spanned two centuries, the *'abids* managed to stay close to the center of political power. That they succeeded as long as they did was due to the relationship that evolved between themselves and their ruling patrons: the Tulunids and Fatimids. These dynastic leaders needed the black soldiers to ward off other aspirants for power and to serve as a counterweight to the *mamluks*, the white slave soldiers. This court-related politics proved rewarding and, in the circumstances, unavoidable for the *'abids,* who were greatly dependent on their masters. They had no roots in

Egyptian society, which both feared and despised this praetorian force. As long as their dynastic patrons remained on the throne, the *'abids* managed to hold on to their position and privileges. Once this condition ceased to exist, their days in power were numbered.

In spite of the importance of slave soldiers in Iraq and Egypt, their use were more widespread in the Maghreb. Black soldiers, acquired in Fezzan, an *entrepot* for some of the trans-Saharan trading routes, formed part of the armies of Tunisian leaders between the ninth and eleventh centuries. Far more significant was the role they played in Morocco. The Almoravide rulers in the eleventh century and their successors, the Almohades, obtained slaves through purchase and conquest for use as their personal military guard. In 1072, Yusuf ben Tachfine, the second of the Almoravide sultans, recruited 250 European horsemen as his personal guard. Then, at his own expense, he bought or recruited 2,000 black Sudanese to become part of his mounted guard—something virtually unheard of in the eastern regions of Islam. (Unlike their dynastic successors, the Almohades, who amassed slaves through warfare, the Almoravides acquired theirs largely through purchase.) Overall, the total number of slaves used at this time for military and other purposes was not very great. Even after the conquest of the Songhay empire by Sultan Moulay Ahmed al-Mansur in 1591, the black population in Morocco was of modest proportions. Between 1500 and 1650, the traffic in black slaves was more important than slavery itself.

This practice was altered by Moulay Ismael, who drastically transformed Morocco's military establishment by creating a professional army of black slave soldiers.[31] Ismael, whose rule spanned a period of more than fifty years (1672–1729), sent emissaries throughout the Sudan and Morocco to acquire slaves to serve him as personal bodyguards and as soldiers in his newly constituted army. His decision to base the military power of the country almost exclusively on black slaves was prompted by the refusal of town and local leaders to provide him with the necessary levies.

Moulay Ismael had his own ideas about the creation of such an *armée de métier*. Thousands of the original recruits were settled on farms, provided with young Negresses, and encouraged to have large families. The sultan's aim was to create an army of young blacks who knew no other life than the one they grew up in and who could be molded into fanatically loyal soldiers. Starting at ten years of age, boys received military training which lasted five years until they were ready for military service. Through breeding and re-cruitment, Moulay Ismael succeeded in building up an army estimated by Moroccan historians to have numbered 150,000 soldiers. Even if the number were a third of this size, as other historians believe, it constituted nonetheless a substantial military force.

However long and valiant their military service, the 'abids remained foreigners in the land. They owed allegiance solely to Moulay Ismael in whose behalf they fought and on whom they depended for their every benefit and pleasure. As a result they were alienated from the country they were honor-bound to defend. Moroccan society barred the door to them. Ownership of land, which defined a man's social status, was denied to them. The people looked down on the 'abids and were resentful that the security of the nation was entrusted to black slaves. Highlighting this feeling was the position taken by the 'ulema, the religious leaders and interpreters of the *shari'a* law. They viewed a standing army of foreign slaves as contrary to the law and, in consequence, refused to inscribe the names of the 'abids in the *diwan*, the military register. These guardians of the law insistently posed the question whether the 'abids were slaves or freemen. If the former, they had no right to take part in a *jihad*, which was the exclusive right of Muslims. On the other hand, if they were free

Muslims, by what right did the sultan have in reducing believers to slaves? Mindful of the need to maintain a strong army and equally conscious of his obligation to uphold his standing as *sharif,* Moulay Ismael, the second of the 'Alawid (Alauite) dynasty which still rules in Morocco today, managed to bring the religious leaders around by his disingenuous statement: "The slaves were declared free, but they were kept under a species of mortmain to provide for the defence of Islam."[32]

The isolation of the *'abids* and their close identification with the sultan created an unbridgeable gap between them and the people. Constrained to live in segregated settlements—the perennial lot of black slave soldiers in Muslim societies—they could not develop a base of popular support. Without fresh conscripts to augment their numbers and their ranks thinned by Moulay Ismael's campaigns to subdue rebellious tribes and capture the Middle and High Atlas, the —*abid* army dwindled in size. This process of dissolution continued unchecked; and by the turn of the twentieth century, the army numbered a bare 4,000 men, a relic of a forgotten past.

## 5.

In Egypt where black slaves had vanished from the army during the centuries of *mamluk* rule, they again reappeared in substantial numbers by the end of the eighteenth century. Louis Frank, the French army medical officer, refers to the fighting skills of black slaves, who, in his estimation, matched those of European soldiers.[33] These qualities were also appreciated by Muhammed Ali, who did much to modernize Egypt during his iron-fisted rule that spanned the better part of the first half of the nineteenth century (1805–49). This Albanian-born military officer, who was sent by the Turks to Egypt to prevent it from breaking away from Ottoman control, confounded his superiors by making it into a virtually independent state. With the help of European advisers, he encouraged the cultivation of cotton, the development of industry, and the creation of a modern army and navy.

As part of this same effort to make Egypt into a modern state, Muhammad Ali dealt a crushing blow to the *mamluks*, an elite corps of soldiers who for centuries had been the power behind the throne. By continuous intrigue, they prevented Egypt from exploiting its substantial resources and becoming a more modern state. In March 1811 he tricked the *mamluks* into attending a feast in the citadel, where they were massacred. While individual *mamluks* continued to serve in the army as officers down through the first half of the century, they ceased to constitute a ruling aristocracy. The destruction of the *mamluks* presaged a similar fate for the Janissary corps in Turkey. Borrowing from the tactic used by his nominal subordinate in Egypt, Sultan Mahmud II, who was bent on modernizing his technologically backward army, had the Janissary corps—4,000 in number—ruthlessly murdered, thereby bringing to an inglorious end this 600-year-old praetorian guard of one time white slaves.

Under Muhammed Ali's instructions, his sons Ibrahim and Ismael carried out far-flung and brutal military campaigns against Ethiopia and the Sudan. To the east, his army seized the Red Sea ports of Suakim and Massawa. Starting in 1820, he sent an army south under Ismael, who conducted a campaign of death and destruction against the defenseless Nubians, occupying Sennar and Kordofan and making Khartoum the capital city of Nubia, which was again made part of Egypt.

The true purpose of this military expedition was to find gold and track down slaves for Muhammed Ali's army and for the slave marts of Egypt. Along the line of march into the Sudan, Ismael's army terrorized the populace and seized thousands as slaves; those prisoners he could not enslave were butchered. Of the estimated 30,000 who were sent down the Nile, only about half managed to make it to Cairo, and many of these were women and children. Death by disease, exhaustion, and maltreatment claimed the others along the road. For his brutality, Ismael paid with his life.[34] After two years of campaigning, with the army demoralized and about to return home, Ismael fell victim to a fire in his own quarters set by a native chief, Mek Nimr, whose people suffered horribly at the hands of the invaders.

Muhammed Ali's campaign into the Sudan was unique in that it introduced a new and barbaric idea of deporting large numbers of people for what were essentially political purposes. It set the pattern for smaller-scale expeditions that were to continue through most of his reign. In 1827 one such expedition was conducted against the Dinkas in the southern Sudan, although without much success. The sturdiest among the captives would be conscripted into the army and the rest handed over to slave dealers and to the inhabitants of the provinces. Under pressure from abroad, Muhammed Ali issued a decree banning further slave-hunting *razzias* in the Sudan. Like many similar orders that were to flow from the pen of Egyptian leaders, this one remained a dead letter. When Dr. Madden, an Englishman, was sent to Egypt in 1840 as a bearer of a letter from the Anti-Slavery Convention to congratulate Muhammed Ali for having abolished slave hunts, he discovered that the edict had never been enforced. Apart from *razzias*, Muhammed Ali obliged the authorities in upper Egypt, Siwa oasis, Nubia, and the Sudan to pay their taxes in the form of slaves, whom he incorporated into his army; this continued for years after the slave trade was officially abolished.[35]

Attempting to arrive at even approximate number of slaves assigned to a particular avocation in one country or another is doomed to failure. Such figures were generally not kept or, if they were, are too insignificant to allow generalizations. A thin ray of light in this impenetrable darkness may be found in regard to the use of military slaves. The penchant of chroniclers to advert to figures—not necessarily accurate—as a way of showing the magnitude of battles or portraying the court retinue does tell us something about the numbers of slaves used for military purposes. The presence of 40,000 blacks in the military service of Ahmad Ibn Tulun, which exceeded the total number of other recruits, clearly indicates that substantial numbers of slaves were involved. No less an observation is valid in considering the very large numbers of slave soldiers who fought in the service of the Fatimids and much later on in the armies of Moulay Ismael and Muhammed Ali. Those who purchased or hunted slaves for this purpose had to come up with slaves who were young, able bodied, and male. Thus, in order to have placed 40,000 slave soldiers at the disposal of Ahmad Ibn Tulun, a far greater number had to be captured or purchased. It does not require a great stretch of the imagination to conclude that blacks in the hundreds of thousands had to be enslaved to meet the quotas for Muslim armies during those periods of Abassid, Egyptian, Tunisian, Moroccan, and Ottoman history. In doing this, the slave traders deprived Africa of one of the most vital and productive elements of its population. In the case of the Sudan, this loss made the country from an early period with history, far more vulnerable to military incursions from Egypt.

While a life as a soldier undoubtedly brought its rewards, it also carried with it no small amount of risk. Apart from the dangers of battle, there was always the latent hostility of the local population, which at times burst forth against the black soldiers. For the latter, at least, these very real dangers could not be compensated for by the promise of being moved into the higher ranks which were traditionally reserved for white soldiers and *mamluks*.

# CHAPTER FOUR

# Sex and Slavery in the Arab World

### 1.

THE MOST COMMON AND ENDURING PURPOSE FOR AC-
quiring slaves in the Arab world was to exploit them for
sexual purposes. Islamic law conferred upon the owner of
slaves full control over their sexual and reproductive functions as well as the fruits of their labor. He had fairly complete sexual access to his female slaves and kept for his own
kinship group the children he sired with them. These women
were nothing less than sexual objects who, with some limitations, were expected to make themselves available to their
owners. To watch over these women, who were carefully
sequestered in the confines of the home, the master added a
eunuch to the complement of his household slaves. The
castrated male became the keeper of his master's beautiful
women. These two opposites—attractive women and cas-

trated men—starkly demonstrated a master's power over the sexual and reproductive functions of his slaves. The marketplace confirmed the high value attached to the sexual aspects of slavery. Eunuchs commanded the highest prices among slaves, followed by young and pretty white women.

Islamic law, as already noted, catered to the sexual interests of a man by allowing him to take as many as four wives at one time and to have as many concubines as his purse allowed. Polygamy was sanctioned as a way of ensuring the benefits of married life to the many women in Arabia whose husbands were killed in the internecine tribal warfare that afflicted the region. By acquiescing to concubinage, Islam endorsed a long-standing practice among Arab men. The status of concubinage was reserved solely for slaves: a free woman could not be taken as a concubine. A story about Mansa Musa, the Muslim ruler of the Mali kingdom in the fourteenth century, is revelatory of the severity of the prohibition against taking free women as concubines. On a visit to Cairo, this otherwise observant monarch was rebuked for his licentious behavior of taking some of the daughters of his subjects as concubines. Taken aback by the public reproach, he inquired whether an exemption was not available for kings.[1] Not even for kings was the reply. In deference to the law, he agreed not to take any more free women into his household as concubines.

The great demand for concubines was reflected in the preponderance of girls and young women who fell victim to the slave traffickers. Africans who tracked down slaves for sale to Muslim markets paid special attention to catching these more desirables in their nets. In the predawn *razzias* on unsuspecting villages, it was not uncommon for the Africans, who often carried out these raids, to kill off many of the men and older women and march off the young women to the assembly points from where they would begin the long trek to the slave market. The fourteenth century traveler, Ibn

Battuta, on setting out from Takedda in the western Sudan to Fez, went by a caravan of six hundred women slaves.[2] Seeing caravans made up largely or exclusively of girls and women was not an uncommon sight on the trade routes linking *bilad as-Sudan* to North Africa. In the mid-nineteenth century, the Latvian-born, German-educated botanist, Georg Schweinfurth, passed on his way what he described as a small slave caravan carrying one hundred and fifty girls.[3] Schweinfurth, who was one of the first two Europeans who attempted to cross the continent from north to south, noted that many slaves died on these long treks across the desert because their captors brought along insufficient food and water for the lengthy journey.

White women were almost always in greater demand than Africans, and Arabs were prepared to pay much higher prices for Circassian and Georgian women from the Caucasus and from Circassian colonies in Asia Minor. After the Russians seized Georgia and Circassia in the early part of the nineteenth century and, as a result of the Treaty of Adrianople in 1829 under which they obtained the fortresses dominating the road into Turkey from Circassia, the traffic in Circassian women came to a virtual halt. This caused the price of Circassian women to shoot up in the slave markets of Constantinople and Cairo. The situation was almost completely reversed in the early 1840s when the Russians, in exchange for a Turkish pledge to cease their attacks on their forts on the eastern side of the Black Sea, quietly agreed not to interfere in the slave traffic. This unrestricted trade brought on a glut in the Constantinople and Cairo markets, where prices for Circassian women brought them in reach of many ordinary Turks and Egyptians. In not a few cases, the slave or concubine status of these women was changed by marriage. Marrying off a son to a slave made good sense in a society where betrothal to a free woman often entailed large expenses, notably in the form of a dowry which the wife kept in the event of divorce. A slave girl, moreover, was usually more submissive than her free sister, and there were no troublesome in-law problems.

By and large, the high cost of white female slaves made them a luxury that only rich Turks, Egyptians, and other Muslims could afford. Others intent on obtaining a concubine had to settle for the "second best," and these were, by large consensus, Abyssinian girls, usually Gallas. These women were much sought after because of their fine lines, grace, and beauty. To this day many Egyptians hold the belief that Ethiopian women possess secret sexual powers. Depending on lightness of skin, attractiveness, and skills, they cost anywhere from a tenth to a third of the price of a Circassian or Georgian woman. It can be seen that in the prevailing scales of value, they occupied a midway position between the white and black slave. As the English chronicler, E. W. Lane, put it: "They themselves . . . think that they differ so little from the white people that they cannot be persuaded to act as servants, with due obedience to their master's wives; and the black (or Negro) slave girl feels exactly in the same manner towards the Abyssinian but is perfectly willing to serve the white ladies."[4]

As long as Circassian, Slavic, Greek, and other white women were available at affordable prices, Arabs preferred them to blacks. Their scarcity value tended to drive up their market value so that by the middle of the sixteenth century white slave women became a luxury that only the ruling sultans, Mamlukes, beys, and the very affluent could afford. From the end of the seventeenth to the middle of the nineteenth century, the average price of a white female slave was four to six times greater than that of a comparable black woman slave. In Egypt, according to Lane, a white slave girl was worth anywhere from three to ten times the price of an Abyssinian.

## 2.

There was no equivalent to this peculiarly Muslim institution in Christianity or Judaism. Christians and Jews owned slaves, although not on a scale comparable to Muslims. However, slave girls were generally not sexually at the disposal of their masters.[5] The Law of Oriental Christianity viewed sexual relations between master and slave as fornication, punishable by excommunication from the church. A child born out of such a relationship was viewed as a disgrace to the owner and was raised as a slave. Illustrating this point was the story of the Caliph Mansur, who sent three beautiful Greek slave girls and 3,000 gold pieces to the physician Georges. Accepting the gift of money, the physician returned the girls with the message that "with such I shall not live in the house, for to us, Christians, only one wife is allowed, and I have one in Belafel." For this, he won the praise and admiration of the caliph.[6]

The institution of slavery as it evolved in the West had no equivalent to concubinage and, hence, created no real demand for female slaves to be used for this purpose. There was, no doubt, a certain amount of cohabitation between whites and their women slaves. Travelers to Brazil or to Portugal's colonies in Africa often drew attention to the not-uncommon practice among white settlers of taking slaves as mistresses or even as wives. Miscegenation was clearly not a taboo among the Portuguese, whose personal relations with blacks were devoid of some of the more virulent strains of racism which infected the behavior of the other European colonizers and slave traders. Easy-going sexual relations with black women were not an indication that the Portuguese colonizers differed from other European settlers in the matter of relations between whites and blacks. Rather, they were drawn along this path because of the unfavorable ratio of

European men to European women and the proportion of whites to nonwhites in the Portuguese African and New World colonies.[7] Here, as in other instances where white slave owners had regular sexual relations with slave women, one should not confuse passion for respect or eroticism with egalitarianism.

Even in the slave states of the antebellum American South, where relations between the races were governed by strict codes of behavior, often stiffened by anti-miscegenation of anti-cohabitation laws, it was not uncommon for slave owners to keep one or more slave girls as mistresses, although rarely as wives. However, this aspect of slavery was incidental to the real purpose of slavery, which was to provide, at an economic price, black slaves to work the cotton fields which were the economic backbone of the South. In this order of things, male slaves, who became the main toilers in the fields, generally commanded a higher price than women slaves of comparable age and health. In contrast, what distinguished the domestic trade in Africa and the export to the Muslim world of young female slaves was the degree to which acquiring concubines was a compelling and conscious motive.[8]

### 3.

Acquiring one or more concubines was an irresistible attraction to men that pervaded all social ranks of Muslim society. After being brought into her master's household, the concubine performed routine domestic chores; it was not uncommon for talented slave women to receive instruction in art, poetry, or singing and then to spend much of their time performing for the benefit of their owners. Notwithstanding the various roles they assumed, the primary purpose of most men in acquiring a concubine was sexual. The concubine offered men a religiously approved way of gratifying their sexual desires and fantasies in ways that were often not possible in normal marital life.

In Islamic society, a man could have no contact at all with his intended wife until the consummation of their marriage. Koranic law, for reasons having to do with female modesty and chastity, forbids women to be in the company of any men, except their husbands or persons so closely related to them as to come within prohibited degrees for marriage. Included in this category were close relatives, slaves, particularly eunuchs, and children too young to be aware of differences of sex. A woman unlike her husband who could avoid the constrictive embrace of a sexually frustrating marriage by taking as many as four wives at any one time and buying as many concubines as he wished, had no such options. She had to live a monogamic life under conditions that placed severe limits on her physical movements in a society which restricted her meeting other men.

Such restrictive courting practices, which few women dared flout, were bound to create, in time, serious strains in marital ties. Personal problems arising from differences in temperament or sexual incompatibility were scarcely avoidable for men and women who were almost strangers to one another upon marriage. The unhappy or sexually frustrated women, rarely a matter of concern to the male-dominant society whose mores she had to follow, had to resign herself to remaining faithful to an uncaring or insensitive husband or to seeking a lover. Adultery, however, when committed by a woman, remained an unpardonable act in Muslim society; under Islamic law it is punishable by death. Such a rule was applied, a *fortiori*, to a woman who owned male slaves as well. While a woman could own slaves in her own right, she was not permitted to have sexual relations with any of them—a restriction that did not apply to her husband. A man who discovered that his wife shared her bed with a slave could have her pay for such a transgression with her life.

In the fabled *The Thousand and One Nights,* such a fate befell the wife of King Shahzaman. The king set out to visit his brother, King Shahriyar, but instead returned home to retrieve something he had forgotten. Coming back to his palace at midnight, he discovered his wife and a Negro slave asleep in his bed. Enraged, King Shahzaman took his sword and slew the two of them as they lay in bed and then went on his journey. The story is instructive because it revealed the double standard that existed for men and women: what was clearly permitted for men was decidedly off-bounds for their wives.

The availability of concubines, moreover, offered a man a measure of relief from the unhappiness of a marriage that was sexually ungratifying. Before purchasing a slave whom he intended to use as a concubine, a man was careful to make sure that she was responsive to his amorous advances. This could be managed in the privacy of special stalls that were set aside in slave markets for the close examination of female slaves by prospective buyers; here men would take liberties with these hapless girls in a manner they would not dream of when courting a woman they wished to marry. In Cairo, despite *hisba* laws regulating the proper and moral conduct of public affairs, including slave market practices, these regulations were often flouted by interested customers of female slaves. This opportunity to choose a concubine after first approaching her in an intimate manner offered for a man a far more promising way of developing a sexually gratifying relationship than with a wife.

Comparing the success of slave girls and free women with men, the Arab essayist al-Jihiz (776–869) observed in an essay entitled "Free Women and Slaves" that the slaves were the better off. "Slave girls," he wrote, "in general have more success with men than free women. Some women seek to explain that by saying that before acquiring a slave a man is able to examine her from every standpoint and get to know her thoroughly, albeit stopping short of the pleasure of an intimate interview with her; he buys her, then, if he thinks she suits him. In the case of a free woman, however, he is limited to consulting other women about her charms; and women know absolutely nothing about feminine beauty, men's requirements, or the qualities to look for. Men, on the other hand, are sounder judges of women. . . ."9

The ubiquitous concubine and the prominent role she occupied in the structured, patriarchal Muslim society, beginning with the family household and reaching into the courts of powerful chiefs and pashas and finally into the seraglio of the sultans of the Ottoman Empire, were inextricable parts of the Islamic world inasmuch as the concubine was part and parcel of domestic life. Because of the special relationship the concubine had with her master, she was often considered a part of the family. As a rule, she was treated with consideration and care and enjoyed many of the amenities of the home. Where a man did not have a wife, it was not uncommon for the concubine to fill in as one and run the household.

Islamic law made provision for concubines so as to assure them minimum rights and to protect their offspring. This protection was necessary because, unlike legitimate wives, they had no legal rights. While a master was duty bound to share his nights with his wives on an equal basis, he had no such obligation to his concubines. A woman disavowed by her husband left the household with her dowry and could return to her family. No similar economic and social safety net was available to the ordinary concubine who was turned out of the household by her master.

Islamic law compensated for these shortcomings by providing concubines a modicum of personal and family safeguards. The law hedged an owner's sexual rights to a concubine by placing the same restrictions of cohabitation on concubinage as it did on marriage. Hence, a Muslim owning two concubines related to one another as sisters was allowed to have sexual relations with but one of the women. If he was attracted to the other as well, he was obliged to sell or part with her. The provisions of the law regarding an *umm walad* fitted in with the special concern for the concubine and the need to protect her from being sold or alienated after she bore her master's child.

In upholding the status of concubines, Islamic law showed compassion and understanding for their vulnerable positions in society. Their gains, however, were acquired at the expense of their masters' lawful wives. Concubinage had the insidious effect of weakening the position of free Muslim women both in affairs of state and at home. After the principle of succession to the Arab caliphate, originally based on elective leadership, was changed to hereditary kingship, concubines gained political power equal to that of the sultan's wives. Henceforth their sons could become the supreme ruler in the Muslim world, as indeed happened within a century of the Prophet's death with the accession of Yazid III to the caliphate. The already weakened societal position of Arab women was now under challenge from a political point of view.

To Arab potentates and the affluent in Muslim society, concubines presented certain advantages that made them more attractive than their free sisters. Marrying the latter required paying out a dowry and extending favors to the family of the bride. In the event of divorce, it might prove necessary to make a property settlement which could be financially burdensome. No such problems arose from parting with a concubine who had no bargaining power. These advantages were not lost on the early Arab caliphs, who increasingly turned to slave women to produce political heirs. Among the bedouins in rural Arabia and in much of West Africa, concubines had a further use. They served their master in expanding his lineage since the children he sired from these women acquired his status.

Concubines successfully competed with wives in ever

more prosaic ways. The availability of new supplies of slaves meant that a fresh young face might an appearance at any time. Added to this advantage of youth, many concubines were instructed to strum a lute, compose a verse, or comport in ways that showed off their beauty and grace. Such young women, who were groomed to please, could stir the imagination of the most jaded prince. It is scarcely surprising that many Arab men preferred the company of these slave girls to that of their wives, who often became neglected and embittered women. A young, attractive concubine who entered the household of her master often became the object, scorn, and hatred of his legitimate wife. The household atmosphere, not surprisingly, was charged with intrigue and rivalry.

### 4.

Inextricably linked with concubinage was the *harim* (Arabic forbidden), an institution that flowered in much of the Islamic world. Strictly speaking, the *harim* was an area of the household set aside solely for women. The practice of secluding women had its origins in Byzantium and Persia and was later adopted by Muhammed, who required his own wives and daughters and those of believers to protect themselves in public by wearing long veils. Later, for reasons of modesty and chastity, women were not allowed in the company of men, except for their husbands and close relatives. Also included in this tightly drawn circle were servants, children, and eunuchs.

A man's wife or wives, his concubines, and their retinue of servants, slaves, and eunuchs made up the *harim,* and their lives revolved around it. In the homes of the very wealthy, there were separate quarters areas or compounds for each of the wives and favorite concubines. White girl slaves imported from the Russian provinces of Georgia and Circassia and parts of the Balkans also adorned the *harims* of wealthy Turks,

Egyptians, and Arabs. Those who could not afford these luxury women were attracted to the bronze-skinned *habasheeyahs*, Ethiopian women who were very much in demand by the voluptuaries of Constantinople, Cairo, and Alexandria. There was a high turnover among these women, who, because of their delicate constitution, frequently succumbed to consumption.

Large *harims* were maintained at the court in Persia during the reign of the Safavids in the seventeenth century and the Khadjars in the nineteenth century. Europeans who traveled to Persia in the seventeenth century noted there were as many as 3,000 eunuchs in the service of the court, an indication of how great were the *harims*. As in Constantinople, the rich imitated their rulers and maintained large *harims* complete with servants, eunuchs, and ordinary slaves.

It was under the pace-setting sultans of Constantinople that the *harim* took on full regal dimensions with all the attendant pomp, ceremony, and intrigue. The *harim* of the seraglio numbered hundreds of concubines who were classified along strict hierarchical rank. These women were ruled over by the sultan's mother through a female superintendent and a large corps of subordinates. Although the *harim* declined in importance after slavery began to die out in Turkey, it persisted into the early twentieth century. On the eve of the overthrow of Abdul-Hamid in 1908 by the reform-minded young Turks, his *harim* contained 370 women and 127 eunuchs.

Wherever Islam spread, the *harim* went along with it. Thus, with the extension of the religion to North and West Africa, the practice of keeping large numbers of slave girls became common. Ibn Battuta observed that the inhabitants of Takedda, a town in West Africa, who frequently visited Egypt and brought back with them some of its finest fabrics and wares, vied "with one another in regard to their number of slaves and serving women. The people of Mali and Walata do the same. They never sell the educated female slaves, or but rarely and at a high price. . . ."¹⁰ Among the twelve "innovations" introduced into the Hausa states in the late fifteenth century by the Bornu ruler, Muhammad Rimfa (1465–99), was the acquisition of a *harim* of a thousand concubines and the appointment of eunuchs to important administrative posts. More common among Muslim rulers was the *harim* of a few hundred young girls. The first minister who ruled in Bornu in the early nineteenth century kept a *harim* that numbered three to four hundred women.

Concubinage and the *harim* made women into a focal point of the Muslim slave trade. Their different uses as domestic, mistress, and sex object assured a continuous demand for young female slaves. In these multiple roles they strengthened the patriarchal family, which is at the basis of Muslim society. The merger of this form of slavery into the structure of family life helped make slavery into a formidable institution in the Islamic world and says much about why it became so difficult to do away with it.

5.

It is scarcely possible to conjure up an image of a *harim* without the eunuch, who was at once a cause of bewilderment and revulsion in the Western world. Muslims, to be sure, were not the first or only people to make use of desexed males. The custom is known to have existed in ancient Persia and China and flourished in the time of the Greeks and Romans. When the Turks first began to seclude their women in *harims*, the Byzantines provided them with eunuchs. Befitting their position of keeper of the master's women, eunuchs were rarely referred to as castrates but by the neutral term of "servant" *(khadim)* or "master" in the sense of teacher. In the early centuries of Islam, the Slavic regions of Europe were the chief source of eunuchs, who were transported as far south as

Spain and re-exported to various parts of the Muslim world. After a while, blacks were better able to recover from the operation, which claimed the lives of many of the white boys who were forced to submit to it.[11]

The need to procure eunuchs outside Muslim lands sprang from the requirements of Islamic law. This very law which forbade Muslims from reducing a coreligionist to slavery understandably barred them from making him into a eunuch. In non-Muslim countries where eunuchs were used, local children were taken for this purpose, whereas in Muslim lands they had to be brought from abroad. The difference between the eunuch population of China, for example, and Turkey and other Muslim countries lay in the all-too visible fact that the desexed boys in China were Chinese while they were anything but Turks in Turkey or Egyptians in Egypt. Islamic law, in addition, prohibited Muslims from performing the operation; and, as a result, castrating young boys became a task that fell to nonbelievers, to be done in their own country. The unending stream of desexed boys who were walked or transported by boat or caravan from their native lands in Europe and later Africa arrived ready made in Muslim countries.

The traffic in eunuchs in Africa is probably as old as the slave traffic itself. In the tenth century, the Maghreb, which was undergoing a period of great prosperity, was importing slaves along with ivory, ebony, and gold dust from the Sudan. In the east there was an unsatisfied demand for slaves—white, black, and mulatto—together with eunuchs, who were provided from the Maghreb and Constantinople. Early on, Ethiopia became the best-known source for eunuchs, who were well appreciated as servants and door keepers of the mosque in Medina. The early sixteenth traveler, Leo Africanus, mentions a present given by the sultan of Fez which was made up entirely of products of the Sudan. These included fifty men and fifty women slaves along with ten eunuchs and an assortment of other goods. Eunuchs were widely used in Africa, particularly where mass slavery flourished, as in Kano in the sixteenth century. There were also appointed to civil service posts in the palaces of kings, and some served in high posts in the military. Nachtigal found eunuchs occupying important places in the administrative system of Bornu, Bagirini, Wadai, and Darfur. They proved attractive to many African and Arab leaders as they were immune to pressure to found a rival dynasty. This motive was uppermost in the mind of the ruler of Muscat, who, around 1800, fearing that his faction-ridden dependency of Zanzibar might break away, appointed eunuchs as his representatives there, dividing civil and military power between them.

The widespread demand for eunuchs was largely accounted for by the increased number and size of *harims*. The very life style of the seraglio and other royal courts in the Muslim world encouraged this growth. Ministers of the court, provincial governors, and high officials, in a show of allegiance to the sovereign, would frequently offer him a gift of a beautiful young slave. The great man, whether he be the sultan in Constantinople, the khedive in Cairo, or the shah in Teheran, would take the woman for his already well stocked *harim* or bestow her on a court favorite.

Thus, the number of eunuchs, known as *aghas,* in the Turkish sultan's household reflected the growing demand for these desexed males. From 20 to 40 black eunuchs in the sixteenth century, the number grew to 200 by the early seventeenth century and doubled by the nineteenth century, at which time there were 1,500 women in the "interior" and "exterior" compartments of the seraglio. The sultan's mother and his chief wife each had fifty eunuchs, and favorite concubines had their own retinues of them; in addition, there were 30 or 40 white eunuchs who served as the gatekeepers.

Eunuchs are best known in the West for their role in

watching over the *harim*. There was no risk that they could be tempted by a woman, and because they owed allegiance to no one other than their master they could be counted on not to betray his trust. Many young castrates served as guards, messengers, and, not uncommonly, as confidantes to their owners. Many were sent to guard the holy ground of the Khaba in Mecca and the tomb of the Prophet in Medina. Owing to their special position, where they lived in a unique world of neither men nor women, their select role as guardian of the *harim* and their isolation from society often imbued them with an intense asceticism and religious zeal. The loss of their manhood seemed to drain away a capacity for human warmth.

As a consequence of the trust and power that many eunuchs acquired, a few were able to rise to positions of considerable authority in the administrative and diplomatic ranks and a few distinguished themselves as military leaders. When Moroccan Sultan Agmad al-Mansur dispatched an army into the Sudan at the end of the sixteenth century to wrest from the Songhay the source of their gold, which was flowing with great abundance into the Maghreb, he appointed a young Andalusian eunuch, Judar, as commander of this force.[12] Not a few eunuchs who served as *harim* guards or held trusted positions were themselves owners of slaves.

Demand generated its own supply. Slave merchants stood ready to buy eunuchs, who could be sold anywhere from twice to ten times the price of ordinary black boys. Constantly rising demand and a relatively inelastic supply placed a premium on the price of eunuchs throughout the Muslim world. Shortly before the turn of the century in Persia, where the use of eunuchs had never quite gained the acceptibility it had in Turkey, upper-class homes payed anywhere from four to six times more for these luxury slaves than for the ordinary variety. Thus, while the price of slaves ranged from £16 to £18 for black females to £24 to £28 for Abyssinians, eunuchs fetched as much as £114 each. Louis Frank, a doctor in Napoleon's army of the Nile, observed that the price was double that of an ordinary black slave.[13] These high prices were due to the scarcity of eunuchs owing to the high mortality rate of the young boys who fell victims to the greed of the slave merchants. In Egypt, where eunuchs were kept by the ruling family of Muhammed Ali and rich Turks, they brought a high price in the slave markets of Cairo and Alexandria. To meet this demand, about one hundred to two hundred boys between the ages of eight and ten were castrated each year in the early nineteenth century at Abotig on the caravan route from the Sudan to Egypt. Among the most skilled of these operators were Coptic priests.

Under the primitive conditions in which castration took place and owing to the unskilled surgery, only a small percentage of the victims survived the operation. A. B. Wylde, who observed the slave trade in the eastern Sudan during the 1880s wrote about a survival rate of one in two hundred. These figures cited by Wylde, who was active in abolitionist circles in England, were undoubtedly gross exaggerated. Mortality among the boys operated on by the Coptic priests in upper Egypt, according to Burckhardt, was two in sixty. The market value of mutilated children, who were between the ages of eight and twelve, rose threefold. "This enormous profit," Burckhardt sardonically noted, "stifles every sentiment of mercy which the traders might otherwise entertain."[14] Low mortality rates were also reported in Mossi and Bornu, both of which enjoyed an international reputation in the eunuch trade.[15] The Mossi, who inhabited the region that is modern-day upper Bourkina Faso, and the Bornuese were known for their skill in desexing males.[16] Apart from catering to local demand, they maintained a large export trade with Turkey, Egypt, and the countries of the Maghreb.

It is more than likely, however, that these survival rates proved the exception rather than the rule. A survival rate of one in ten, which Barth[17] had observed during his travels in Africa, probably came closest to the actual figures. Even allowing for such a rate, the number of young boys who fell victim to this barbaric practice over the centuries was undoubtedly of a high order. Usually, the operation, when performed on blacks, involved complete amputation of the scrotum and penis or as the expression went "level with the abdomen."[18] By contrast, far more consideration was given in operating on white children. The latter often retained the ability to perform coitus and not a few even took wives and concubines.

The rising demand for eunuchs in the nineteenth century caused small manufactories where the operation took place to spring up along the slave trade routes. Slaves were obtained in the upper reaches of the White Nile, chiefly Kordofan, Darfur and Dongola, as well as Lake Chad. Others were taken from various regions of Abyssinia, where they proceeded to the Red Sea ports of Massawa and Suakin to begin the weary journey to the main slave emporiums in the Middle East, notably Jeddah, Medina, Constantinople, and Beirut. The White Nile blacks were transported by one of two established routes. Batches of them would be crammed into small boats which would take them up the Nile to Alexandria; others would be made to cross the Sahara, partly on foot, partly by camel, until they reached the coast at Tripoli, Tunis, or Morocco.

The transport of slaves across the entire length of these routes, which was hazardous even for healthy slaves, posed unacceptably high risks to the ailing eunuchs who would be just recovering from the horrors of their operations. Special rest places had to be established en route to the slave markets. Along the Nile, these were at Gondokoro and Khartoum, and at such places as Kebabo and Marzuk in the Fezzan region on the Sahara route. It was during the layovers at these and other designated places that the black boys were castrated.

Later on, after Egyptian authorities proscribed these "road-side" operations, eunuchs were imported "ready made" from Kordofan and Darfur.

To most Muslims, making a black child into a eunuch raised no more of a problem than enslaving a young girl for a life in a *harim*. If there were misgivings, these were easily put out of mind by the people who were long accustomed to the sight of eunuchs. Those who served in the seraglio or in the courts of other Muslim rules in Egypt, Persia, Tunisia, and Morocco commanded a degree of respect among ordinary people. His station in life, it was always felt, had to be far superior to anything he might have known in Africa. The pain suffered by a child in losing his virility was, at least in Muslim eyes, more than offset by the benefits he gained in this servile state. Some Muslims might well have argued that their eunuchs were no worse off than the gelded soprani of the Sistine chapel, "the musical glory and the moral shame" of the papal choirs. Eunuchs themselves did not constitute an aggrieved group because, by the time they grew up, they could remember no other way of life. A great many even had no recollection of the operation. This point was made to the French medical officer, Dr. Louis Frank, who took a personal interest in the well being of the black slaves in Egypt while serving there with Napoleon's Army of the Nile. In his memoir on this sensitive subject, Frank wrote: "I often talked with eunuchs in Cairo, but none of them were willing to give me reliable information about the operation that they had undergone; they always evaded the question and tried to convince me that they could not remember it at all."[19]

To Westerners, on the other hand, eunuchs evoked a sense of wonder and revulsion. They appeared as strangely oriental figures with their pointed turbans and flowing robes of striped silk, fussily acting out their roles as guardians of the seraglio. In another, and more fundamental, sense, Western-ers saw in the eunuch all the hideous aspects of the Muslim slave trade, made all the more abhorrent because the fate of a eunuch was reserved only for a non-Muslim boy.

Slavery in the Islamic world was not always exclusively linked to blacks. In the early centuries of Islam, large numbers of whites in the Balkans and Asia became victims of the slave traffic or were captured in *razzias*. Unlike religion, race was never a limiting factor for enslaving people. Circassian concubines and white slave soldiers from Slavic countries were conspicuous in Egypt and Turkey until the last decades of the nineteenth century. As white slaves became scarcer, however, they become a luxury in which only the wealthiest could indulge themselves. In time, the multiracial character of slavery in the Arab world virtually ceased to exist and became almost exclusively black. In this respect, it differed little from slavery in the New World.

The association in the Arab mind of black people with slavery can be seen in the language itself. By medieval times, white slaves were known as *mamluks*, an Arabic word meaning "owned," while the term *'abd* was reserved for black slaves. In time, the word *'abd* lost its exclusive meaning and came to mean a black person regardless whether he was slave or free. This semantic evolution of the word *'abd* from a social to ethnic designation undoubtedly derived from the popular image of the black person in Arab history as a slave. This is the opposite course taken by the English word "slave," which started out laden with ethnic meaning and ultimately became a social term.[20]

As long as slavery maintained a multiracial cast, Arab and Turkish slave owner favored white slaves over blacks in so far as work assignments and what might be called career prospects were concerned. White slave girls were preferred as concubines over black girls; and among the latter, the fairer-complexioned Abyssinians were shown partiality over their darker-skinned African sisters. This order of racial preference is captured in a number of paintings of the *harim* by an assortment of Western artists who portray the white slave woman as the central figure in the secluded quarter. *L'odalisque et l'esclave* by the nineteenth century French painter Jean-Auguste-Dominique Ingres, heavy in erotic overtones, shows a reclining nude white odalisque being attended by a slightly dark-complexioned slave woman who is playing a string instrument—and nearby in the background stands a watchful black eunuch. Racial considerations also figured importantly in the distribution of assignments in the Arab-maintained slave armies. The better and more prestigious posts in the cavalry were set aside for the *mamluks* while the *'abids* were restricted to serving as lowly foot soldiers or performing menial chores. In time, this favoritism disappeared, but only because slavery itself became an overwhelmingly black institution. However, as long as there were enough white slaves on hand, blacks suffered from racial prejudice.

The negative attitudes displayed by Arabs towards blacks were rooted in feelings of racial prejudice and cultural superiority. Although Islam as a religion has been singularly free of racism, the Arabs—like many other peoples—have not been immune to this form of prejudice. Many Arabs were of the view that blacks were racially inferior people, a point of view that found expression in the writings of a number of early Arab writers and scholars. While some Arab scholars wrote about blacks in a compassionate way, a larger number revealed critical, if not outright hostile, feelings.[21] Those who harbored such sentiments toward these people from the South considered blacks to be primitive and ignorant people, untrustworthy, and lacking in the human graces. Some writers dwelt upon the physical features of blacks, complaining of their wooly hair, smelly bodies, ungainly facial features, and lack of self-control. Arab writers also had little good to say of the whites whom they enslaved—Turks, Slavs, and Mongols. For these barbarians of the North, as well as those of the

South (the Buja, Zanj, and other peoples of Africa), who possessed no faith of their own worthy of mention, enslavement and attendant conversion to Islam were a delivery from a low form of existence to a high civilization. Little matter whether these people wished to give up the life they knew and undergo such a radical social transformation.

Interestingly, the Arabs had a much higher regard for the peoples they encountered in the East and West. As sophisticated people whose ships and caravans had traveled far and wide, the Arabs acknowledged gradations of civilization among nonbelievers. In the East lay the ancient civilizations of pagan China and India in which they saw redeeming qualities. And in the West was the Christian world, which represented a rival faith and competing world order. Christians, along with Jews, because of their monotheistic faith which was accorded recognized status in the eyes of Islam, were not to be enslaved. This was not the case for the barbarians of the north and south.

Attributing personal and moral characteristics to different peoples along arbitrary East-West and North-South lines was fairly widespread among Muslim scholars in the early years of Islam. At a time when beliefs were uninformed by genetic and biological sciences, climate was considered to be a decisive element in shaping human behavior. It was the view of many Muslim scholars that the social behavior and physical characteristics of people inhabiting lands of extreme temperatures were adversely affected by these climatic conditions. The ninth century essayist al-Jahiz summed up this view in a sentence: "If the country is cold, they are undercooked in the womb; if the country is hot, they are burnt in the womb." The tenth century writer, Ibn al-Faqih, as a standard for the best formed people, dwelt at great length on this theory: "The people of Iraq have sound minds, commendable passions, balanced natures and high proficiency in every art, together with well-proportioned limbs, well-compounded humors, and a pale brown color which is the most apt and proper colour. They are the ones done to a turn in the womb. They do not come out with something between blond, buff, blanded and leprous coloring, such as the infants dropped from the wombs of the women of the Slavs and others of similar light complexion; nor are they they overdone in the womb until they are burnt, so that the child comes out something between black and murky, malodorous, stinking, wholly-haired, with uneven limbs, deficient mind and depraved passions, such as the Zanj, the Ethiopians, and other blacks who resemble them. The Iraqis are neither half-baked dough not burnt crust, but between the two."[22]

Similar views are to be found in the writings of Muslim scholars living as far apart as Persia and Spain. Sa'id al-Andalusi, a *qadi* who lived in Toledo in the eleventh century, likened Indians, Persians, Chaldeans, Greeks, Romans, Egyptians, Arabs, and Jews to people who cultivated the sciences and contributed to learning. Even the Chinese and Turks, he grants, were not without some distinction in these spheres. On the other hand, he contemptuously dismisses the northern and southern peoples "who are more like beasts than like men." Even the most primitive sedentary people, Sa'id held, were ruled by a king and lived up to a religious law. The only exception to this natural order "are some dwellers in the steppes and inhabitants of the deserts and wilderness, such as the rabble of Bujja, the savages of Ghana, the scum of the Zanj, and their likes."[23] Strikingly, Sa'id held no such view when speaking of the fairer-skinned barbarians of the North.

While these and other writers lumped the barbarians of the North and South together as fit subject for enslavement, they often drew a distinction between them. They spoke more approvingly of the whites and disparagingly of the blacks. The former were often credited with having useful skills and better human qualities and more deserving of a place in the higher ranks of the slave hierarchy. By contrasts, the blacks, with few exceptions, were considered as lacking in these qualities and suitable only for the least rewarding and dirtiest tasks. In comparing the qualities of white and black slaves, the great Arab scholar and man of letters, Ibn Khaldun (1332–1406), wrote:

> The only people who accept slavery are the Negroes (Sudan), owing to their low degree of humanity and their proximity to the animal stage. Other persons who accept the status of slave do so as a means of attaining high rank or power, as is the case with the Mameluke [mamluk] Turks in the East and with those Franks and Galicians who enter the service of the state [in Spain].[24]

The view expressed by Ibn Khaldun on the comparative virtues of black and white slaves reflected a racist attitude that was already widespread in the Arab world. As he would have it, blacks were accepting of slave status on account of human deficiencies while whites proved to be willing recruits to slavery in order to get ahead in life. Here, coming from no less a personage than Ibn Khaldun, was the old canard of blacks being primitive and shiftless people and totally unlike the industrious and career-minded whites.

Racist views expressed by Arab scholars tapped a deep root in public attitudes towards blacks. Indeed, given the widespread existence of slavery in the Arab world over so many centuries, it would have been surprising that such feelings did not exist. In considering cause and effect between racism and slavery, there can be little doubt, as Eric Williams observed in his study of slavery, that: "Slavery was not born of racism, rather racism was the consequence of slavery."[25] Because of the very nature of the unequal relationship between master and slave, the work and behavior of the slave rarely matched the owner's expectations. Slavery did not bring out the best in people, either owner or slave. The slave was often considered an ingrate and not worthy of the benefits bestowed on him. By nature, he was hopelessly lazy and shiftless, devoid of principles, and given to fornication. "Is there anything," asked Egyptian writer al-Abshihi (1388–1446), "more vile than black slaves, of less good and more evil than they? As for the mulatto, if you show kindness to one of them all your life and in every way, he will not be grateful, and it will be as if you had done nothing for him. The better you treat him, the more insolent he will be, the worse you treat him, the more humble and submissive."[26]

Stereotypes of the personal habits and cleanliness of blacks also abounded. They were often depicted as not keeping clean and giving off a foul odor. Ibn Butlan, whose guidebook on slavery offered practical advice to prospective slave owners, described Zanj women in the most derogatory manner. The blacker the women, he wrote, "the uglier their faces and more pointed their teeth. . . . Dancing and rhythm are instinctive and ingrained in them. Since their utterance is uncouth, they are compensated with song and dance. . . . They can endure hard work . . . but there is no pleasure to be got from them, because of the smell of their armpits and the coarseness of their bodies."[27]

Considering the prominent role played by concubines in the lives of Arab men, it should not be surprising that the erotic behavior of blacks was a subject of intense interest. This was reflected in early Arabic poetry and literature, where blacks are depicted as possessed of great sexual prowess and unbridled sexuality. These stereotypes are not limited to males alone. Black women are portrayed as having irresistible sexual appeal and an unquenchable appetite for sex.[28] Al-Jariz, said by some of his biographers to be of African descent, quotes some verses attributed to the eighth century poet Farazdaq, "the great connoisseur of women":

How many a tender daughter of the Zanj
    walks about with a hotly burning oven
        as broad as a drinking bowl.[29]

What is striking about much of these writings is the inclination to depict black women at once physically repulsive and sexually attractive.

That Arabs enslaved blacks on a large scale over the course of many centuries has to say something of how they considered them as a people. Uprooting them from their families and society and transporting them across vast distances of ocean and desert resulted in untold numbers dying and in psychological trauma for many who survived the ordeal. The brutalization of people on so large a scale could only be sustained where the victims were worthy of servile status. Indeed, the Arabs had always considered Africans as specially suited to be their servants.[30] They were hard working, accepting of their station, and, except for rare occasions, not given to rebellion.

# CHAPTER FIVE

# Early Muslim Traffic in Slaves

## 1.

ISLAM, BY SANCTIONING SLAVERY, GAVE TREMENDOUS IM-
petus to its growth and, as a consequence, sparked the development of the slave trade along transcontinental lines.
Initially, the greatest number of slaves were obtained through
military conquest in central Asia, Africa, and eastern Europe.
Islam's intermittent wars of conquest, which continued
through the Middle Ages, produced an almost unending
stream of male and female prisoners, many of whom were
made into slaves. The allure of acquiring slaves became for
many of the faithful as compelling a reason to embark on a
*jihad* as the religious imperative of extending the frontiers of
Islam.

Waging warfare in the quest for slaves was not limited to
land battles; there were also the unending depredations of

marauders at seas. Piracy in the Mediterranean, often indistinguishable from privateering, and augmented by surprise *razzias* against the Christian seaboard, yielded a continuous supply of slaves to the adjacent North African lands "to an extent which varied at different periods but was always considerable."[1] Mediterranean Christendom, stretching from Spain to Byzantium, responded in kind with retaliatory action on land and sea. The captives, often referred to as "Moors" and "Saracens," were put to work in the fields and in homes or in the galleys of ships. Those who did not manage to escape or be ransomed blended into the local population after a gradual process of conversion to Christianity.

The traffic in slaves to Muslim lands was by no means a monopoly of Muslim traders and plunderers. Europeans, especially during the early Middle Ages, had staked out a strong interest in the sale of slaves to Muslim countries. The import of slaves through commercial channels began to compete early on with the forcible methods associated with battlefield conquest and *razzias*. Christian merchants in Venice, much to the indignation of the papacy, carried on in the middle of the eighth century an active trade in slaves with the rapidly expanding Muslim empire, whose growing wealth created a near insatiable demand for this human commodity. At the time, although Venice was under the nominal rule of Byzantium, which prohibited this kind of trade, its enterprising merchants paid no heed. In 847 they even procured slaves in Rome for sale to North Africa, which had become a thriving market for European goods. So flagrant did this traffic in slaves become by the early ninth century that Leo V, the Byzantine emperor, issued a decree forbidding his subjects, and the Venetians in particular, from trading with Egypt and Syria.

At about this time there developed in central and eastern Europe a growing trade in "Slavs" who were sold to Muslim countries. Jewish merchants also took part in the Slav traffic that moved across central and western Europe during the ninth and tenth centuries. Later on, the *mamluks* in Egypt acquired slaves from Slavic countries, usually by means of Genoese and Venetian trading posts in the Crimea. Georgians were also much in demand in the Middle East slave markets. The Seljuk Turks, whose empire in the thirteenth century extended to Syria, Armenia, and Persia, acquired them along with other whites by purchase, kidnapping, and plunder for the purpose of selling them in their far-flung holdings.[2]

Slavs, who were esteemed for their qualities to make good soldiers and servants, were particularly in demand as eunuchs. They were highly prized in Iraq in the ninth century where most white eunuchs, according to al-Jahiz, were Slavs. Another indication of the strong demand for them was the high proportion of Slavs among the eunuchs imported into and re-exported from Muslim Spain during the early Middle Ages.

## 2.

For a better part of the Middle Ages, Europe served as a valuable source of slaves who were prized in the Muslim world as soldiers, concubines, and eunuchs. It would not long compete with Africa in this trade if only because Christian Europe, with few exceptions, rejected the notion that its people could be enslaved, particularly for the despised Muslim world. In the greatest part of black Africa, by contrast, there were few governments or chiefs that could interpose their authority against the merchants who arrived by caravan and ship in quest of slaves. Lamentably, many African chiefs often became middlemen in the trade by rounding up inhabitants of nearby villages and exchanging them for an assortment of manufactured wares. Where such working arrangements were entered into, Christian and Muslim traders had no need to resort to forcible means to acquire slaves but would purchase them from Africans.

Black Africa, or as it was known in Arabic as *bilad-as-Sudan*, "the country of black people," offered a vast hunting ground for the slave traders. It comprised the great belt of savannah that stretches across Africa from the Atlantic to the Red Sea. It was bounded on the north by the Sahara desert and to the south by the tropical forest. The Niger, which flows for most of its course through this vast region, formed the western configuration, offering a natural connecting link for the people who made their lives along this mighty waterway. This is the area that was once identified as the center of such important states as Ghana, Mali, and Gao, which at the zenith of their power were formidable empires.

Raiding for slaves in the *bilad-as-Sudan* can be traced to the fourth millenium when King Seneferu of Egypt penetrated Nubia as far south as the fourth cataract of the Nile, where slaves were captured in the area where the White and Blue Niles cross. Such forays were frequently undertaken by the dynastic families who ruled Egypt down through the centuries. Slaves were also sent north as tribute to the Egyptian rulers.[3] For some six hundred years a famous treaty, known as the *bakt* (Latin *pactium?*), regulated economic and military matters between the Muslim rulers of Egypt and the Christian kings of Nubia. A provision of the *bakt* stipulated that 442 slaves be sent each year to Cairo, to be distributed as follows: 365 were assigned to the public treasury, 40 to the governor of Cairo, 20 for his assistant in Aswan, 5 for the magistrate of the town, and one for each of the 12 notaries. The small number of slaves taken by the Egyptian authorities was undoubtedly a fraction of the annual shipment sent north for private use. There was no provision in the treaty preventing Egyptian slave merchants from sending their caravans to Nubia, where they were free to ply their trade.

Caravans laden with their precious cargoes followed well

traveled routes. Slaves destined for the Egyptian trade, for example, were shipped down the Nile, while those consigned to Arabia and points east took the route that led to Suakin, Assab, and other Red Sea ports, where they were placed on boats for the short trip to Arabia. Traders with connections with North African markets directed their caravans north, marching their slaves across the vast expanse of the Sahara desert.

Until very recently, many Western scholars were of the view that black Africa's technological backwardness stemmed from its lack of contact with the Mediterranean world, an isolation imposed on it by the impenetrability of the desert. In fact, the Sahara was not a barrier to trade but offered well traveled routes that connected the Sudan with the Maghreb. Although the extremes in temperature, lack of water, sandstorms, and periodic insecurity made travel across the desert a hazardous venture, it did not deter the merchants who saw profit to be made from such a journey. Traffic was moving across the desert as early as 1000 B.C., when chariots were drawn from North Africa into the Sudan along clearly defined western and central routes. The first led from Morocco through Zemmour and Adrar to the banks of the Senegal and the Niger, while the other followed a path from Tripoli through Ghadames, Ghat, and Hoggar to Gao in the Niger.[4] By the fifth century B.C. the Carthaginians were trading directly with black Africa, bringing home wild animals, notably monkeys, lions, panthers, and elephants, and precious stones and slaves. Three centuries later, the Saharan trade centered on the Tripoli-Fezzan-Bornu route and contributed much to Carthage's riches. Although traffic on these different routes continued to develop through the centuries, it took on very large dimensions only after the Arabs and Berbers introduced large numbers of dromedary camels into North Africa in the middle of the fourth century A.D.

The development of these routes stimulated considerable

economic activity at their northern and southern termini. Many towns in North Africa, notably Kairouan in Tunisia, Murzuq in the Fezzan, Tahert in the mountains of central Algeria, and Sijilmasa in southern Morocco, began to flourish. Trading cities along the great grasslands region of West Africa began to emerge. What information there is shows that the Soninke inhabitants of Ghana developed this state by the fifth century into a formidable empire and, through vassal states, controlled the lucrative trade in gold and salt. The measure of prosperity of this state in the tenth century was attested to by the Arab writer, Ibn Hawkal. In his eyes, the king of Ghana was "the richest sovereign on earth . . . he possesses great wealth and reserves of gold that have been extracted since early times to the advantage of former kings and his own."

The empire was succeeded in the western Sudan by Mali and Songhay, while more to the east in the Lake Chad region lay Kanem-Bornu, in important respects the greatest of these empires. The state of Kanem owed its prosperity to the trans-Saharan trade. It is not by chance that it was situated at the southern terminus of a major long-distance caravan route that passed through Fezzan and Kawar. Domination of Fezzan made it possible to control the north-south trade (Maghreb/Tripoli-Kanem-Bornu) and the east-west routes (Egypt-Ghana/Mali/Songhay).

Caravans traveling from the western Sudan to the Maghreb were laden with a variety of wares that usually included gold, salt, ivory, and, occasionally, wild animals; slaves were almost always part of the consignment. The late ninth century Arab historian and geographer, Al'Yakubi, observed that Berber traders brought back black slaves, probably from Kanem to Zawila, the capital of the Fezzan.[5] These fair-skinned people, who converted to Islam in the eighth century, were among the most practiced slave traders, maintaining this vocation right into the nineteenth century.[6]

When Al'Yakubi recorded his observations, the Maghreb was on the threshold of a period of great prosperity. Large tracts of land that had fallen into disuse were again made productive because of the introduction of an elaborate system of irrigation. The manufacture of cotton, woolen cloth, and silk were revived, bringing renewed prosperity to Tripoli, Sfax, Tunis, and Gabes. What probably was the most profitable part of the Maghreb's thriving economy was the trade it carried on with the Sudan for the importation of slaves, ivory, ebony, and gold dust. Ibn Hawkal provides a clear description of the country in the tenth century when he tells us that "the Maghreb is chiefly remarkable for black slaves . . . (the white slaves come from a quarter of Andalus) . . . and coral, and ambergis, and gold, and honey, and silk, and seal-skins." Great numbers of these slaves were shipped to the eastern Islamic world to meet the enormous demand for Christian, black, and mulatto slaves and for eunuchs. Most of the slaves from the Sudan passed through Kairouan, the richest city in the Maghreb.[7]

The prosperity that enveloped the Maghreb in the tenth and part of the eleventh century was also in evidence in a new state that emerged in its eastern section, in an area that includes modern Tunisia and part of Algeria. The importance of this state, which is known in early Arabic as Ifriqiya, can be better appreciated by recalling that it was used as a base by the Fatimids in their conquest of Egypt in 969. Like other governments in the Maghreb, the court in Ifriqiya depended on the trans-Sahara trade as an important source of its wealth. The state reached the height of its prosperity in 1050, after which time it rapidly declined, falling victim to the Arab Hillali invaders.

Gold and slaves were the two main imports into Ifriqiya; a part of these slaves were the *'abid sudan,* slave soldiers who came from the Sudan via Zawila in the Fezzan.[8] It is possible that these *'abid* represented the beginning of the corps of

Sudanese soldiers that lasted until the demise of the state in 1050. While some were undoubtedly part of the Sultan's personal guard and would have been mounted, the bulk of them served as foot soldiers.

Most of the slaves that came up from Zawila were intended for military purposes but were used for household tasks or exported. Ibn Hawkal reports of the shipment to the east of *khadam,* a general Arabic term meaning servants or slaves; those who were re-exported usually received some form of training to prepare them for their new life. The majority, however, stayed in Ifriqiya and were absorbed in the economy. Ibn Hawkal supplies the interesting information that parts of Cape Bon in Tunisia that proved unhealthy for strangers posed no difficulties for black slaves, who readily adapted to the environment and worked with good cheer. This might suggest that these slaves were used as squatters and laborers for the colonization of marginal lands.

An important source of information on the trans-Saharan trade comes from Leo Africanus, who was born in Granada in 1495 of Moorish parents. In his book, the *History and Description of Africa,*[9] which is based on his extensive travels through Africa, Africanus supplies some information of the extraordinary trade that was being carried on between the Barbary Coast and the Sudan. Increased security in the desert tempted many merchants to venture the trip to the Sudan. They took with them European cloth, sugar grown in Sus in southern Morocco, clothing, brass vessels, books, and, most importantly, horses. In exchange, they brought back gold, civet, and slaves. The merchants who traveled to Bornu, according to Leo Africanus, often had to wait a whole year before the king rounded up a sufficient number of slaves. What this suggests is that the king's raids against the pagan people living to the south of his kingdom did not yield enough slaves to meet the demand of the North Africans. Ironically, when Kanem-Bornu fell on hard times, its inhabitants were also sold into slavery by external enemies despite the fact that most of them had been Muslims since the thirteenth century.

In Bornu, Africanus found that the sultan would exchange only slaves for horses despite an abundance of gold. Slaves were in plentiful supply owing to the sultan's frequent slave raiding against his neighbors. One horse brought the Arab merchants anywhere from fifteen to twenty slaves. Initially, the Barbary merchants were averse to accepting payment in human currency, preferring gold, which explains why they were first drawn to the Sudan. It was not long before they came only for slaves and would accept no other form of payment.

The large number of slaves that flowed to the Maghreb made them useful as gifts for royalty, to be given to loyal followers and deserving subjects. Leo Africanus mentions a present given by the sultan of Fez to a local chief which included slaves and products of the Sudan. The following are the details of this expensive gift, which Africanus happily took the trouble to record:

> Fiftie men slaues, and fiftie women slaues brought out of the land of the Negros, tenne enuches, twelue camels, one Giraffa, sixteen ciuet-cats, one pound of ciuet, a pound of amber [ambergris] and almost six hundreth skins of a certaine beast called by them Elamt [Addax gazelle], whereof they make their shieldes, eurie skin being woorth at Fez, eight ducates; twentie of the men slaues cost twentie ducates a peece, and so did fifteene of the women slaues; euery eunch was valued at fortie, eury camell at fifties, and eury ciuet-cat at two hundreth ducates: and a pound of ciuet and amber is solde at Fez for threescore ducates.[10]

The narrative is interesting because it provides a good idea of the relative value of slaves and suggests the extent to which blacks were enslaved to meet the growing demand of the northern market.

From early on in recorded history until the last slave caravan crossed the dessert to Libya in 1929, the trans-Saharan connection served as a major network for funneling slaves into the Maghreb from the Sudan. Until the nineteenth century, when reliable figures on this trade became available, it is possible only to conjecture about the actual numbers brought north on the different routes that made up this trading network. A slight indication of the volume may be gleaned from the writings of contemporary observers. When Ibn Battuta set off from Takedda to Tuat, he observed that the caravan he was traveling with carried six hundred women slaves. The story is of interest if only because it reveals the carrying capacity of a single caravan, which Ibn Battuta did not think to be unusual; more significantly, it suggests that based on such a load factor the actual number of slaves transported to the Maghreb in the course of a year may have run into a few or more thousand if one assumes that numerous caravans, big and small, were moving back and forth across the desert. There was a constant demand for slaves in the Maghreb for export to the eastern Arab countries and to Constantinople and for the local market. With the growth of prosperity, slaves were in demand as domestics and concubines by the Arab-Berber aristocracy and the many prosperous merchants, and as soldiers for the sultans in Morocco and Tunisia. The trans-Saharan trade in slaves as well as gold had become the lifeblood for the numerous Barbary ports and a source of wealth for the merchant class, who looked upon the Sudan as an Eldorado.

The ebb and flow of traffic, to be sure, was affected by general economic trends in the north and, more importantly, by political conditions in the Sudan and security along the routes. Nowhere was this more dramatically in evidence than along the western route. The anarchy that prevailed following the overthrow of the Songhay empire in the early 1590s by the armies of El Mansur and the failure of the Moroccans to follow up their victory by establishing effective administrative control over their newly acquired domain brought about an end to this important route. The insecurity let loose by the Moroccan conquest had the effect of "kill[ing] the goose that more less literally laid the golden eggs."[11]

Over the centuries, as shall be seen later on, other routes were disrupted by political instability in the Sudan or in the Maghreb. Traffic on the Tripoli-Fezzan-Bornu route, which became the most important trading thoroughfare in the Sahara following the destruction of the Songhay empire until the 1820s, came to a virtual halt as a result of the Tchadian wars in the late 1830s and the takeover of Tripoli and the Fezzan by the army of the Turkish sultan. Part of this traffic was taken up by the Wadai-Benghazi and Sudan routes, suggesting that the closing down of a profitable route did not necessarily imply the stoppage of trade but simply its displacement along more secure avenues. To the extent that these developments occurred, they were bound to put a temporary crimp in the caravan trade and, as a result, cause the traffic in slaves to fall off.

The historical evidence demonstrates that certain of these routes remained commercially active down through the last century and even into the first quarter of the present one.[12] So large did the traffic in slaves bulk in the trans-Saharan trade during the nineteenth century that at times it was not very far behind the more formidable East Coast slave trade. In 1858 the British consul-general in Tripoli reported that the slave trade accounted for "more than two-thirds of the value of all the caravan trade." The number of slaves annually shipped to the Maghreb at about that time was, according to consular reports and explorers' accounts, estimated at about 9,500.[13] This was roughly half the amount being sent to the East African coast at the time and about 13 percent of the total involved in the transatlantic slave trade.

**3.**

Important as the trans-Saharan trade figured in the slave trade, it was greatly overshadowed by the traffic in slaves that centered on Africa's East Coast. The earliest surviving description of the coast is contained in a guidebook known as the *Periplus* (circumvention or sailing around) *of the Erythraen Sea,* as the Greeks and Romans called the Indian Ocean. Written by an anonymous Greek sailor about A.D. 110, the *Periplus,* in the manner of such guides, describes the voyage through the Red Sea and down the East Coast, enumerating landmarks, harbors, and coastal towns, notably those where the possibilities for trade were favorable. This would appear to establish the existence of trading stations along the coast starting from Opone, now Ras Hafun, as far south as modern Tanzania, although the town of Rhapta, which delimits the farthest bounds known to the author, has yet to be located.

The *Periplus* offers brief glimpses of the local population and products available for trade. The inhabitants are described as belonging to the Negroid race, being "men of practical habits, very great in stature," and living under a tribal system where there were "separate chiefs for each place." Somewhere near present-day Mocha, Arabs came and settled, intermarrying with the natives and staking out a major role in trade. These merchants purchased from visiting Arab ships a variety of manufactured goods, primarily "the lances, made especially for them at Mouze, hatchets, swords, awls, and many kinds of small glass vessels, and at the same places wine and not a little wheat, not for trade, but to serve for getting the good-will of the savages." In exchange, they sold great quantities of ivory, tortoiseshell, palm oil, and rhinoceros horn, which, when ground into powder, was used as an aphrodisiac. What was available for trade apparently did not differ much from town to town.

The nature of the trade, which in essence constituted an

exchange between East Africa's raw material and human resources for the manufactured goods of the northern lands, indicates a low level in socioeconomic and technological development. This exchange was very much in keeping with today's pattern of trade of the developing countries of East Africa which still involves the sale of raw materials for the manufactured goods of Western countries.

Out of Opone came another form of trade which would be a curse on Africa for centuries to come. This was the traffic in slaves. The coast near Opone, the author of the *Periplus* informs us, produces "slaves of the better sort which are brought to Egypt in increasing numbers." In subsequent centuries, the trade may have extended farther down the coast and reached into the Comoro Islands. In any event, there are reports of Zanji slaves reaching China as early as the seventh century A.D.[14]

Between the time we are familiar with in the *Periplus* and the turning point marked by the tenth century, there are no source materials about the East Coast, which the Greeks referred to as *Azania* and the Arabs as *Sawahil*. There is strong evidence that a regular trade in slaves and other commodities had been going on between Persian-ruled Mesopotamia and the coast. The Sassanian kings who ruled in Mesopotamia, modern-day Iraq, had made Persia into a formidable sea power which reached as far as the western half of the Indian Ocean. The destruction of the Sassanian military power by invading Arab armies at the battle of Nehavend in 642 brought an end to the empire and to the collapse of Persia, which was incorporated into the rapidly expanding Arab-Muslim empire.

During the heyday of Sassanian maritime power, Persian ships appeared to have traveled regularly to the East Coast. Their interest lay in securing ivory, tortoiseshells, and slaves. Slaves were acquired by the late Sassanian kings apparently to serve as a praetorian guard. This was the period of the

Abbasid caliphates in Baghdad, who, as part of their ambitious goal of reviving their empire, decided to desalinate the marshlands of southern Iraq for the cultivation of sugar cane. For this large development project, large numbers of slaves were needed, most of whom were brought from East Africa. The back-breaking labor caused great unrest among the slaves, who were said to have revolted for the first time around 696. An insurrection of far greater proportions took place in 869 when the Persian adventurer, Al-Kabith, called on the slaves to fight for their freedom. Thousands responded to his call; and in the year 871 he led them in the capture and sacking of Basra. The swath of death and destruction he left had so terrorized the population that, when the tenth century geographer Al-Masudi visited the country forty years later, he was told that "the chief of the black slaves" had caused the death by famine or the sword of at least a million people.[15] The revolts were ultimately suppressed, but by their resistance the slaves managed to bring to an end one of the few cases of mass rural exploitation based on slave labor in Muslim history.

Who were these slaves and where did they come from? Some information to these questions can be gleaned from the *Geography* of Ptolemy, apparently written in the second century, to which additions and emendations were made by geographers in fifth century Alexandria. Ptolemy refers to "man-eating Ethiopians" who lived to the south of Rhapta. These were probably people of Bantu Negroid origin. These people, who probably pressed north over the succeeding centuries, lived along the coastal region stretching from Sofala in present-day Mozambique, to the north of Mogadishu in Somalia. This is what roughly corresponds to the land of the Zanj of Arab geographers. There can be little doubt that the slaves who were shipped to Mesopotamia, Persia, and as far off as India and China during the period from about the ninth to the fourteenth century came from the land of the Zanj.

Much of what is known about the Zanj coast and about its inhabitants has been reconstructed from the accounts of Arab geographers.[16] This period of Abbasid rule in Baghdad witnessed the flowering of Arab learning, whose origins can be traced to the Hellenistic culture which the Arabs inherited from the late Roman empire. Greek literature, which was translated into Eastern languages by the Oriental Christian churches, had a profound effect on the intellectual outlook of Arab writers. To no subject did they make a greater contribution during this period than to geography. Ptolemy's geographic treatise, which appeared in the second century and was translated into Arabic in the sixth century, was one such work whose influence was widely felt among Arab travelers and geographers.

That Arabs evinced a keen interest in geography should not be surprising. This was a period of growing travel and increasing commercial activity. The spread of Islam under the driving force of the Ummayad rulers (634 to 750) created a vast Muslim community. This community was fast becoming conscious of history in general and of its own history in particular and its place in the world. It was only natural to learn about this emerging society, chart its place in the universe, and describe the people who inhabited these various lands. The Muslim traveler, moreover, could expect great hospitality even in the most isolated communities of the faithful located in infidel lands. The celebrated fourteenth-century traveler, Ibn Battuta, whose extensive travels brought him to virtually every then-known part of the Muslim world, experienced a friendly reception from the Muslim inhabitants of Mogadishu.

A further incentive to travel and study geography was the *hadj,* or pilgrimage to Mecca, a religious obligation for all believers who had the means and strength to perform it. Countless caravans of pilgrims annually set out for the holy city from all parts of the Muslim and non-Muslim world. There these strangers met on a common ground where they were able to exchange ideas and information about each others' lands and customs.

The accounts of the Arab geographers of the East Coast for this period are discursive and, with few exceptions, do not concentrate on the countries or peoples in the area. To some extent, the information is based on personal observation; more commonly, it is derived from older accounts of other travelers from towns along the coast and the adjacent islands. Mogadishu, Kilwa, Pate, Lamu, Malindi, Mombasa, Brava, and Sofala are among the better known of these towns. By the fifteenth century, there were thirty-seven urban settlements, all of which had their own mosques, decorated sometimes with exquisite Persian art. According to archaelogical evidence, many of the towns were laid out in regular streets, and the houses constructed by the Arabs were made of stone and mortar, with large windows and terraces, doors and frames of wood, and spacious courts and gardens.

There is no conclusive evidence that Arabs or Persians were largely responsible for the founding of these towns. It would appear that urban life evolved among the Bantu-speaking Negroid population who inhabited the region long before the arrival of foreign settlers. The latter, made up mainly of Arabs but including Persians and Indians as well, developed trading posts and gradually settled in the towns, enriching them through trade and architecture and by propagating Islam. Through the establishment of trading posts, the Arabs came into daily contact with the Negroid population. Over a period of time, there was a fusion of peoples, culture, and language, with the foreign settlers intermarrying with the local population and speaking their language.[19] Arab influence, however, appeared to have a most formidable impact on Swahili culture. Although Arabic was the official language in these coastal towns, it mixed with the local Bantu speech, out of which emerged Swahili. This language, rich in tradition and imagery, is today the *lingua franca* in an area that covers a large part of East Africa.

Of special importance were the relations that developed between the Arab settlers and the Negro population. Evidence of such ties, which is scant, is derived from Muslim or Arab sources; what they do reveal, however, is that the Arabs occupied a dominant position. Taking note of this relationship, one Arab writer of the tenth century, Abou Ziad-Hassan, observed that the Zanj people were given to fighting "but the Arabs exercise a great ascendancy over them. Whence man of this nation sees an Arab, he prostrates himself before him."[20] A similar observation was penned by El-Idrisi, whose interests were not confined to the East Coast alone but extended to the West African countries of Ghana, Tekrur, and Kuku (Gao). "The Zanj," he wrote, "are in great fear and awe of the Arabs, so much so that when they see an Arab trader or traveler they bow down before him and treat him with great respect, and say in their language: 'Greetings O people from the land of the dates!' Those who travel to this country steal the children of the Zanj with dates, lure them with dates and lead them from place to place, until they seize them, take them out of the country, and transport them to their own countries. The Zanj people have great numbers but little gear. The ruler of the island of Kish in the sea of 'Uman raids the Zanj with his ships and takes many captives."

These slave-trading and raiding proclivities of the Arabs did not prevent them, as was previously noted, from forging close bonds with the Zanj people. Actually, their slave-trading activities may have had the support of local chiefs who connived with the Arabs in the capture and sale of their fellow blacks. As traders, the Arabs had an interesting number of manufactured artifacts to offer in exchange for slaves as well as gold and ivory. The willingness of blacks to cooperate with the Arabs in such an exchange was born out by Al 'Yakubi, who compiled a useful record of Nubia, the adjoining Beja people, and the kingdom of Kanem situated on Lake Chad. He also describes the kingdoms of Ghana and Kuku, which at that time were the two states in the western Sudan. In one particularly revealing passage, he observed: "They [the Arabs] export black slaves . . . belonging to the tribes of Mira, Zaghawa, Maruwa and other black races who are near to them and whom they capture. I hear that the black kings sell blacks, without pretext and without war. . . ."[21] Ibn Battuta, who visited farther down the coast in Kilwa in the fourteenth century, wrote that its sultan carried out frequent raids in search of slaves. His efforts were evidently crowned with success as he lavished them on passing guests as gifts.

The practice described by Al 'Yakubi was not, as shall be observed on numerous occasions later on, restricted to any particular part of Africa where Arab traders ventured or limited to any definite time period. In considerable measure, the primary acquisition of slaves was carried out by local chiefs and merchants who then exchanged their captives for products that these traders brought with them. El-Idrisi also took note of the practice among blacks to carry out raids against neighboring villages for the purpose of making off with captives who would then be sold as slaves. "The people of Lemlem," he observed, "are perpetually being invaded by their neighbours, who take them as slaves . . . and carry them off to their own lands to sell them by the dozens to the merchants. Every year great numbers of them are sent off to the Western Maghreb." After being marched across the Saharan desert, these primitive forest tribesmen from Ghana were then sold in the slave marts of Wargla and other towns in this part of the Maghreb.

# 4.

Trade, to the virtual exclusion of all other activities, was the vocation of the Arabs living on the East Coast.[22] This was the sole purpose for their contacts with the upland tribes. No attempt was made to subjugate the local population as was done centuries later by the Portuguese, French, English, Dutch, and the other European colonizers who lorded it over the black population. To the extent that Arabs took up arms at this time it was for keeping open trading routes or preventing interference with their activities—not for the sake of conquest or dominion. Seashore merchants, they revealed no curiosity in exploring the interior. This they began to do by the early decades of the nineteenth century when the mushrooming demand for slaves and ivory impelled them to push into the interior. As early settlers at the turn of the new millenium, the Arabs were interested in markets across the sea in Arabia, the Persian Gulf, and as far east as India than in the dark continent to their back.

A look at the map will readily explain why the earliest traders, as well as invaders, came from this part of the world. It is probable that the Hindus were trading with East Africa and settling on the coast as early as the sixth century B.C. The straight course over the Indian Ocean from Mombasa to Bombay is 2,500 miles, about the length of the Mediterranean. And from Zanzibar to Aden the distance is 1,700 miles and about 2,200 miles to Oman. By contrast, the route between Europe and the coast before the Suez Canal was cut was 8,000 miles. These distances between the coast and the East would have been exceedingly difficult to traverse were it not for the monsoon winds.[23] The northeast monsoon, which blows at its strongest from December to March, carried ships as far south as Madagascar to the Malibar coast, while the southwest monsoon brought sailing vessels from

India to the East African coast between from about June to September. These alternating winds, which were discovered by the Greek navigator Hippalus, were chiefly responsible for bringing East Africa into the trading orbit of the Persian Gulf and India. Early on, Arab merchants and sailors learned about the monsoon (Arabic: *mauwism*, meaning market or holiday), realizing that their dhows could be blown south to East Africa by this wind in December and after a few months, during which time they could conduct trade, driven back with the wind's change in direction. Until the coming of steam, the monsoon was responsible for the development of Africa's East Coast ports and their sharing in the changing patterns of the Indian Ocean trade.

East Coast trade with markets in Arabia and Persia and also with India and China increased in scope from the tenth to the fourteenth centuries. Masudi referred to increasing demand for ivory, whose softness made it perfect for medieval carvings. Export of rhinoceros horn and tortoiseshell as well as copper ingots from Katanga were also part of the expanding and increasingly diverse trade. Another such staple was gold. Kilwa, one of the most important of the coastal towns, owed much of its growth to its starting in the late twelfth century of the trade route that brought Zimbabwe gold north from Sofala, not far from Beira in what is now Mozambique. Throughout the twelfth century, western Europe became an increasingly important market for this precious metal. The gold for the first coins struck in London's mint during the reign of Henry III came from Africa.

Yet another important staple for which there was a strong foreign demand was slaves. The primary markets were located in Arabia and the Persian Gulf. The Arab *Kitab al-Ajaib al-Hind*, written during the middle of the tenth century, noted that 200 slaves were exported annually from East Africa to Oman. It appeared that most of these came from the northern part of the Horn of Africa. Not for nothing did the

Arabs call the northern Somali coast *Ras Assir* (the cape of slaves).[24] The *Kitab al-Ajaib al-Hind,* one of the earliest documents of this period of Islam, stated that visitors to East Africa from Oman preyed on its inhabitants, in words that rang familiar to those of El-Idrisi, by ". . . stealing their children and enticing them away by offering them fruits. They carry the children from place to place and finally take possession of them and carry them off to their own country."[25]

By the beginning of the fifteenth century, the East Coast had achieved a modest degree of urban growth. Along the coastal strip between the Kilwa group of islands and Mogadishu, some thirty-seven towns managed to develop and maintain a degree of prosperity and urbanity. Because they were more conscious of their differences than what they shared in common, they were never able to unite into a single confederation or state. Several of these towns, notably Kilwa and Mogadishu and to a lesser extent, Mombasa, prospered. Islam, which managed to take hold on the coast in the thirteenth century, was the religion that people of these towns professed. When Ibn Battuta came to the coast in 1331, he chose to visit Kilwa and Mogadishu. He could not help observe the piety of its inhabitants.

No less significant, Ibn Battuta was made aware of the large number of slaves that made up their populations. The sultan of Kilwa, he noted, carried out frequent raids in search of slaves. So plentiful were they that he presented twenty of them as a gift to an indigent *fakir* from Yemen. Both Kilwa and Mogadishu, in fact, owed part of their prosperity to the slaving activities carried on by their sultans. Mombasa, too, attained a high level of material progress because its hinterland was a catchment area for slaves and ivory. Arab-owned ships from the Red Sea took on slaves at the Comoro Islands from Muslim traders. The islands, which benefited from these activities, had become in the fifteenth century, in the words of one writer, "slave-trade centres and stores of human flesh between Africa and Arabia."[26]

Under the impact of expanding trade, the Indian Ocean had, during this period, come under different influences. Traders were regularly moving back and forth between the Far East and the African East Coast to the tempo of the monsoon winds. From the twelfth to the end of the fifteenth century, Muslim traders gained control of the Indian Ocean trade, coming from such diverse places as India, the Persian Gulf, and Arabia. A considerable trade in slaves developed between India and the East Coast. At the very beginning of the thirteenth century an Islamic empire was created in the northwest of India, with its capital in Delhi. Within a century, the Delhi sultans were pushing southwest to the coast and finally conquered the Deccan. In 1334 the Deccan became for a short period the capital of their empire. During this time, Muslim as well as some Hindu merchants reached the African East Coast. These traders were instrumental in bringing ivory from modern-day Tanzania and gold from Zimbabwe and Indonesian spices to Egyptian and Syrian ports. Eastward another pattern of trade had taken hold. New markets had opened in China and India for African ivory, while in Islamic India there was a growing demand for slaves.[27]

Slaves achieved significant prominence in Gujarat and the Deccan areas. Much in demand were the *habshis* or *siddis* from Ethiopia, who served as soldiers and sailors. From 1459 to 1474 King Barbuk of Bengal possessed some 8,000 of these warrior slaves, most of whom were apparently taken from the slave marts of present-day Tanzania.[28] In a manner traditional of these praetorian guards, they were heavy into political intrigue. When King Fath Shah attempted to curb their power, the *habshis* reacted by killing him. Two slave soldiers of African origin briefly ruled over Bengal toward the end of the fifteenth century. Their power soon waned when an

Asian became sovereign and they were forced to take refuge in the Deccan.[29]

The East Coast also fell in the trading orbit of China. As early as the tenth century, Chinese geographers were aware of Po Pa Li, a country located in the western sea peopled by black and ferocious people of Mon Lin. It is believed that Po Pa Li was situated somewhere along the Somali coast and that Mon Lin was Malindi, one of the towns strung out along the coast.[30] Chinese writing of the medieval period referred to Arabs bringing blacks to their countries as slaves, who, if taken to China, would be worth their weight in aromatic wood.[31] In the eighth century, two black women were presented to the emperor, and in the early twelfth century it was noted that affluent people in Canton possessed slaves.

# CHAPTER SIX

# Slavery on the Frontiers of Araby: 1500–1800

## 1.

BY THE TIME VASCO DA GAMA'S FLEET PENETRATED INTO the Indian Ocean in 1498, the slave trade had become a major factor in the economic, political, and social orders in large parts of Africa. Along the East Coast, the highlands of Ethiopia, and the northern savanna that stretched from the headwaters of the Senegal River in the west to Lake Chad in the east, enslavement was a common enough reality which found sanction in custom and in law. In Muslim Africa, there was a great demand for servile labor, not only to serve as household help, concubines, and soldiers, but to work the fields and toil in mines as well. African chiefs and merchants met this growing demand by enslaving great numbers of people by means of violence, guile, and trade. Through these methods they stoked the demand for slaves in foreign markets, notably the Maghreb, Arabia, the Persian Gulf region, and India. Available evidence suggests that within Muslim Africa, a slave mode of production had developed.[1]

Slavery, as originally practiced in most of Africa, was usually benign in character and often indistinguishable from the serfdom that was widespread in medieval Europe. Although not much is known about the internal African slave trade, it appeared to have been limited to transactions carried out on a narrow local scale.[2] Slavery was a way of reintegrating into society people who had been cast adrift from family and community by wars and natural disasters. The structure and organization of African society rarely allowed for isolation or identity outside the family. In its ideal form, the African community is rooted in the family, which provides its members with a sense of well being and order. Those who acquired slaves gave their new charges a new identity and a sense of belonging.

This traditional approach to enslavement broke down in the face of growing demands at home and abroad for servile labor. With the coming of the Europeans, the volume of slave exports swelled to huge numbers, leading to profound dislocations in African society. For many chiefs and traders, the material benefits of participating in the trading opportunities offered by the Europeans proved irresistible. As demand for slaves from these foreigners escalated, it was no longer possible to meet them through localized raiding and trading practices. Raiding for slaves, as a result, was extended beyond neighboring tribes and became a grimmer and more murderous activity. In the cycle of war, devastation, and ensuing famine, community life could barely survive. In periods of famine, chiefs intensified their raiding so as to acquire slaves whom they exchanged for food; families bartered their children for food and protection. In this state of endemic violence, the air was rent with the wails of the victims.

While the mushrooming export of slaves to the New World quickly outdistanced the traffic to North Africa and the Muslim heartland, this centuries-old trade continued to develop apace. Beginning in the latter part of the eighteenth and early nineteenth centuries, it received a fillip from the demand for slaves in the French-owned Mascarene Islands in the Indian Ocean and from the Omani-controlled islands of Zanzibar and Pemba.

The extension of the slave trade to the northern savanna, Ethiopia, and along the East Coast was facilitated by religious and economic factors. The pervasive growth of Islam in the states and cities located in these regions provided a favorable ideological climate for enslavement and the traffic in slaves. What heightened the salience of this factor was that the major foreign markets of these regions for slaves were in North Africa and the Middle East. This made it easier for Muslim merchants who controlled this traffic, not only in Islamized Africa but in Christian Ethiopia, to dispose of their human merchandise in foreign markets. Bound by a commonly shared religion, exporters and importers undoubtedly had fewer difficulties in establishing a relationship of trust and, where difficulties arose, in accepting the jurisdiction of *shari'a* courts.

Thus, by the thirteenth century, by which time Islam was integral to the life of most city-states along the East Coast, the traffic in slaves for domestic use and overseas trade to Arabia, the Persian Gulf, and India was a routine commercial activity. Over the succeeding three centuries, the participation of such Islamic states as Ghana, Songhay, Sennar, and Adal in the slave trade occurred at a time when Islam was making deep inroads into sub-Saharan Africa. In large measure, this came about through the zealous efforts of Arab and Berber traders who traveled by caravan across the Sahara

carrying both the message of the Prophet along with Mediterranean and European wares in exchange for gold and
slaves.[3]

Just as interstate warfare and domestic insurrection have
spawned in the contemporary African scene armies of refugees, similar as well as other forms of violence claimed vast
numbers of slaves in different periods of African history.
Whereas much of the violence in present-day African can be
traced to the conflicting claims of nationalism and tribalism,
the underlying reasons for enslavement in Muslim Africa
could be found in Koranic-based laws legitimizing slavery.
Slave-generating violence ranged in scale from locally inspired *razzias* to full-fledged interstate warfare. To meet the
burgeoning demand for servile labor for local domestic use
and export, attacking hill and forest pagans became a major
dry-weather occupation of Muslim tribes in the western
Sudan. Not uncommonly, raids of this sort were marked by
savagery against the captives. Those who could not be sold
because of age or infirmity or were found to be undesirable
by the conquering tribesmen were often put to death. Very
often, this was done in the name of religion.[4] Over the
centuries, the number of people who were enslaved and
murdered as a result of these individual forays had to run in
the hundreds of thousands, if not millions.

Although the figures can never be known, the toll of those
enslaved in *jihads* or *pseudo-jihads* had to be very great indeed.
Great numbers of people were taken as slaves during the
intermittent religious wars between Muslims and Christians
that ravaged the Nile valley and Ethiopian highlands in the
sixteenth century. A *jihad,* mounted from the Islamic sultanate of Adal from the 1520s to the 1540s, temporarily overran
Ethiopia and resulted in the deportation of thousands of
slaves across the Red Sea into Arabia.[5] Thereafter, it was the
Muslims' turn to be enslaved following a recovery by Ethiopia which checked the Muslim advance.

During Morocco's drawn-out military campaign against Songhay that led to the collapse of this Muslim empire, Moroccans took slaves as their rightful spoils of victory. This time, however, many of the victims were Muslims, whose enslavement is proscribed by Koranic law. It was as a result of this massive violation of the religious law that the famous Islamic scholar from Timbuktu, Ahmed Baba, wrote his treatise on the enslavement of blacks in which he warned that the taking of slaves was admissible only within the context of a holy war and only if the slaves were not Muslims.

That Ahmed Baba saw fit to raise his voice against enslavement of Muslims by fellow coreligionists was a clear indication how widespread the abuse had become. In actual fact, this practice fell within a familiar pattern that could be traced back centuries before Ahmed Baba condemned it and was very much in evidence for centuries afterward. Bornu's Muslim king Uthman ibn Idris, in a letter to the *mamluk* government of Egypt dated 1391–92, protested the action of Arab raiding parties of enslaving free Muslims, even members of the royal family, and "selling them to the slave dealers of Egypt, Syria and elsewhere, and keeping some of them for themselves. . . ."

What evidence there is about the size of the early slave population in Muslim Africa comes mainly from travelers to these regions. For the most part, there is agreement that, despite the dearth of statistics and the difficulty in distinguishing between free people and slaves, the latter comprised a substantial part of the overall population and, in some areas, may have been a majority.[6] This conclusion appears to be valid for the nineteenth century when information on the size of the slave population and its distribution among the population is more reliable. Stories abound of individuals who owned hundreds and in some cases several thousand slaves. What is more certain was that there were a great many small slaveholders. It was not uncommon even for people of limited means to own one or two slaves in Bornu. Owning a few slaves was particularly important in the rural areas where a division of labor was scarcely known and households had to be self-sufficient if they were to survive.

In sub-Saharan Africa, slavery tended to conform to the Islamic model that used slaves in *harims,* the household, the military, and government. Thus, not unlike the use of slaves in the Middle East, many servile laborers in sub-Saharan Africa catered to the consumption and leisure needs of their owners or were employed by local rulers to reinforce the existing social order. This was particularly important in black Africa where retaining an extensive retinue of luxury slaves, numerous concubines, and elaborate courts served as important symbols of power.

In overwhelmingly rural sub-Saharan Africa, however, neither the government nor the people could afford to keep slaves mainly for consumption purposes. Manpower was desperately needed in agriculture and mining. In West Africa, it has to be understood, land was always more abundant than labor and slavery provided an effective means for mobilizing manpower for economic development. Not uncommonly, slaves were settled on large estates and farmed for merchants and officials under conditions that bore some resemblance to plantation life in later America or contemporary European feudal estates. Prior to its destruction, the rulers of the Songhay empire settled large numbers of slaves along the Niger River and succeeded in transforming the Niger valley into a rich agricultural area. The use of such estates in the western Sudan adumbrated the development in Zanzibar three centuries later of a plantation economy for growing cloves.

The rich gold and copper mines of the western Sudan provided yet another source of employment for slave labor. Slaves were known to have worked in subterranean gold mines in Senegal where they and their wives and children spent virtually their entire lives. In Tegehazza, the Saharan town known for its salt works, slaves worked alongside freemen in mining this precious commodity. The mines, as Ibn Battuta informs us, supplied salt for much of the populace of the western Sudan. "The Sudanese," he wrote, "come all the way here [Teghazza] to replenish their salt supplies." An indication of its value was that it served as currency for the Sudanese, just like gold and silver. Those who had the misfortune of working under the harsh conditions of this bleak Saharan town quickly experienced the brutish and impersonal nature of slave life which was generally unknown to most slaves in Muslim Africa.

A much underrated role played by slaves in Africa was as caravan workers. Indeed, it has been argued that the absence of an adequate system of transportation was one of the most important reasons for the persistence of slavery until the introduction of rail and motorized transportation.[7] Leo Africanus mentions that slaves substituted as beasts of burden in carrying supplies for caravans in search of gold over paths considered too hazardous for camels. They also served as guards for the protection of merchants of Agades who traveled the dangerous route between Kano and Bornu. Not infrequently, they were pressed into service in slave-bearing caravans to guard against escape by slaves who were being taken to market. Because of their reliability and experience, slaves attained command position on caravans, notably in the East African trade.

African slaves played a useful role in accompanying their masters on the arduous pilgrimage to Mecca, known as the *hadj*. This act is incumbent upon all Muslims who are possessed with the means to carry out such a journey. Its purpose is to provide Muslims with a conception of Islam as a universal religion and the consciousness of sharing a common religious heritage. The name of Mansa Musa, the colorful ruler of Mali, conjures up one of the most celebrated of such pilgrimages. When he set out in 1324 on the journey, the emperor was preceded by 500 slaves, each bearing a staff of gold weighing 500 *mitkal,* or six pounds.[8] When lesser souls undertook the journey, they did so, to be sure, with none of this pomp but not without a covey of slaves of their own.

A long and hazardous trip made having such traveling companions a necessity; apart from the forbidding distances, there were the natural obstacles of desert and mountain crossings and lurking brigands. The path taken by Mansa Musa, which was commonly used by pilgrims at the time of the great Sudanic states, led north across the Sahara, then turned east to Egypt, and finally took a southward direction to the *hijaz.* A return journey of this sort, which covered over ten thousand kilometers, took many years to complete.

Slaves were taken along to serve as porters and guards and to tend to their masters' personal needs. One such need was cash. Owners, using some of their slaves as a kind of traveler's check, sold them when they had a need for money or goods.[9] This practice, which can be traced back centuries, carried over well into the twentieth century. British and French colonial authorities found the sale of slaves accompanying pilgrims and disguised as servants or fellow pilgrims difficult to control. As late as 1960, some Tuareg notables were reported to have sold some slaves in Arabia to defray part of the expense of the pilgrimage.

The sale of so many slaves from different parts of Muslim Africa as well as from India and Java helped assure a continuing rich and varied supply of servile labor in the slave markets of Mecca and Jeddah. Pilgrims arriving from Iraq, Syria, Persia, and other parts of the Middle East frequented these markets, and many brought back with them newly purchased slaves.[10]

There can be little doubt that slavery and the slave trade in the states and empires that made up West Sudan Africa were entrenched institutions as far back as the eleventh century.

There is no way of knowing, however, whether these two institutions were indigenous to the region or developed as a consequence of the trans-Saharan trade in slaves. There is, by contrast, convincing evidence that in the Guinean area there was a mutually reinforcing relationship between the growth of the domestic market in slaves and in the external demand for this human commodity. The evidence for upper Guinea, which takes in the Gambia and present-day Liberia, shows that domestic slavery and trade in slaves developed in response to the European demand for servile labor for the Americas and were not indigenous systems upon which an export trade was erected.[11] Here, something of a cause and effect relationship may be said to have existed.

In the West Sudanic states, no such relationship could be said to have existed. Slavery and the local traffic in slaves were important for economic development and were only incidental to the economy.[12] Such exports, to the extent they were carried on, could undoubtedly be traced to the entrepreneurial endeavors of public officials or private individuals who were engaged in the export of slaves, and probably other commodities, as a way of amassing wealth. In East Africa, which was another major source of exports to the Muslim world, it was far more likely that this external traffic was the motor that kept the slave trade in high gear.

## 2.

The spotty information available about the export of slaves from Africa to the Arab world makes any assessments of the volume of this traffic and the time period it covered subject to a considerable margin of error. Not surprisingly, this narrow factual base has become a broad launching pad for exaggerated claims about the number of slaves shipped out of Africa and the time frame in which the trade ran. This is particularly true of the traffic that came out of East Africa. The English historian, Reginald Coupland, writing in 1938 trumpeted the claim that the trade went on unimpeded on a grand scale for at least two millenia. Striking a comparison between the European and Arab slave trades, he wrote:

> Now the European Slave Trade did not begin till the sixteenth century, it did not reach its full volume till the eighteenth, and in the course of the nineteenth it was suppressed. But the Arab Slave Trade, as has been seen, began before the Christian Era, and did not stop till some fifty years ago; and though its output in any single year can never have reached the highest figures of the European trade, the total number of Africans it exported from first to last through all those centuries must have been prodigious.[13]

This sweeping claim has been laid open to serious challenge by E. A. Alpers, G. S. P. Freeman-Grenville, and other historians and can no longer be taken seriously. These historians have propagated something of a contrary view by minimizing the significance of the pre-seventeenth century slave traffic originating from the East Coast. In undercutting the Coupland thesis, Freeman-Grenville takes an equally untenable position that the export of slaves from the East Coast did not begin until the Omani intervention in the mid-seventeenth century.[14]

Upon close scrutiny, this point of view simply does not hold up. As has already been seen,[15] slaves had been traded across the Indian Ocean for centuries before the Omani influence was felt on the East Coast, although clearly not in the numbers suggested by Coupland. Gervase Mathew, writing in the same volume as Freeman-Grenville, made note of the increase in transoceanic trade in such commodities as ivory, iron, rhinoceros horn, amber, and leopard skin and concluded that slaves were also part of this trade. "The slave trade," he wrote, "was probably a constant factor; there are many references to Zanji slaves."[16] Part of this trade was directed toward Arabia and the Persian Gulf as well as to India. East African slaves were being shipped to the gulf, notably to Bahrain, between the tenth and twelfth centuries. And R. B. Serjeant, using the *Hadrami Chronicles*, confirms that slaves from East Africa were being exported to Arabia long before the arrival of the Portuguese at the end of the fifteenth century.[17]

The Portuguese conquest of East Africa was the first example of the brutal use of military force by a European power for imperial purposes. Conceived by d'Albuquerque, the plan was designed to maintain Portugal's precarious foothold in India. D'Albuquerque, who became viceroy of India, was of the view that this foothold which was centered in Goa could become a permanent maritime and Christian power only if Portugal maintained a permanent fleet in the Indian Ocean. This "lifeline to India" concept, which was quite bold for its time, posited that Portugal must gain control of three strategic points. One was Socotra, which would serve as a base for ventures into the Red Sea; the second was Hormuz, which guarded the entrance into the Persian Gulf and was itself a major market for spices and other eastern products; and the last was Malacca, whose location at the western end of the Chinese trade would allow Portuguese ships to control all the trade, mostly spices, across the Bay of Bengal.

This bold design, which Portugal managed to carry off, had little chance of succeeding unless Lisbon established bases along the East Coast to provision her ships on their long journey to India. It was within the context of this forward strategy that Portugal set out to conquer the coast. This it did with great savagery over the nine-year period between 1500-09.[18] In quick succession, the peaceful and prosperous Arab towns were called upon to submit and pay a yearly tribute to the king of Portugal or face destruction. In 1505, a small armada of ships under d'Almeida, the newly named viceroy of India, forced Kilwa and Sofala to accept Portuguese overlordship. When Mombasa refused to bow to the threat, as it was to do so often during the two hundred years of Portuguese rule, it was attacked and put to the torch. As it turned out, none of these towns became the headquarters of the Portuguese on the coast. The Portuguese found it more to their liking to rule from Mozambique, which they colonized in 1507.

Measured against these strategic goals, Portuguese policy under Prince Henry the Navigator was to strengthen its imperial and commercial links with the East. In this scheme of things, the East Coast was essentially to serve as a way station along the route to India. In promoting trade with Arabia and India, gold and ivory figured most prominently and not slaves. An important but underrated reason behind Lisbon's policy to clear a path to the East was to break Muslim sea power in the Indian Ocean and, in so doing, outflank Islam. Portugal wished to destroy the belief that *mare indicum* equalled *mare islamicum*. Thus, the opening to the East so vigorously pursued by the Portuguese was nearly as much an effort to promote a religious crusade as it was a plan to acquire new riches. This was a latter-day counterpart to the Islamic dogma of *dar al-harb*.

The Portuguese, to be sure, had no qualms about trafficking in slaves when it suited their purposes. During the sixteenth and seventeenth centuries, Portuguese ships carried small numbers of slaves to India, and part of their American market was supplied from the East Coast as well. Actually, the numbers never amounted to much even after Portugal lifted its ban in 1645 against slave exports from the East Coast to Brazil. Rough seas at the Cape and the long journey made such a journey risky and expensive. Only later on, with the coming of fast ships and diminished supplies from the West Coast, did the East Coast assume importance.

Interestingly enough, there were times when the Portuguese resorted to the slave markets in Madagascar and the Comoro Islands rather than buying slaves from their East Coast possessions.[19] High profits were what probably attracted them to the Comoros, an archipelago consisting of four islands which lies in the Mozambique channel roughly between Madagascar and Mozambique. It was reported that slaves were being sold there for nine or ten reales of eight to the Portuguese, who were expected to realize ten times that amount in other markets. It is unlikely that many of these were taken to the slave markets of Middle East countries. The devout Portuguese, who viewed Islam as an implacable foe of Christianity, understood only too well that slaves sold to Muslims usually adopted the faith of their masters.

While the Portuguese themselves were not carrying on much of a trade in slaves from the East Coast to the Middle East, this did not mean that such a trade was languishing. One Gaspar de Santo Bernadino wrote in 1606 the following remarks about his visit to the northern coast of Kenya:

When we reached Pate we were informed that some Moors from Arabia had arrived in a small vessel for the purpose of bartering for African boys whom they carried off to their country. There the boys were made to follow the Moorish religion and treated as slaves for the rest of their lives. Six of them had already been purchased.[20]

What this tells us is that merchants from Arabia and the Persian Gulf set sail in ships that took advantage of the northeast monsoon in November and, after acquiring slaves in any one of the coastal towns, departed for home with the setting-in of the southwest monsoons in April or May. There is evidence that this was the pattern of trade between Comoro merchants and traders from Arabia. In 1655, it was recounted, Peter Mundy "happed on a poore vessell with matte sailes. Shee came from Messalagia on the west side of the maine of St. Lawrence . . . bound for the Red Sea; her merchants Arabians, her merchandise slaves, about 300 of St. Lawrence aforesaid."[21] Over the years, Arab merchants developed close maritime and commercial contacts with towns along the coast from Faza in the north to Kilwa in the south and were able to identify major sources of supply for the slave trade.

These contacts, which, over the years, coalesced into trading networks dominated by Omani Arabs and Swahilis, undoubtedly provided much of the motive force in maintaining the coast's position as a supplier of slaves during the period of Portuguese ascendancy. This was probably no easy matter considering the monopolistic trading practices of the Portuguese and the frequent disruption of normal life resulting from their unwanted presence. In the approximately two hundred years of this rule, which stretched from 1500 to 1700, estimated total exports—based on scanty evidence—were two hundred thousand slaves, or on the order of one thousand per year for the entire coast.[22]

### 3.

Whether judged from the point of view of the colonizers or of the Arabs, little good can be said to have come out of Portuguese colonial practices in East Africa. The Portuguese imposed themselves by force on the indigenous population with little consideration for their interests or aspirations. True to its colonialist mentality, Lisbon sought to extract a maximum of profit from the towns of the coast through monopolistic or restrictive trading practices. In the circumstances, this proved to be as profitless to the inhabitants as it was to the architects of the shortsighted policy. The effect of this was to hasten the decline of Portuguese rule by inciting the hostility of the population against the colonial authorities and prompting the people to turn to Oman for assistance to oust the hated colonial oppressors.

Oman was a rising star in Arabia and was soon to demonstrate that it was a force to be reckoned with in East Africa. In 1650 the Omanis, under the Imam Sultan ibn Saif, ejected the Portuguese from Muscat and from the entire Arabian seaboard. This dealt a crushing blow to Portugal's waning power in the Indian Ocean; barely twenty years earlier, the Persians had driven Lisbon from Hormuz. News of Oman's victory encouraged the Arabs of the coast to turn to the imam for support. Mombasa, long a thorn in Portugal's side, sent a delegation to Muscat to complain of "the iron yoke and the injustices . . . that weighed upon them, and the evil deeds of all sorts committed there." In 1652 the imam sent a small squadron of ships to attack Pate and Zanzibar and succeeded in defeating the Portuguese garrison. This was the beginning of Omani involvement on the East Coast. Eight years later, at the invitation of Pate, the Omanis descended upon the coast and attacked and captured Faza and Mombasa but not the formidable Fort Jesus. Ever bolder, the imam, who by now had assembled an efficient navy, carried his attack farther south and in 1669 attacked Mozambique and almost succeeded in storming it.

In the following three decades, growing Omani naval superiority had shown itself in individual engagements against the Portuguese. This was clearly not enough to deliver the people of the East Coast from the tyranny of their colonial masters. In 1696, Saif ibn Sultan, the son of Imam Sultan ibn Saif, assembled a large fleet to attack Mombasa, whose twenty-five-hundred-man defending force had already been warned of his approach. After a thirty-three-month siege, the Omanis wore down the defenders, who fought to the last man, and raised the flag of victory. The Portuguese made a brief military comeback by retaking the fort in 1728 thanks to feuding between the Omani governors in Mombasa and

Zanzibar and the outbreak of civil unrest in Muscat. In the face of this threat, the Omanis closed ranks and in the following year drove the Portuguese from the redoubt. Thereafter, the Portuguese made no serious attempt to extend their political power north of the Ruvuma River.

It was not long before the Omanis had settled in that they incurred the wrath of a great many of the merchants and inhabitants of Mombasa, Kilwa, and other towns. The new imperialists turned out to be no less grasping and rapacious than their predecessors.[23] Exhausted by years of fighting, moreover, they proved too weak to deal with the economic problems inherited by the Arabs and Swahilis following the departure of the Portuguese. In Kilwa, the sultan chafed at the presence of an Omani garrison which wreaked havoc with the town's long-established pattern of trade. What made these problems even more intolerable was the high-handed manner in which the Omanis treated the local inhabitants, making many long for the day to see a return of Portuguese rule.

The death of the redoubtable Saif ibn Sultan in 1711 added to these difficulties by confronting the Omanis with an intractable succession crisis that remained unresolved for thirty years. This power vacuum developed at a sensitive time when Saif was maneuvering to consolidate his power in the newly won territories by securing the allegiance of the local rulers. The crisis was finally resolved in 1741 with the replacement of the Yoruba dynasty by that of the Busaidi, and the election three years later of Ahmad ibn Said al-Busaidi.

The coming to power of Ahmad ibn Busaidi (1744–84), the founder of the Omani Busaidi dynasty, had a salutary effect in restoring a measure of Omani authority on the coast. The small fleet of warships he despatched in 1744 to the coast served as a reminder to the local leaders that Omani suzerainty had to be acknowledged. Kilwa, anxious to restore its trading position, was quick to offer its allegiance. This contrasted with the response from Mombasa where the Omani-derived Mazrui family denounced the new ruler as a usurperer. This marked the beginning of a bitter rivalry between the Busaidi and Mazrui houses for control of the trade and politics of the northern Swahili coast.

The extension of Omani political power to the East Coast had important political implications for the future growth of the slave trade. Muscat looked with favor upon this form of commerce as it had long served as an *entrepot* for slaves arriving from the coast who were then shipped to different points in Arabia, the Persian Gulf, Iraq, Syria, and India. Importing slaves was an important source of revenue for Muscat; left in Omani hands, it held out far greater promise for growth. The changed political environment could only facilitate this process. As the coast entered a period of greater political stability under the aegis of Busaidi rule, it attracted more Indian merchant capitalists—known as Banyans—who, during the seventeenth and eighteenth centuries, marked out a predominant role in financing the closely linked traffic in ivory, cloth, and slave trade. Such venture capital was to prove indispensable for underwriting large-scale slaving operations, which the Arabs became dependent upon for the success of their slave trade activities. Indifferent to political boundaries, the Banyans also operated to the south of Cape Delgado by assisting the struggling Portuguese authorities in Mozambique to levy taxes.

Against this background of generally improving political and financial developments, there were indications that the northern slave trade, that is, the traffic directed toward the Arab heartland, Persia, and India, increased substantially. The imam took measures to assert a firmer control over Zanzibar and, in so doing, helped stimulate trade along the Kilwa coast. Ships arriving from India docked at Zanzibar and offered their goods to merchants who came from towns running the length of the coast in exchange for ivory and slaves. According to an account of the French adventurer, Jean-Vincent Morice, writing in 1776, the trade between the coast and Zanzibar proceeded as follows:

> When the ships from India arrive in December, January, or February, all the Moors from Kilwa, Mafia, Mombasa, and Pate go to Zanzibar to buy cargoes and distribute them subsequently in their districts in exchange for ivory tusks, provisions and slaves. In March and April all the Moors and Arabs come to the Kingdom of Kilwa to trade there for slaves, for Kilwa is the assembly point for all the slaves who come from the mainland.[24]

How long this pattern of trade in slaves had been going on was not revealed by Morice. Quite possibly, it went back to 1744 when Kilwa offered fealty to the new Busaidi sovereign. Trafficking in slaves also most probably figured in the quickened pace of Arab trade that developed along the coast to the south of Kilwa and opposite the Kerimba Islands during the 1760s.

Starting in 1735, the East African slave trade, which until the seventeenth century formed part of the traffic across the Red Sea, branched out and took on dramatically new dimensions. That year, La Bourdonnais was appointed governor general of the long-neglected Mascarene Islands—Ile de France (Mauritius) and Ile de Bourbon (Réunion)—which are situated some thirteen-hundred kilometers to the east of Madagascar. The new governor general, an ambitious man who had a vision of making Mauritius into an important naval base for attacking the British in India, set out to develop the island. He constructed roads, bridges, and government facilities and created a new capital in St. Louis. And as a way of promoting the prosperity of the inhabitants and attracting new settlers, he encouraged coffee and sugar growing, established cotton and indigo factories, and introduced manioc from Brazil.

To work the coffee and sugar plantations, whose output increased by leaps and bounds with each succeeding year, La Bourdonnais cast about for a secure source of slave labor.[25] He initially turned to Madagascar, the nearest and richest source, but soon dropped this plan because of the hostility of the local chiefs. The resourceful Frenchman then turned to Mozambique, which officially was barred to all foreign traders. Through judicious bribing, French traders were able to penetrate the official barrier and purchase the slaves they needed. By the end of the eighteenth century, there were approximately one hundred thousand slaves in the Mascarene Islands, as against a white and half-white population that was barely a fifth of that size.

La Bourdonnais' hope of bringing in large numbers of slaves proved illusory, with barely one or two thousand arriving in the first five years of his administration. This trickle virtually dried up in the 1740s and 1750s when Portuguese officials closely enforced royal decrees forbidding foreign ships from trading in Mozambique. The Portuguese were not anxious to encourage the presence of another imperial power near their African preserve. Their efforts to impose an embargo on the sale of slaves prompted the French to shift their attention to Ibo, the principle port of the Kerimba Islands.

It was not until the 1770s that the pace of slave exports from East Africa to Ile de France and Ile de Bourbon picked up sharply. Reversing past policy, the Portuguese were now only to happy to allow French ships to trade in slaves. In the thirteen years between 1781 and 1794, official figures show that 46,461 slaves embarked on Portuguese and foreign ships, mostly French, or approximately 3,600 per year. French slave traders were also doing a brisk business in Kilwa. This was largely abetted by the activities of Morice who, as a result of his own experiences in Kilwa, tried to induce the French government to set up a slave-trading center there. Although nothing came of this scheme because it threatened to bring France into open competition with Oman, the opportunistic Morice succeeded in 1776 in signing his well-known treaty of one hundred years with the sultan of Kilwa which allowed him a monopoly of slaves at twenty piastres each, with the sultan receiving a duty of two piastres. He contracted to supply Morice with a minimum of 1,000 slaves per year. Most of these slaves were destined for the Mascarene Islands, but Morice managed to ship some of them to the French Antilles. In the three years between 1787 and 1790, a total of 4,193 slaves arrived in Ile de France under this agreement.

Kilwa's growing importance in the slave trade was what persuaded Ahmad ibn Busaidi to appoint his own governor there after the island attempted to throw off his rule in 1780. As Omani influence along the coast became stronger, there was less opportunity for direct trading by foreigners at the mainland ports which were under the direct control of the Busaidis. This could be taken as an indication that the Omanis, after having established their presence on the coast for nearly a century, were ever more anxious, despite the limited power at their disposal, to influence the direction of events.

## 4.

Thanks to the work of Philip D. Curtin, there is a reasonably sound estimate of the number of slaves shipped across the Atlantic.[26] Based on his analysis of the data and relevant information, Curtin advanced a figure of eleven million slaves for this trade. By contrast, aggregate estimates ventured by historians for the trans-Sharan, East African, and the Red Sea traffic to the Muslim heartland are, by all admission, rudimentary in the extreme. There is, notably, for the trans-Saharan trade, the previously mentioned work of Ralph

A. Austen, who does not hesitate to acknowledge that he is not the Curtin of the Sahara. Yet his very tentative conclusions, based on a most cautious approach befitting the meagerness of the data, do offer some rough indication of the magnitude of this trade.

According to these very rough estimates, the export trade across the Sahara, the Red Sea, and the Indian Ocean for the period up to 1600 totaled 7,220,000.[27] Taken by major trade routes, this breaks down to 4,820,000 for the trans-Saharan for the period 650–1600, and 2,400,000 for the Red Sea and East Coast for the relatively shorter time span of 800–1600. Estimates for the Red Sea and East Coast routes break down to 1,600,000 and 800,000, respectively. The trans-Saharan traffic, by this reckoning, accounted for about two-thirds of the exports while the share of the Red Sea trade represented about 22 percent and that of the East Coast 11 percent. On an annual basis, an estimated average of 5,000 slaves made their way across the half a dozen routes that, at different times, cut across the desert, while 2,000 slaves passed through ports along the Red Sea and another 1,000 were embarked on ships from East Coast ports. This represented an average annual figure of 8,000 slaves who were exported to the Arab world.

The picture begins to change somewhat for the two-hundred-year period running from 1600 to 1800. For the seventeenth century, there was, according to Austen's and other estimates, an increase in the trans-Saharan trade from 550,000 to 700,000 while traffic along the Red Sea and East Coast remained stable. The rise in the trans-Saharan trade is undoubtedly attributable, in part, to the breakup of the Songhay empire, which generated in its wake the enslavement of large numbers of people and their forced transport to Morocco. Such a phenomenon, as has been observed, was an ineluctable consequence of warfare in Africa. According to these same estimates, there was in the eighteenth century a fourfold jump in the East Coast trade, which rose from

100,000 to 400,000, while traffic along the trans-Saharan and Red Sea routes remained unchanged at 700,000 and 200,000, respectively. The rise in East Coast exports can be traced to an increase in slaving activities by Omanis, who were consolidating their power along the mainland ports and in Zanzibar, and the energetic role played by the French in filling their manpower needs in the Mascarene Islands. For this time span, these three routes yielded an approximate total of 2,000,000 slaves, or an average of about 10,000 per year.

Substantial as these figures are, they fall short of providing a fuller picture of numbers enslaved. Of those who fell into the hands of the slave trader, a great many died before they left Africa. Again, it will never be possible to know the number of those who fell on the wayside during the long forced marches to the coast or on board the crowded dhows that sailed from Zanzibar, Pemba, and mainland ports to the markets in Arabia. Although there had been a tendency by abolitionists and their supporters to exaggerate the numbers of such deaths, there can be little doubt they were substantial. Losses from death have been estimated at about 10 to 14 percent en route to ports of departure and about 6 to 10 percent at ports of departure.

Deaths were common during the march to the port of embarkation. The incidence of death tended to vary directly with the length of the march. According to one study dealing with the Atlantic trade, 40 percent of the slaves bought in the interior of Angola died before reaching the coast in the six months between initial purchase and delivery.[28] Comparable, if not greater, incidences of mortality probably occurred on the marches across the inhospital climate of the Sahara where extremes of heat and cold alternate between day and night and where water and natural shelter are scarce.

Malnutrition during marches, resulting from pitiful food rations, caused many of the slaves to succumb to illness and injury. Those who fell behind were usually dealt with harshly by the armed guards who either killed the stragglers or left them behind.

Male slaves also suffered terribly because they were yoked together with forked sticks or chained together so as to prevent them from escaping. Women and children were usually spared this fate because there was less risk they would bolt for freedom.

There were, throughout the Islamic slave trade, identifiable trends regarding age and sex ratios of the exported slave population that remained fairly constant. Slaves were generally very young, with very few past thirty. A majority of them were young women and girls, reflecting the requirements of the Arab market for household help and concubines. This preference showed up in the price differential between male and females. Males, unless they were castrated, were cheaper than females of comparable age. The sex-ratio trends for the Atlantic trade ran in the opposite direction, with males generally outnumbering females because of the work requirements on plantations and in mines. This was reflected in the higher price that males went for at slave auctions.

# CHAPTER SEVEN

# Heyday of the Slave Trade: 1800–1900

## 1.

BY THE DAWN OF THE NINETEENTH CENTURY, THE TRAFFIC in slaves out of Africa had reached huge proportions. The greatest human migration before the mass movement of Europeans overseas in the middle of the nineteenth century was well underway. This traffic, after falling off in the last decade of the eighteenth and the first decade of the nineteenth century because of the war in Europe, surged ahead. For a while, the transatlantic trade regained its previous level, while the traffic in slaves originating in the East Coast entered a period of sustained growth. Caravan traffic across the Sahara and the stream of slaves that passed through Red Sea ports were to reach new records before tapering off. Within Africa and the islands lying off the East Coast and in the Indian Ocean, the introduction of new crops transformed the political economy and resulted in a more systematic enslavement of people and a more intensive exploitation of slave labor. There was, in line with these changes, a pronounced tendency to emphasize the production aspect of slavery.

The mushrooming traffic in slaves, whose hideous workings were becoming known to the public, triggered a counterreaction which, for the first time in the history of slavery, sought nothing less than an end to this nefarious trade. In the last decades of the eighteenth century, reformers in a number of countries, many of whose citizens were deeply involved in the trade, secured the adoption of laws that either abolished the slave trade or limited its scope. The United States adopted restrictive legislation in 1791 and 1794; Denmark outlawed the trade in 1802; and in Great Britain, whose slave merchants battened on the trade like those of no other nation, Parliament enacted a law in 1807 making it illegal for its citizens to participate in the trade. The United States followed in the same direction in 1808, the year the British law took effect.

Despite initial setbacks, half-hearted attempts at enforcement, and widespread smuggling, these prohibitory laws made their mark. Great Britain, which took the lead in the attack against the slave trade, urged other European and New World nations to take part in the campaign. The upshot of this was that a number of countries, including Portugal, Spain, and France, entered into treaties pledging them to put down the slave trade. In the face of these efforts, the days of the transatlantic trade were numbered. It took decades, however, before the attack against the slave trade was expanded into a campaign for the abolition of slavery.

Some fifteen years were to pass following Britain's enactment of its ordinance against the slave trade before it turned its attention to the traffic in slaves in the Muslim world. Britain's efforts in this direction were initially directed towards East Africa but were gradually extended to include the

Persian Gulf, North Africa, Arabia, and the Ottoman Empire. The strategy employed for suppressing the trade was again mainly diplomatic in nature. Treaties were signed with the countries implicated in the trade committing them to adopt measures that would bring about its abolition.

This diplomatic assault against the slave trade, stiffened as it was by a small roving squadron of the British navy, was not without its results. It impeded somewhat the regular flow of slaves and raised the risks of doing business. In spite of these gains, it was generally acknowledged that the movement of slaves from Africa to the slave markets of Arabia and the Persian Gulf was little affected by these stratagems. Muslim leaders, with some exceptions, were not sympathetic to the cause they were resigned to pursue, and the people of influence who surrounded them were unreservedly hostile. In this environment, the slave trader's cunning, his network of connections, and his ruthless pursuit of pecuniary gain made him an elusive target.

The anti-slave trade campaign, paradoxically, probably had a greater effect in stimulating the demand for slaves within Africa than in curtailing their shipment to foreign markets. Now that exports were subject to a certain amount of financial risk and judicial penalities, more slaves became available for the local market. This had the effect of pushing down prices for slave labor, thereby encouraging more of a use for it in the growing "legitimate" commerce.

In the eyes of many scholars, missionaries, and government officials, there was a difference between the slave trade, which they regarded as illegal, and commerce in "legitimate" goods such as rubber, cloves, ivory, copal, ostrich feathers, and gum arabic, which they actively encouraged. These products were being exported alongside slaves, and their share of the market was growing. For abolitionists, this shift in trading patterns carried great significance. They argued, with good reason, that the increased suppression of the slave trade and the growth in "legitimate" trade would sound the death knell of slavery because merchants would prefer investing their money in commodities that found an expanding market in the industrialized countries. Impeccable as this logic was, it was flawed in an important respect. The "legitimate" trade that abolitionists wanted to substitute for the slave trade was almost always a commerce in the products of slave labor; much of the "legitimate" goods was grown or transported by slaves. Rubber and copal collected by slaves on the mainland were "legitimate," as were the cloves grown by slaves on Zanzibar and Pemba. As the abolitionists finally came to understand, the extension of commerce in "legitimate" goods made their goal less attainable since it served to push up the demand for slaves.

## 2.

For many centuries, the need of the Arab and Western worlds for the products of Africa and the mercantile instincts of the people to the north and south of the Sahara combined to make trade a potent force in the development of the northwestern corner of the continent. Trade bridged the Sahara, one of the foremost natural barriers to human intercourse, and linked the Sudan to the Maghreb. This commerce was a cynosure for merchants from the Christian and Muslim worlds whose ships filled the ports of the rugged Barbary Coast from Tripoli to Agadir. For the people of the Sudan, trade from across the desert brought highly prized merchandise and the culture of Islam, which inspired their social and political development. In exchange, the traders from the north carried back with them the exotic products of the Sudan along with gold and slaves.

There were four main routes that connected the north to the south over which this traffic passed. In the west lay the Morocco-Taodeni-Timbuktu route, with its important

Mabruk-Tuat branch; in the center was the Ghadames-Air-Kano route to Hausa land; more to the east was situated the Tripoli-Fezzan-Kawar route with its terminus in Bornu; and last was the Cyrenaica-Kufra-Wadai route.[1] For want of statistical information, it is not possible to gauge the volume of traffic that passed over these routes, which were among the oldest highways in the world. Such information that exists before 1850, particularly in the accounts of European travelers, is impressionistic. The main features of the trade can be detected but not the total volume that passed over any one route.

The ebb and flow of traffic was determined by political conditions in the Sudan and security along the routes. For both these reasons, the Morocco-Timbuktu route could not realize its full potential. Security, which was severely affected by anarchic conditions that prevailed in the western Sudan following the breakup of the Songhay empire, continued to remain a problem right into the nineteenth century. When conditions were favorable, slaves were one of the more important commodities that were transported across the route. In the late seventeenth and early eighteenth centuries, the powerful Moroccan Sultan Moulay Ismael imported thousands of slaves from the Sudan to fill the ranks of his standing army.[2] The traffic in military slaves was discontinued by Moulay Ismael's successors following his death because of their tendency to take part in the civil strife that plagued Morocco in the first half of the eighteenth century. As traffic in military slaves tapered off, overall trade declined. The route, nonetheless, continued to play an important role for the exchange of Sudanese gold for the salt of Teghazza. With the return of political stability to Morocco, this western route experienced a resurgence in traffic in the 1880s. Hundreds of slaves were reaching Morocco toward the end of the decade from Timbuktu.[3]

The other three routes and their branch roads were also

traveled by slaves. After the fall of the Songhay empire, the political center of gravity in the Sudan shifted eastward, from the Niger River to Lake Chad. Its power was such that it succeeded in dominating the regions of the Sahara as far west as the southern boundaries of the Fezzan. As a result, the Fezzan-Bornu road became the most heavily traveled of the roads, a position that it held until 1820. Although this route carried much salt southward from Bilma, its main purpose was for the transport of slaves.[4] This route, which started from an area extending from Lake Chad westward to Hausa land, followed a northerly direction to Agades; from there, it was a twenty-five day journey by foot to Ghat. The caravans, including those bringing slaves from as far as Darfur, would converge on the Fezzan. There they would be taken in hand by Tuaregs, who then shepherded their charges either to Tripolitania via Murzuq or to Ghadames by way of Ghat.

At Ghadames, an important staging point, the caravans would split up, some bound for Morocco and others following a straight northerly direction to Tunis. Those who managed to survive the trek from Kano to Tunis covered a distance of three thousand kilometers. For many, the adventure was not yet over. From Tunis or Tripoli, they were dispatched on waiting ships to Constantinople or to the Levant, where they were sold for a fourth or fifth time.[5]

The fourth and last route that comprised the network of major thoroughfares that linked the Barbary Coast and the Sudan ran from Benghazi via Kufra to Wadai.[6] The safety and growth of the route were due to a unique set of circumstances largely having to do with the introduction of the Sanusi order into Cyrenaica in 1843 by its founder Muhammed ibn 'Ali al-Sanusi. In promoting the rapid spread of the brotherhood, known as the *tariqa,* al-Sanusi encouraged the bedouin tribes in the region to maintain peace and order. *Zawiyas* (lodges) were constructed along the route to serve as hospices for pilgrims and traders. The governors of these lodges, because of their responsibility in maintaining them, were quick to become involved in trade. The British vice counsul in Benghazi attested to these activities when he reported in 1876:

> The caravan route from Banghazi to Wadai is shorter and less dangerous than any other and the community of Marabouts, of the recently formed order of Es-Senousy, are building mosques and digging wells at regular intervals along the route with the object of securing the safety of the caravans. [7]

These measures combined to make the Benghazi-Kufra–Wadai route the safest in the Sahara. The route proved its worth as a safe and profitable alternative to the older Tripoli-Bornu road, which had fallen into disuse because of the depredations of the *condottiere* Rabih in the area south of Lake Chad. This state of affairs was borne out in the observations of the great French scholars and travelers, Gautier and Chudeau, who noted that while the Fezzan-Bornu route was hardly used, large caravans were departing from Benghazi for Wadai laden mainly with guns and ammunition which were to be bartered for slaves. [8]

Slaves, ivory, and ostrich feathers made up the bulk of the exports from Wadai. There is evidence that slaves constituted the lion's share of the trade although its volume and value are not known. [9] Precise information about this traffic did not show up in consular reports because of its illegal and hence clandestine nature. The slave trade was formally abolished in Tunisia and Algeria in 1846 and in Tripoli in 1853. France had successfully suppressed the trade by mid-century and in so doing reduced the traffic to local exchanges. The rulers in Tunis and Tripoli adopted a tolerant attitude because they derive illicit gains from the trade, which also generated taxes for the state coffers.

Actually, many of the slaves transported along this eastern

route never reached the coast. Some were given as alms to the Sanusiya; and not a few of these converted to Islam, joined the brotherhood, and settled near the *zawiyas*, where they worked the land. A good number of the captives were taken from Kufra or Jalu to the slave markets in Egypt. This become more and more common after the Mahdist state in the Sudan disrupted traffic on the Nile and along the *darb al-arb'in* (the forty-day road) from Asyut to Darfur after 1885.

## 3.

Although the precise number of slaves who were marched across the Sahara into a life of bondage is not known, the figure must run high. The various travelers and explorers who spent much time traveling from town to town in the desert commented on the extent of the slave trade. The German explorer, Henry Barth, to whom we owe much for revealing the secrets of the interior of northern Africa, witnessed the departure for Fezzan of a caravan of seven hundred fifty slaves, who, he remarked, were still at that time the main export of Bornu.[10] The English explorer, James Richardson, who together with Barth explored the region, reported in 1846 that without slaves the Bornu caravan traffic would hardly exist. A little more than a decade later, the British consul general in Tripoli observed that the slave trade made up "more than two-thirds of the value of all the caravan trade. . . ."[11] By this time, Ottoman Tripoli, whose trade network covered much of the Middle East, had become an important center for the export of slaves.

Reports of these and other travelers and consular officials have provided the basis of differing estimates of the number of slaves exported from the four main trading routes to the Mediterranean. Approximations of this sort, as has been previously noted, have to be approached with caution as they are subject to a considerable margin of error. Thomas Fowell

Buxton, the English abolitionist leader, whose campaign against slavery in the Muslim world induced the British government to take action against the trans-Saharan slave trade, estimated its volume at 20,000 per year.[12] Mauny considered this a minimum figure and believed it was probably far in excess of it. This French historian estimates annual exports at 20,000, or 2 million a century.[13] He asserts, without substantiation, that similar numbers were exported across the desert for the preceding seventeen centuries during which this northern trade is known to have existed or certainly during the twelve centuries following the Arab conquest of North Africa. The 34 million or 24 million blacks suggested by Mauny's reckoning would undoubtedly have made a lasting impact on the demographic and racial composition of North Africa and the Middle East, and there is scant evidence for this. Along more realistic lines, Boahen estimates the number of slaves taken across the desert in the first half of the nineteenth century at about 10,000 per year, as compared with the approximately 70,000 who were transported across the Atlantic Ocean at the beginning of the century.[14] Austen, following a more rigorous analysis and review of available data and accounts of travelers, arrives at the not too dissimilar figure of 1,200,000 for the century, or 12,000 a year.[15]

That so many slaves could be transported across the Sahara was a tribute to the skills of those who led the caravans and to the network of roads that sustained commerce and communications in a most hostile environment. For the merchants, the routes, despite many hazards, proved themselves by offering the shortest and safest means for the transport of merchandise. For the slaves, however, the trip across these same roads, which usually took from sixty to seventy days, was an ordeal that many did not survive. It is not possible to calculate a mortality rate since it is not known how many slaves, over time, embarked on this forced march and the actual numbers who reached the final destination. By a number of accounts, for each slave who reached the journey's end, three or four died on the way. Usually, they fell victim to the burning sun or freezing cold of the night or to the tortures of thirst, hunger, and exhaustion.

Centuries of traffic on the trans-Saharan roads did not diminish the hazards of traveling on them. In 1805 a caravan of 2,000 men and 1,800 camels making its way on the Teghazza-Timbuktu route perished of thirst—not a man or beast having survived.[16] Slave caravans, made up as they were with many women and children, were particularly vulnerable to such tragedies. On a trip back from Tibesti in the Tchad region, Nachtigal passed a spring in whose immediate vicinity were camel skeletons and the bones of people, the apparent remains of a slave caravan that came to grief when this source of water ran dry.[17] Europeans who traveled the Fezzan-Kawar route often recorded with horror the human skeletons with which it was strewn. Blanched bones, usually those of women and children, were often piled up around wells, the telltale monument of a desperate effort to reach water.

While on the road, slaves often fell victim to disease or were killed or captured by marauding bands of brigands. The privations of the journey and short rations, often the result of indifference or penny-pinching attitudes of cost-minded merchants, made many of the slaves susceptible to illness and disease. Moving from one disease environment to another in a debilitated physical condition made slaves ready victims of contagious diseases such as cholera and smallpox. An epidemic among slaves in transit, whether by land or sea, was much to be feared. A caravan afflicted by smallpox might be condemned to wander in the desert, like a plague ship, shunned by all.

It was in the interests of the merchants, whose capital was tied to the fate of the caravan, that the slaves be decently treated while in transit. A heavy loss in life could easily turn an otherwise lucrative venture into a financial disaster. Slaves delivered in good condition to Benghazi and Tripoli usually yielded a return of 300 to 500 percent. It was the lure of such enormous profits that led so many merchants to hazard the trip to the Sudan. What logic dictated, however, was not easily attainable on the road. Once a caravan set out on the journey home, the slaves came more under the control of the caravan leaders and their outriders whose primary concern was to keep the caravan moving towards its destination. The lash of a whip, or worse, was what kept the sick and weak slaves from falling behind. Where slave owners were not sufficiently attentive to the needs of their newly acquired human merchandise, the slave drivers, who were responsible for the slaves only while in transit and for moving them from place to place at so much per head, were likely to press them hard until they reached their final destination.

## 4.

Toward the end of the 1830s, the horrors of the trans-Saharan trade had aroused public opinion in England, prompting demands that action be taken to bring it to an end. Prior to this, the Colonial Office, a bulwark of conservatisim, evinced a mild interest in dealing with this branch of the slave trade, only to pull back when genuine opportunities for action were suggested. The truth of the matter was that, while the government had adopted a position second to no other in the struggle against the Atlantic trade, it revealed a pusillanimous attitude in regard to the Saharan and Mediterranean trade.[18] One slave crusade was about all the country could manage at a time.

Beginning in 1840 this policy was to undergo a marked change. With strong public backing, the government launched a concerted diplomatic attack on the slave trade in

Tunis, Morocco, Tripoli, and the Ottoman Empire. The guiding spirit behind this campaign was Foreign Secretary Henry Palmerston, a committed abolitionist. In this struggle, he had the backing of two invaluable allies, Thomas Fowell Buxton and the British and Foreign Anti-Slavery Society, which was formed in 1839. Buxton, the spiritual heir to Wilberforce, was largely responsible for bringing the trans-Saharan slave trade into the public limelight.

In tackling the slave trade question in these Muslim countries, Great Britain encountered difficulties that it rarely came up against in its dealings with European states implicated in the Atlantic trade. Unlike the latter countries, which were committed to the principle of abolition, political authorities in the Barbary States and in the Ottoman Empire saw nothing wrong with slavery and trafficking in slaves. Muslim leaders, in pleading for understanding on this issue with Western politicians, warned that their thrones, if not their lives, were at risk if they were to abolish the slave trade. Even if committed to such a course, their writ did not run very far as the officials responsible for implementing such a policy were themselves often counted among the slave traders.

It was in Tunis that the British struck their first blow against the slave trade and slavery in the Muslim world. By the end of the 1830s the bey depended on British support to fend off French colonial ambitions and to forestall attempts by the Turks to restore political control over the regency, which was nominally part of the sagging Ottoman Empire. Only a short time before, the sultan had dispatched a military force to occupy Tripoli, from whence he removed the ruling pasha. It was rumored in Constantinople that the sultan would do the same in Tunis in order to reassert Ottoman control. It was against this political background that the bey acted with alacrity when told by Sir Thomas Reade, the British consul in Tunis, that nothing would be more "gratifying not only to the British Government itself, but to the

British nation generally" than the abolition of the slave trade and slavery.

Within a short time, the bey abolished slave markets in the country and prohibited the public sale of slaves. In April 1842 he outlawed the importation of new slaves into the country. The crowning act came in January 1846 when the bey issued a decree freeing all slaves in the country and declaring slavery itself illegal.

This bold action was warmly received in England where the Anti-Slavery Society sent the bey a message of congratulations. These words of appreciation, as it turned out, were premature as both slavery and the slave trade continued unchecked. Slaves of Sudanese origin, although in reduced numbers, were regularly smuggled into the country, where they found a ready market. Of these, many were Muslim women born of free Muslim parents, whose enslavement was in contravention to Islamic law.[19] Almost thirty years later, and acting almost as if the 1846 decree were never issued, the British prevailed upon the bey to include in the Anglo-Tunisian Treaty of 1875 a clause outlawing slavery. How effective this provision was can be gauged by the fact that the English consulate at the entrance of the *souks* in the Arab medina became a haven for escaped slaves. In June 1880 the British consul reported that five Negro women had taken refuge in the consulate.[20] By this time, however, there were signs that both slavery and the slave trade were disappearing. In 1887 the bey freed the women slaves in his *harim*. Three years later, France, which by then had taken possession of the country as a protectorate, obliged the bey to issue a decree inaugurating a system of penalties for anyone having bought, sold, or held a human being in slavery.

Palmerston's diplomatic efforts in Morocco turned out to be singularly unsuccessful. When the British consul general in Morocco appealed to the sultan to stamp out the trade in his dominion, he was flatly turned down. The sultan pointed out as the "making of slaves and trading therewith" were approved by the Koran, which "admits not either to addition or diminution," it was beyond his power to abolish the traffic or restrict it in any way."[21] Palmerston was not about to challenge the sultan for the simple reason that he needed his cooperation in maintaining the status quo in the region. Thus, in the case of Morocco, it was the sultan's strong political position rather than any religious principle that allowed him to defy the British.

There the matter was allowed to rest until the 1880s when the Moroccan slave trade attracted attention in Europe. Lurid reports circulated about the sale of very young children, many of whom were said to have been separated from their parents. The Anti-Slavery Society took the matter up with gusto, and questions were raised in Parliament about the holding of slaves by persons under British protection. Much stress was laid on the fact that there were public sales of slaves in seaports "almost within sight of a British possession."

The British position towards Morocco had changed very little over the past forty years. Because of Morocco's strategic position on the Straits of Gibraltar, London was anxious to preserve the country's political independence and to prevent its coasts from falling into the hands of rival powers. In London, there was concern of possible European, particularly French, intervention in the sharifian state. The Foreign Office was therefore reluctant to press the sultan on so sensitive a matter as that of slavery. Nonetheless, it did make a "friendly" appeal that he consider abolition. He rejected this as unrealistic. In a frank and revealing statement, the sultan explained why abolition was not possible:

> It would endanger us with our subjects, for it touches, not on customs alone, but also religion. This Empire is not as other countries, which are civilized and whose inhabitants dwell in cities; they . . . are mostly Bedouins and Nomads, and do not

always occupy the same place, . . . but change with every wind. They cannot be bound by anything; and it is very difficult for them to forsake their customs—much more so to forsake what concerns their religion. They do not obey what is ordered them—they obey in words, but not in deeds. If their obedience in acts is required, troops and an army must be sent to them, until they obey though with repugnance, and then when the troops are withdrawn they revert to their customs.[22]

The sultan's unwillingness to cooperate was a blow to the abolitionists and a setback for the campaign against the trade, which was showing signs of winding down. Morocco was not an exporter of slaves but had always been an important importer. Most slaves arrived in the country from the south by way of Tuat and Tindoff. Estimates by contemporary observers of the actual numbers differed greatly. The British consul general, who was anxious to play down the matter, reported that about 300 to 500 were brought in annually, while the Anti-Slavery Society, which believed there were 50,000 slaves in the sharifian kingdom, claimed the yearly figure to be 4,000[23]—a grossly inflated figure considering that the trans-Saharan trade was in decline. Whatever the actual numbers, Great Britain would do nothing about the trade in view of its own diplomatic interests and the sultan's refusal to take any action. The situation continued unchanged until the French occupation in 1912 put an end to both the institution of slavery and the traffic in slaves.[24]

## 5.

The diplomatic attack against the Turkish slave trade over-shadowed events in Tunis and Morocco. On Europe's diplomatic chessboard, Turkey and its tottering empire were considered as important assets in maintaining the balance of power on the continent. By the 1830s, Great Britain had become committed to maintaining the territorial integrity of Turkey's far-flung empire. Further weakening of it would upset the balance of power in eastern Europe and whet Russian and French territorial ambitions. Of immediate concern were Russian designs in the Balkans and French colonial aims in North Africa. Palmerston's stated aim was not only to maintain the territorial integrity of the empire but "reforming it to make it more capable of resisting its enemies and able to play its part in the balance of power in eastern Europe."

This policy was put to an early test in 1840 following demands by Buxton and the Anti-Slavery Society that Turkey be pressured into proscribing the slave trade. Nothing came of this as the Foreign Office was fearful lest it undermine the *Porte's* position by pursuing such a course. Shades of the British dilemma in Morocco! London's anti-slavery aims became hostage to its avowed policy of keeping the Ottoman Empire intact.

This timid attitude soon gave way to a more forthright approach that did yield results. The impetus for this shift in tactics was provided by disturbing accounts of large numbers of slaves dying along the trans-Saharan routes. These grisly reports were dispatched by James Richardson during his travels in the Sahara and were widely circulated by the Anti-Slavery Society. To remedy this deplorable state of affairs, he recommended closing down the slave markets in Tripoli and Constantinople. An indirect and perhaps more cogent consideration than Richardson's accounts militating in favor of some form of action was a partial British success against the slave trade in East Africa. Under a treaty signed in 1845 between the British government and Seyyid Said, the ruler of Zanzibar, the imam agreed not to permit the sale of slaves from his African dominions to Arabia and the Persian Gulf. (See section 8.) He also allowed British naval ships to enforce the treaty in the Persian Gulf and the Red Sea. It was soon recognized that the treaty, which took effect on January 1,

1847, would be difficult to implement unless Turkey and Persia issued *firmans,* or decrees, prohibiting their respective ports in the regions from importing slaves. In 1842 the British resident at Bushire estimated that four thousand to five thousand slaves were sold annually in the Persian Gulf. As long as these ports remained open to slaves from Said's domain, traders from the East Coast would be encouraged to take the risk of running British naval patrols.

A response from Constantinople was not long in coming. Reluctant to antagonize the British, the sultan complied by closing down the slave markets in Constantinople and issuing the required *firman.*[25] The shah, however, refused to go along, invoking the familiar religious argument about slavery. Only after stern measures were threatened did he come around and agree to close his ports to slave imports from East Africa.

The outcome was the first victory for the British in their diplomatic campaign against the slave trade in the Ottoman Empire. Although the agreement with the *Porte* was limited to the Persian Gulf, it set an important precedent that would later be extended to the trade in the Mediterranean. The sultan's decision was even weightier in terms of its religious implications inasmuch as it was the first taken by a Muslim leader of his stature against the slave trade. The results also demonstrated that a firm stand against the trade need not be inconsistent with Britain's goal of maintaining the integrity of the Ottoman Empire.

With this record of success behind it, the British government once again reverted to its cautious ways. It was not long, however, before it was shaken by new reports on the horrors of the trans-Saharan slave trade. F. H. Gilbert, the vice consul in Tripoli, sent back a report about a slave caravan out of Wadai which suffered a high loss of life. In a particular eight-day journey, thirty-two slaves had died or were left to their fate because of "the swelling of their feet in traversing the hot sands." The only way to deal with the problem, he advised Palmerston, who was to close down Tripoli as a slave-exporting port. Turkey, he noted, had already accepted the principle of forbidding the importation of slaves from Africa to the Persian Gulf. Pursuing this analogy, Gilbert observed: "The trade in slaves through Tripoli and other ports in the Mediterranean to Constantinople and the Levant is open to every objection which existed to the trade from the East Coast of Africa to the Persian Gulf."[26] Gilbert's proposal, were it to be adopted, would deal a severe blow to the trans-Saharan slave trade. The sultan conveniently chose to address a strong warning to the governor of Tripoli to see to it that the atrocities reported by Gilbert not be allowed to occur again. The vizirial order was sure to remain a dead letter because those responsible for implementing it were themselves involved in the trade.

The slave trade across the Sahara had a rhythm of its own that was little affected by the exchanges of diplomatic correspondence between London and Constantinople. Reports would come in revealing a high incidence of deaths on slave caravans, growing slave exports from Tripoli and Benghazi to the Levant, often on ships flying the Turkish flag, and continued complicity of Turkish officials in the trade itself. The reports were then routinely forwarded to the British ambassador in Constantinople, who would bring them to the attention of the sultan. Invariably, he issued instructions to correct the abuses, which for the most part were observed in the breach.

Events during the Crimean War (1854–56) put a new face on these matters. In September 1854, Canning, the British ambassador in Constantinople, informed the government that the Turks had taken advantage of the invasion of the eastern shores of the Black Sea by English and French troops to revive the trade in white slaves. This let loose a feeling of disgust in Britain and France that Turks were enslaving and selling Christians at a time when Christian armies were defending Muslim Turkey. Anticipating a strong Western reaction, the sultan almost immediately issued an order abolishing the trade in white slaves. This decision to extend the principle contained in the 1847 *firman* abolishing the slave trade in the Persian Gulf to the Black Sea was an important victory in the uphill struggle to abolish the slave trade in the Ottoman Empire. The circle would be closed once this principle was extended to the Mediterranean.

In 1855 evidence was building up of numerous shipments of slaves from Tripoli and Benghazi to Crete, a fueling station for ships plying between Barbary ports and the Levant. There were, in addition, alarming accounts of slaves being disembarked from Turkish ships at Rhodes and Mytilene. This information was put to good use at the end of the Crimean War when Clarendon, the foreign secretary, informed the sultan that "he could do nothing more acceptable to Her Majesty's Government and to the British nation than to adopt measure which should be really effectual for putting an end to the Slave Trade." The *Porte*, deeply indebted to England and France for the role they played in the war, could hardly do less. In January 1857 he issued a *firman* prohibiting the slave traffic in the Mediterranean and outlawing the sale of slaves in Tripoli. The *firman*, which laid down penalties for noncompliance, was to be enforced throughout Turkey and its dominions with the exception of the Hijaz, where, it was feared, its enforcement would provoke a violent reaction. What the decree meant was that slavery was left untouched but that the sale and purchase of slaves were now illegal.

Little time passed before it was realized that the sultan's *firman* was mainly observed in the breach. Barely a year after its issuance, the acting British consul general in Tripoli referred to it as "a mere fiction," and five years later his successor described it as "a solemn mockery." Throughout the remainder of the century reports trickled in from different parts of the empire describing flagrant violations of the *firman*. This was not surprising inasmuch as the decree was issued at the instance of foreign powers and not at the request of the people. Slavery, as it was clearly understood in the Muslim world, could not perpetuate itself without being sustained by a continuous flow of fresh supplies from African sources. Slave populations in the Muslim world, because of high mortality rates and the practice of manumission, did not maintain their numbers. The slave trade, as a result, continued to operate albeit in a more discrete manner and on a reduced scale. Officials, in return for the usual *bakshish*, tended to turn a blind eye to the practice. Only when the demand for slaves dried up with the abolition of slavery by the Turkish government in 1889 did the traffic itself come to an end. That this trade died hard can be seen from the reports of the British and Italian Anti-Slavery Societies which told of slaves being shipped from Benghazi to the Levant as late as 1907 to 1910. Its final demise did not come about until the Italian occupation of Cyrenaica in 1911.

The end of the slave trade across the desert dealt a severe blow to the trans-Saharan routes. This trade alone accounted for half of all exports across the Sahara; and as it declined, so did the overall volume and value of trade. What accounted for this drop was not so much the enforcement of the anti-slave trade treaties, which was sporadic at best, as the introduction of more attractive modes of transportation and commercial opportunities. Once European goods began to reach the markets of Hausa land and other inland markets from the 1850s onward at cheaper prices and greater quantities from West African ports, the days of the caravan routes were numbered. The camel was no match for the steamship. These new routes not only were cheaper and swifter but led to the demand for new agricultural products which generated great wealth which exceeded by far such traditional desert exports as gold, ivory, ostrich feathers, and slaves.[27] By the time the partition of the continent was completed, the caravan routes had become irrelevant to the West African and North African trade.

Great Britain's dogged diplomatic campaign helped bring about the end of the slave trade, at least on paper, in North Africa, save for Morocco, and throughout the Ottoman Empire with the exception of the Hijaz. The dominant theme of this campaign, however, was the elevation of political interest over humanitarian concerns; where the two conflicted, the British government showed no hesitation in sacrificing the latter in favor of the former. In Tunis, success came quickly with a minimum of effort because the government had little to lose by pressing for abolition and the bey had everything to gain by acceding to London's wishes. In Morocco, by contrast, no serious effort was made to end the slave trade lest this undermine British strategic interests in the country. The same attitude colored British thinking towards the *Porte,* who succeeded in holding off the British for almost fifteen years. For much the same reason, the British refused to enter into a treaty with the *Porte* to ensure the implementation of the 1857 *firman.* But for the unremitting efforts of the Anti-Slavery Society and the sultan's ill-starred action in reviving the traffic in Christian slaves, the campaign against the slave trade might have been called off, as it was in Morocco, or have taken many more years before it bore fruit.

This protracted phase of the diplomatic campaign against the slave trade brought out a revealing aspect about Islamic law on slavery that showed it to be more supple than traditionalists would have one believe. In Tunis, political expedience carried the day: the bey outlawed the slave trade and then slavery, thereby shattering the centuries-old belief that Koranic law governing slavery and, by implication, condoning the traffic in human beings could not be tampered with. In Turkey the sultan's action to issue the *firman* banning the slave trade removed a major impediment that had blocked reform and thereby made it easier later on for Muslim leaders in Persia, Egypt, Oman, and elsewhere to declare the traffic illegal.

## 6.

It has been estimated that the export of slaves from Africa to the Islamic lands of North Africa and the Middle East involved the movement of approximately two million people.[28] About half of this mass of humanity, or one million people, were taken from the upper Nile valley and Abyssinia (modern-day Ethiopia). In both these regions there was the same pattern of slave raiding and trade that prevailed in the rest of Africa. About half of these one million slaves were taken to Egypt by way of the desert or down the Nile while the other half was sent to ports on the Red Sea for export to Arabia and the Persian Gulf. The origins of this trade, as has already been seen, go back many centuries. Ottoman records show that slaves were being shipped to Turkey and Egypt from Suakin following the annexation of this Red Sea port by the Ottoman in 1556–57.[29]

Egypt's geographic location made it convenient to draw slaves from black Africa, particularly after its conquest of the Sudan in the early nineteenth century. Bornu and Wadai served as a major source of slaves for the Egyptian market. They were shipped there via Libya and the western desert along one of several available roads. The principle trading route, however, was one that led out of Darfur and which was in use since the end of the seventeenth century.[30] The annual caravan from Darfur was the largest of any that reached Egypt, and its principle merchandise was slaves. Another route reached out from Sennar. Here blacks taken as captives in raids into Abyssinia and the Nuba mountain region were sold to dealers who transported them either down the Nile to the well organized slave market of Cairo or over to Suakin for shipment to Arabia and the Persian Gulf. Suakin was already one of the great slave ports whose traffic turned the Red Sea into a major artery for the slave trade.

The captives taken in the southern Sudan included such proud Nilotic people as the Shilluk, the Nuer, and the Dinka, who were easy prey to the ravages caused by Egyptian colonization and European commercial exploitation. The great majority of these enslaved peoples were youths under fifteen years of age; most of them were girls. The Swiss traveler, Jean Louis Burckhardt, who traveled by slave caravan from Shendi to Suakin, recounts in his diary that many of the girls were prostituted by the slave traders or given over to nocturnal scenes of "the most shameless indecency."[31] By the early nineteenth century, Shendi, which had become a center for the internal trade of the various regions of the eastern Sudan as well as for the export trade, was one of the largest slave markets in the central Sudan. Burckhardt noted that some 5,000 slaves annually passed through this ramshackle town," of whom 2,500 are carried off by the Souakin merchants, and 1,500 by those of Egypt" and the rest by bedouins and nearby traders.

By the time the slaves reached Egypt's well organized slave markets, the slaves had changed hands three or four times and by then their nationality was unknown. The *jellaba,* or slave traders, would simply identify them by the nationality of the country from which they were exported; Egyptians knew little and cared less about the birthplace of the slaves they had purchased. For example, slaves coming from different regions of the Sudan were arbitrarily assigned a national identity such as *at-Tungurawi* or *al-Furi,* regardless of whether they actually were from the Tungur or Fur nations.[32]

The type of work performed by slaves in Egypt fairly well conformed to the range of tasks carried out by slave labor in most of the Arab world. To a large extent, this was identified with domestic service and concubinage, which generated a continuing demand for young female slaves. Periodic government drives to fill the ranks of the army with slave soldiers also kept up the demand for young male slaves. Muhammed Ali's brutal campaigns into the southern Sudan to secure slaves for the *jihadiyya,* or army of slave soldiers, were discussed in a previous chapter. A distinguishing characteristic of slavery in Egypt was that it often entailed the use of slaves for agricultural and outdoor purposes. There was a pronounced tendency, as well, among the rich (often referred to as Turko-Egyptians) and middle class people to own slaves as status symbols, much the same as rich people in Europe hired servants. In addition to the established uses for slaves, there was also a practice of using them as a form of currency. On Egypt's southern frontiers, government authorities frequently used slaves to pay functionaries and suppliers. As late as 1881, Egyptian military authorities in Fashoda were selling slaves to raise tax money.

There was, as a result of these requirements, a steady demand for slaves from the private and public sectors. Nor was this restricted to the upper reaches of Egyptian society. Many people, including shopkeepers, bedouins, *fellahin,* clerks, government employees, all ranks of army officers, the clergy, doctors, and others were generally in the market for slaves.[33] Christians and Jews also kept slaves, a right that was denied them in Turkey. The high turnover in the slave population owing to the practice of manumission, the susceptibility of slaves to contagious diseases, and the slave tradition of the ruling class, itself composed of former slaves, had the effect of intensifying the demand for slave labor.

In spite of numerous reports by British and French consular agents and travelers accounts, the number of slaves brought to Egypt during the nineteenth century remains shrouded in mystery. Estimates of slave imports do, however, provide rough indications of the volume of the trade for certain periods. In the early 1820s, large numbers of slaves were introduced into Egypt. In 1820, Muhammed Ali set a goal of 20,000 recruits for the *jihadiyya* that was not met because of the high death rate of the slaves during the desert crossing and in training camps from contagious diseases and dysentery. Three years later the target was raised to 30,000 recruits. In a message of encouragement to his soldiers, Muhammed Ali reminded them of the importance of their mission. "You are aware," he wrote, "the end of all our efforts and this expense is to procure Negroes. Please show zeal in carrying out our wishes in this capital matter."[34] The destructive raids against the Shilluk and Dinka in the Nile flood plain in the south and against Sudanic people elsewhere bore grim testimony to the zeal with which they carried out this command. These slave campaigns were continued during the 1830s as Muhammed Ali needed as many soldiers as possible for his far-flung military operations in Syria and Arabia. By the end of the decade, approximately 10,000 to 12,000 slaves were entering Egypt each year.

There was a sharp decline in slave imports over the next two decades, with the trade averaging about 5,000 to 6,000 a year. A reversal of this trend set in during the 1860s when the cotton boom caused a dramatic surge in demand for agricultural labor. The estimated annual inflow of slaves was on the order of 25,000 to 30,000. The irony of it was that this near-unquenchable demand for slaves undoubtedly grew out, in part, from President Lincoln's decision during the American Civil War to blockade Confederate ports, thereby closing Europe off from its traditional source of cotton. Egyptian cotton growers rushed to buy slaves to work their rapidly expanding cotton fields.

As long as Muhammed Ali held power, the slave trade remained an unquestioned feature of Egyptian life. Although from time to time, Muhammed Ali expressed opposition to slavery, he refused to curtail or abolish it on the familiar grounds that the practice was in conformity with Islam. The first attempt to break with it was made by the Khedive Said who issued an order in December 1854 banning the importation of slaves into Egypt from the Sudan. Behind this approach was the flawed premise that the slave trade could be eliminated by striking at the traders and interdicting the main slave routes without abolishing slavery around which the demand for slaves revolved.

This strategy proved utterly ineffectual against the army of Arab, Sudanese, and European traders who dominated the slave trade through the length and breadth of the upper Nile. To judge by Said's oft-stated pledges to enforce the decree, it was evidence that it had little effect. As the trade shifted westward to the populous Bahr el-Ghazal region which Arab slavers from Darfur turned into a "slave preserve," the volume of slaves brought to the slave markets grew. In the 1860s the region was exporting 4,000 to 6,000 slaves a year, a figure that was partially confirmed by the anti-slavery river patrols who seized some 3,500 captives between June 1864 and February 1866. Estimates for 1867 placed total exports from the Sudan at between 10,000 and 30,000, with half being shipped overland down the Nile valley and across the Sahara desert and the other half being taken to Red Sea ports. The accounts of the British explorers Speke and Grant, on their way home from Uganda, and those of Samuel Baker, who traveled up the Nile the same year, bear out the huge dimensions of the trade.

That the trade could continue to expand in the face of laws that branded it illegal is not difficult to understand.[35] There were powerful vested interests that brooked no opposition to this lucrative trade. Poorly paid officials were easily corrupted by venal groups. There was also no provision for the confiscated slaves. Although they should have been repatriated at the expense of the traders, they were taken to Khartoum, where they were pressed into the army. The government itself was thus led into a veiled form of slave recruitment. Ismael himself did not set a good example as he was one of Egypt's largest slave owners. As for slavery in the Sudan, he was well aware that his officials were deeply involved in the trade or deriving ill-gotten gains from it. A shrewd political leader, he realized how deeply rooted slavery was in the Sudan and how important the traffic in slaves was to Egyptian society.

Officially, Ismael was committed to doing away with the slave trade, and his public utterances on this subject led public opinion in the West to take him at his word. Abolition of the slave trade had become the great political cry in North America and in Europe, and Ismael understood he would have to join the campaign if he was to continue to receive Western support for his extravagant economic schemes and for his political ambitions in the southern Sudan, East Africa, and Abyssinia.

In a masterful stroke, Ismael named Samuel Baker, the British explorer, to mount an expedition which was to annex the upper Nile to Egypt, suppress the slave trade, and open the great lakes to navigation.[36] The appointment of Baker, whose exploits in the upper Nile valley and discovery of Lake Albert had made him a household name in Britain, was seen as an earnest indication of Ismael's intention to put down the slave trade. In taking up this challenge, Baker was confronted with the impossible task of taking on an army of some 5,000 Arab slave traders who were shipping some 50,000 slaves a year down the Nile. From his own travels, Baker could be under no illusions about the monumental nature of the assignment he willingly accepted from Ismael whom he believed to be a decent and sincere man. He had observed firsthand how Egyptian officials in Khartoum had connived in maintaining the trade and the disintegrative effect slave raiding had on Shilluk society. When Baker completed his mission in Euqatoria in 1873, he somewhat naively believed he had suppressed the slave trade. What he succeeded in doing was to banish the slave trade from the river but only to leave it more flourishing than ever in the desert.

The next to accept the challenge in Equatoria was Charles George Gordon, another in that breed of British soldier—adventurer whose exploits in Asia and Africa were so much part of the Victorian era. With a dedicated staff of Europeans, Gordon resolved to suppress the *razzias* and the slave trade, hoping that domestic slavery would simply die away.[37] Although he was a man of great courage and possessed of superb qualities of leadership, Gordon lacked tact in dealing with the slave-trading tribes. He entered upon the campaign against the slavers with great zeal. Hundreds of *jellabas* were expelled from their *zeribas,* or fortified encampments, in southern Darfur. After a particularly difficult campaign against the slave traders in the Bahr el-Ghazal region, which Gordon was at one point ready to abandon, he succeeded in defeating Sulaiman, one of the greatest slavers in the area, and scattered many of the lesser *jellabas.* In the wake of these harsh measures a wave of discontent spread over the river areas of the Sudan, which was later swept up in the rising tide of Mahdism.

Despite some successes, Gordon was unable to overcome the influence of the slave traders, win over a sullen and uncooperative bureaucracy who remained unreconciled to having Europeans holding top posts, and allay the suspicions of the southern tribes. Through his valiant efforts, Gordon managed to hamper the trade, but he fell far short of eliminating it. He won limited battles against the slavers, big and small, but lost the war against the slave trade. By his own estimates, 80,000 to 100,000 slaves were exported between 1875 and 1879. Discouraged by his lack of progress, Gordon resigned from the Egyptian service in 1880, a year after Ismael, his patron and supporter, had been deposed.

The slave trade in the Sudan had by now attracted a good deal of attention in England. As opposed to the considerable progress that successive British governments had achieved against the trade in North Africa, Turkey, and the East African Coast, its record in the Sudan and in Egypt was blank. Failure to act was undermining efforts to reduce slave imports into the Persian Gulf. Slave traders were taking slaves from Red Sea ports and bringing them to the Gulf and Arabia after their sources in the East African Coast began drying up as a result of the British-Zanzibar accord in 1873 outlawing the slave trade.

In 1877 the Convention for the Suppression of the Slave Trade was signed by the British and Egyptian governments outlawing the trade in Negro and Abyssinian slaves.[38] Slave dealers were to be severely punished and their slaves set free. British vessels in the Red Sea were empowered to stop ships and set free any slaves found on board. Any person depriving a freed slave of his freedom or taking from him his certificate of manumission would be punished as a slave dealer. The prohibition of selling slaves from family to family would take effect in Egypt after seven years and in the Sudan after twelve years. Similarly, the trade in white slaves would be made illegal after seven years. Under the treaty, four special *bureaux* were established in Cairo, Alexandria, the Delta, and upper Egypt to register manumissions and to find work for freed slaves and schools for the children among them. Despite some progress by the *bureaux* in manumitting slaves, the treaty still fell far short of its intended objectives. The slave trade continued unchecked in the Sudan. Gordon, who had been appointed governor general of the whole of the Sudan, stated in 1879 that the treaty's provisions governing the export of slaves from the country could no longer be enforced. After the Mahdi overran the country, the treaty, insofar as it effected the Sudan, was a dead letter.

Following the British occupation of Egypt in 1883, progress picked up in implementing the treaty. The activities of the manumission *bureaux* increased, and by 1889 they had freed 18,000 slaves. More and more of these freed slaves were able to find work in the cities, thereby eliminating an important reason for holding back on manumission. As the power of the workers' guilds declined, conditions were being created for the emergence of a free labor market in Egypt. One-time owners of slaves came to appreciate that free labor was cheaper and less troublesome than slave labor. Given these changing economic conditions and attitudes, slavery was becoming moribund. As early as 1891, Cromer, the British resident, could write in his annual report, that few slaves were left in private homes. In 1895 a new Convention between Great Britain and Egypt for the Suppression of Slavery and the Slave Trade was signed in Cairo. This agreement, and accompanying legislation that provided stiff penalties for those engaged in the trade, ended the long history of slavery and the slave trade in Egypt.

While Egypt was in the throes of freeing itself from slavery and the slave trade, quite another story was unfolding to the south. The British government, following the occupation of Egypt in 1883, disclaimed all responsibility for the far-flung empire which Ismael had claimed to rule beyond the Egyptian frontier. It was decided not to oppose the rising tide of Mahdism but to withdraw the threatened Egyptian garrisons from the Sudan and leave the country to its fate. This was to have been Gordon's last assignment, but it came to a tragic end. The destruction of the forces under Gordon's command at Khartoum in 1885 signaled a triumph for the Muslim revolt and, for the time being, sealed the end of Egyptian influence in the country.

The trade received an enormous impetus after the captrue by the mahdi of Bahr el-Ghazal, an important source for slaves. Slave traders who had been in hiding quickly flocked to the Madhi's standard. The great strength of the Mahdi was fed by a fierce hatred by the people for the brutal and corrupt Egyptian rule and their fanatical opposition to British-led efforts to destroy the slave trade. Even many slaves were attracted to this charismatic leader after he adjured slave owners to treat their charges according to the precepts of Islamic law. This benign approach was short lived. Little time passed before the Khalifa, the Mahdi's successor, re-established the slave trade in all its vigor. Slave caravans from Dervish territory in the Nile valley converged on the Red Sea, where bedouins arranged for the shipment of their human cargoes to Arabia. A. B. Wylde, sometime British consul in Jeddah, reported in 1887 that slaves—males, females and eunuchs—were never so numerous and cheap in the Red Sea area.[39]

Meanwhile in England, there was growing agitation for a new campaign to reclaim the Sudan. A desire to wash away the stain of Gordon's death was an important factor behind this feeling as were fears that other European countries might be tempted to occupy the country. It was against this background that an Anglo-Egyptian force was assembled under Colonel Kitchener to march on Omdurman to put an end to Mahdism. The Khalifa's 50,000 soldiers, many of whom were armed with nothing more than spears, were no match for the firepower of the British army. The Arab force was totally destroyed in what a war correspondent described as ". . . not a battle but an execution."

With the Sudan recovered, the British and the Egyptians quickly set about to bring slavery and the slave trade there to an end. The great progress achieved in Egypt toward the realization of these goals over the previous fifteen years did much to facilitate this task. The basis for abolishing the slave trade and slavery in the Sudan was established in the Anglo-Egyptian declaration of January 1899 which governed the future administration of the Sudan. One provision of the declaration prohibited, with immediate effect, the import and export of slaves. Domestic slavery, on the other hand, was to be gradually phased out. For example, those born in the Sudan after the reoccupation could not be enslaved. Kitchener, who became governor general of the Sudan, issued a directive to district governors that stated: "Slavery is not recognized in the Sudan," but added that "as long as service is willingly rendered by servants to masters it is unnecessary to interfere in the conditions existing between them."[40] Given the entrenched position of slavery in the country, it was to be expected that opposition to these antislavery measures would develop. Cases of slave trading were frequently uncovered. In 1906 the governor of Talodi was murdered along with forty Sudanese soldiers while attempting to suppress slavery. In that same year, Arab opposition to the slavery ordinances assumed near insurrectionary proportions in southern Kordofan after authorities set about to free and return to their homes one hundred twenty women and children who were held as slaves. However, the traffic in slaves disappeared; and slavery itself gradually withered away, although it took some years before its final demise.

## 7.

The success of the Busaidi clan in making good its claim to rule in Oman paved the way by the end of the eighteenth century for the assertion of direct Omani control over its mostly nominal East African possessions. The guiding force behind this move was Seyyid Said Ibn Sultan, who at the tender age of fifteen became ruler of Oman after dispatching his half-brother by a knife, thereby thwarting a plot to have him succeed to the throne. Said, a grandson of the founder of the Busaidi royal line, held power for fifty years and succeeded in the course of this time to make Zanzibar into an important island-state whose economic influence and political power extended the length of the Swahili coast. In the spirit of his predecessor, Said eschewed the title of Iman, which carried strong religious connotations, but styled himself Seyyid, meaning lord or master. Since 1795 the imamite had become a purely religious office distinct from secular power. It was as a secular ruler, using political and military power to achieve economic and imperial goals that Said saw himself, an image that was strengthened by styling himself Seyyid of Zanzibar.

A number of motives help explain Said's decision to concentrate power and authority in Zanzibar rather than in Muscat. In doing this, he continued in the tradition of his predecessors, who, in chasing the Portuguese from Mombasa and limiting their power to Mozambique, were impelled to create an overseas empire. Like the Portuguese, French, and English, Omani rulers extended their horizons to distant lands in search of fortune and land. Pursuit of imperial power was not, however, a prime factor in coming to Africa. The Omanis were not out to create an empire based on military power and a state structure. They were simply too small in numbers to carry off such a feat. They could not hope to succeed at such statecraft where the far more powerful Portuguese had failed. What the Omanis set out to accomplish was to build a trading empire based on the politically autonomous towns and ports of the coast whose leaders offered fealty and loyalty without compromising their own long-acquired rights. The most important part of this trading system was the traffic in slaves.[42] It was against this background that Zanzibar became the center of Omani activity in East Africa and developed as the pivot of the slave trade.

The East African trade, as has already been seen, received a powerful stimulus from the activities of French slavers starting in the last quarter of the eighteenth century. By the end of the century there were about 100,000 slaves in Bourbon and Ile de France as against a relative handful fifty years earlier. Between 1811 and 1821, according to Nicholls, slaves were being shipped from the coast to the Mascarene Islands at the rate of about 5,000 a year, or a total of 50,000 for the decade.

About half of these came from the Swahili coast where the
Omanis held sway.[43] In spite of legal restriction imposed by
the Moresby Treaty (1822) forbidding the sale of slaves to
Christians from Said's dominions, the trade continued
through the first half of the century. In addition to the Mascarene Island trade, Spaniards and Portuguese were buying
slaves from the Swahili coast, notably from Kilwa, although
in smaller numbers. These slaves, which were shipped
around the Cape to the Americas, accounted for a substantial
total of the proportion taken from the coast during the first
four decades of the century, after which their numbers fell off
appreciably. The effect of European demand for slaves, as
well as for ivory, was to stimulate economic activity up and
down the coast. The Omanis, along with other Arabs, contributed to and benefited from the rising fortunes of the coast
by trading in slaves.

Accompanying this increased economic activity was a pronounced tendency by Omani rulers to emphasize their political authority on the coast. Renewed attempts to intrude
political power stemmed from both political and economic
considerations. There was a long-standing concern over the
politically free-wheeling activities of the sultans in the coastal
towns who did not pass up an opportunity to chip away at or
even challenge Omani suzerainty. In 1785, Oman managed to
reestablish its political authority over Kilwa, from which it
had been ousted a number of years earlier. Perhaps of greater
moment was the concern among the more traditional Arab
slave traders and their Indian creditors to tighten up on the
market and supply of slaves. Rising European demand undoubtedly contributed to the sharp rise in prices for slaves
during the last two decades of the eighteenth century. In
Kilwa the price had gone up from $25 a head to $40 in 1802.
This was not in the interest of the northern Arabs who were
competing in same markets. It was also a source of concern
to the Omanis as well. They purchased slaves in Kilwa for the

Muscat market and for their growing needs in Zanzibar. Thus, increased political control could be seen as a way of stabilizing the market by bringing increased numbers of slaves from the hinterlands and keeping a closer watch over European purchasers. As part of this strategy, duties on exports would be raised so as to assure maximum revenues.

It was this objective of commanding the growing revenues generated by the slave trade along the coast that provided another reason to Omani leaders to assert authority there. Revenues were growing and there was little doubt that much of this bonanza was derived from the expanding slave trade. In 1804 French Captain Dallon complained about the extortionate duty of $11 per head that was extracted from his compatriots by Zanzibari authorities. In Kilwa the duty was somewhat less. Assuming an average duty of $10 per head on the 2,500 slaves who were exported annually from the Swahili coast to the Europeans for the period 1811–21, Said's treasury stood to benefit by $25,000 a year.[44] This represented a third of his income from the coast in 1818. This made Said very much alive to the potential value of the coast and spurred him to fasten his sovereignty on Brava, Lamu, and Pate in the early 1820s. These duties did not include the substantial revenues derived from slave exports to Zanzibar (and Pemba) and to the northern destinations, that is, Arabia, the Persian Gulf, and India. In the Arab heartland, where slavery was a deeply entrenched institution, its survival could be assured only by the continuous influx of substantial numbers of slaves. Slavery had also taken root in Zanzibar long before it became a necessity in the 1830s and 1840s to sustain the clove plantations. The British naval officer, Captain Smee, who visited Zanzibar in 1811 observed that quite a few Arabs owned as many as 800 to 900 slaves. He considered that about three-quarters of the island's 200,000 population was made up of servile labor. A lively trade in slaves was going on, according to Smee, with 6,000 to 10,000 being exported each year to Muscat, India, and the Mascarene Islands.[45]

As trade routes in the interior expanded, the distribution system for slaves and ivory underwent marked changes. Kilwa no longer shipped slaves directly to overseas markets but was reduced to routing them to Zanzibar, which became the primary point in the assembly and export of slaves. Slave merchants now flocked to the Zanzibar market for this human commodity. Captain Smee, who observed that market in operation, described how large numbers of slaves paraded past the merchants who were anxious to pick out the best of the lot. His account bears the hallmark of a man trained to report only what he observed:

> When any of them strikes a spectator's fancy, the line immediately stops, and a process of examination ensues which for minuteness is unequalled in any cattle market in Europe. The intending purchaser having [discovered] that there is no defect . . . of speech, hearing, etc., that there is no disease present and that the slave does not snore in sleeping, which is counted a very great fault, next proceeds to examine the person: the mouth and teeth are first inspected, and afterwards every part of the body in succession. . . . The slave is then made to walk or run a little way to show that there is no defect about the feet; after which, if the price is agreed to, they are stripped of their finery and delivered over to their future master. I have frequently counted between twenty and thirty of these files in the market at one time, some of which contained about thirty [slaves]. Women with children newly born hanging at their breasts and others so old they can scarcely walk are sometimes seen dragged about in this manner . . . some groups appeared so ill fed that their bones appeared as if ready to penetrate the skin.[46]

Under the attentive care of Seyyid, Zanzibar grew from an insignificant little town, rarely visited by shipping except to take on water and provisions, to the principle port on the western shores of the Indian Ocean, the chief *entrepot* of the African-Asiatic trade, and the home of the greatest slave market in the East. The *entrepot* role was more a consequence of geography than of deliberate choice.[47] During the long period between the defeat of the Portuguese and the subjugation of the Mazrui family, the Omanis had intended to make Mombasa into the center of their emerging empire. Had they conquered the town, it still could not have competed with Zanzibar in becoming the pivot of Omani trade. Zanzibar, with its commodious harbor, was on the main line to most of the trade routes into the interior whereas Mombasa was far up the coast and inaccessible to most slave and ivory caravans. The island was also endowed with natural resources, notably timber, coconuts, and money cowries. Seyyid also appreciated the immense fertility of Zanzibar's soil, which was ideal for developing the lucrative clove culture. To his keen eye, Zanzibar had the added virtue of being settled by Arab families who did not hold back in their loyalty to him.

As long as Great Britain tolerated the East African slave trade, Zanzibar remained in the forefront of this commerce. Estimates of this trade vary considerably because they are based, with a few exceptions, on incomplete and often contradictory accounts. If the quantitative information leaves much to be desired, the impressions it creates, however, are unmistakable. The numbers of slaves shipped from the coast to Zanzibar and from there to northern destinations for most of the century were substantial indeed.

Most estimates of the number of slaves who passed from the coast to Zanzibar and to points north each year for the period between 1800 and 1870 range from 6,000 to 20,000, although the latter figure is undoubtedly inflated for the first three decades of the century. According to Martin and Ryan,[48] the figures for each of the first three decades ranged from 60,000 to 65,000. There is a 50 percent jump in exports during the 1830s to 95,000 and a virtual doubling of this figure in the following decade. Between 1840 and 1849, about 187,000 slaves were shipped from the coast to Zanzibar and to Arabia, the Persian Gulf, and India. There is a moderate fall off to 176,000 during the 1850s but a resurgence in the numbers over the next sixteen years. In the 1860s, about 207,000 were shipped; and between 1870 and 1876, the year the slave trade was abolished in Zanzibar, 300,000 slaves were sent to the island and to the northern destinations. These figures give a total East African Arab slave trade of 1,257,100.

According to this same study, about 55 percent of the slaves sent to Zanzibar were retained there for local needs and the remainder were exported to the northern destinations. Thus, average decennial imports from East Africa into Arabia, Persia and India from 1800 to 1829 were 25,000, with the figure rising to 35,000 for the 1830s, 40,000 for the 1840s, 65,000 for the 1850s, and 20,000 for the first three years of the seventies. Applying a 9 percent transit mortality rate increases the sum of these figures from 390,200 slaves to 424,100.

Average annual figures used by Martin and Ryan in arriving at total numbers, which they readily acknowledge to be "guesstimates," may very well be excessively low. Reliable estimates given in the 1840s for the number of East African slaves sent north are sharply at variance with those used by these two researchers. Loarer estimated that before 1846, 7,000 to 8,000 slaves were exported to the northern destinations. Estimates that Hamerton gave before 1846 are double those offered by Loarer. He claimed that 20,000 slaves were brought to Zanzibar each year, and of these 13,000 to 15,000 were exported to the Red Sea, Arabia, the Persian Gulf, and India.[49] For the 1850s there are average annual estimates that exceed the figures given for the 1840s. According to one report, in 1856, the year Said died, 15,000 slaves were taken from Zanzibar to the Persian Gulf and 2,500 to the Red Sea. These and other figures, in the view of Nicholls, suggest that despite year to year fluctuations the northward market by the 1840s "was accepting about 15,000 slaves annually."[50]

The boom in the East Coast slave trade was fueled primarily by the development of the clove culture in Zanzibar and to a far lesser extent in Pemba and Pate. Cloves were first introduced to Zanzibar in 1819 with the encouragement of Said, but production only began to hit its peak in the 1840s and then leveled off after the 1850s after a decline in prices set in.[51] The planting, picking, and harvesting of cloves, which yielded two crops a year, were labor-intensive operations requiring a large and disciplined work force. An annual 30 percent attrition rate due to high mortality and desertions usually meant that the slave population had to be renewed after three or four years. A substantial amount of the clove production came from a few large plantations, some of which were worked by as many as 4,000 to 6,000 slaves. As late as the 1890s, the sultan owned a number of large estates employing 6,000 slaves. Members of the Busaidi family and other prominent Arab and Swahili proprietors owned plantations that required the labor of hundreds of slaves. Most *mashambas,* or plantations, however, were owned by small farmers who used about 40 slaves.

As the clove trees began yielding large harvests in the 1840s, this began to transform the social structure of Zanzibar. Heretofore, Omani traders looked down on agriculture. Now these traders became farmers, and slave traders became slave owners. A slave system gradually emerged in Zanzibar and in other parts of East Africa, notably Pemba and Malindi, where the ownership of slaves and land defined the principle social groups in society. As ownership of slaves became more important, Zanzibaris regarded them more as a part of the social order and less as a commodity to sell.

The great demands for slaves placed severe strains on traditional methods for acquiring them. Initially, slaves were to be found in abundance in the coastal hinterlands; but by the beginning of the nineteenth century, Yao and even some Malawi slaves were brought to Kilwa, as were Nyamwezi to the north. Many of these slaves were the traditional by-product of the internecine tribal wars. After a while, a new form of warfare developed whose sole purpose was to acquire slaves who would then be sold at the coast. This was greatly facilitated by the introduction of firearms.[52] In the late 1830s the acquisition of firearms from Arab slave traders enabled the Sangu to become a major force in south-central Tanganyka and to carry out slave raids against the nearby population. Zanzibar Arabs would promise leaders of the Zigua a certain number of muskets in exchange for slaves, which would prompt them to attack neighboring villages and then send the survivors to the Zanzibar slave markets. A not uncommon tactic was for the Arabs to come to an area, stir up trouble between different chiefs, and then wait for the victor to sell them the slaves taken in battle.

The Arabs began penetrating the interior in small numbers by the start of the third decade, usually following routes pioneered by Africans of the interior.[53] This was a radical change in their pattern of settlement, which for centuries found them indifferent to everything beyond the thin coastal fringe with its towns and plantations. The lure of great profits, which could run as much as 500 percent from the slave and ivory trade, proved irresistible. By the 1830s small numbers of Arabs pushed up to and beyond Lake Tanganyka. Gradually, they founded communities around the shores of the lake in such towns as Tabora and Ujiji. These and other Arab communities were not interested in taking territory but to trade with the Africans.

Where the Arabs came up against a centralized state, it was the Africans who defined the terms of this trade.[54] This was the case with the Buganda, one of the most highly centralized of the African states. A profitable trade developed since the arms and cloth offered by the Arabs were much sought after by the Buganda, who provided slavery and ivory in return. Quite another situation arose when the Arabs moved into an area where there existed no centralized political authority to rein in their quest after slaves and ivory. Such was the case in the eastern Congo in the region known as Manyema, which was rich in ivory. Here the Arabs spread their authority by establishing principalities ruled by powerful traders, the most famous of whom was Tipu Tip. Armed with rifles and aided by local people such as the Myamwezi, the Arabs carried out devastating raids for ivory and slaves. One of the great traders in ivory and an unrepentant slaver, Muhammid bin Hamid, better known as Tipu Tip, carved out a political empire in the upper Congo where he reigned supreme during the 1880s and early 1890s. This system of raiding and trading endured until the Belgians of the Congo Free State defeated the Arabs in battle and destroyed the last vestiges of their power.[55]

## 8.

British attempts to curb the East African slave trade preceded by a number of years their diplomatic attack against it in North Africa, Turkey, and the Persian Gulf. Along the Swahili coast as elsewhere, the British campaign against the Muslim-controlled traffic revealed a strong mixture of political self-interest and diplomatic concerns. The British first took up the issue with Seyyid when they first became aware that slaves were being taken from his dominions to India. This indeed, was a centuries-old traffic, but those who carried it on were now in violation of the 1808 Act for the Abolition of the British Slave Trade. The act applied to the transport of slaves into India and other British possessions.

After numerous efforts by the Indian government to bring a halt to the traffic, it was decided in 1812 to bring the matter directly to Seyyid. The British governor in Bombay addressed a request to him that he put his subjects on notice that the import of slaves into India was illegal and that they be urged to end the practice. Napean, the British governor, even went so far to urge Seyyid that he emulate the principal powers of Europe and abolish the entire slave trade. This request apparently struck Seyyid as so odd that he did not bother himself to respond.

The British request bore few results. Seyyid was not about to sacrifice the revenues he derived from the trade or antagonize his subjects for the sake of British legal propriety. There was little inclination for that matter by the British to push Seyyid too hard lest he ally himself with the French.[56] It was only after the destruction of French power in the Indian Ocean that the British first took the timid step of raising the matter with Seyyid. This was no more than a polite request as the British did not wish to complicate problems for the young ruler with his subjects.

The first serious attempt to bring the traffic under control came not from British authorities in Bombay but from the governor of Mauritius, Sir Robert Farquhar. Before this island of French sugar growers had fallen to the British during the Napoleonic wars, it was the practice to import slaves from Madagascar and from Seyyid's East Coast domains. Now such imports were no longer legal. Caught between the need to abolish the traffic and the wrath of the French settlers, Farquhar decided to end the trade by striking at its source. He concluded a treaty with Radama, the ruler of Madagascar, to prohibit the sale of slaves to Europeans. Having closed one source of the trade, Farquhar enlisted the support of the government in Bombay in 1821 to prevail upon Seyyid to take similar measures in his dominions. The authorities in Bombay had come under increased pressure to do something following publication of a report by the African Institution in London on the Zanzibar slave trade claiming that 10,000 slaves were being sent each year to India,

Muscat, Bourbon, and Mauritius.[57] When Seyyid was confronted by this joint request from the British government in Bombay and Farquhar, he could not ignore it.

Shrewd politican that he was, the Omani ruler realized that refusal to cooperate could cost him British goodwill without which he would have to stand alone against his foes in Muscat and in East Africa. In the summer of 1822, Captain Fairfax Moresby was dispatched to Oman to negotiate a treaty with Seyyid.

Under terms of the accord concluded between Seyyid and Moresby, the sale of slaves in his dominions to "Christians of every description" and the transport of slaves in Arab vessels to European possessions were forbidden.[58] Seyyid's vessels were enjoined from carrying slaves south of Cape Delgado, thereby preventing their sale to Mauritius, and east of a line from Diu Head (in India) to near Socotra, thereby forbidding their shipment to India. Enforcement of the treaty's provisions was to be assumed by ships of the British navy.

This was the first of a number of fateful encounters that Seyyid and his successors were to have with agents of the British government concerning the delicate matter of restricting the slave trade. The Omanis were made to understand that British friendship, which they were much in need of, had to be repaid in the hard currency of slave trade reform. As it turned out, the price was not as steep as Seyyid had feared. The Indian Ocean was too vast and British cruisers too few in numbers to permit an effective vigilance of the many vessels that made their way from Zanzibar to Mauritius and to India. Evidence was soon not wanting that the provisions of the Moresby Treaty were being flouted.[59]

There the matter of the Indian Ocean slave trade would have probably rested for some time had it not been for the bizarre episode involving an officer of the Royal Navy on the East African Coast. On a voyage from the Cape to Zanzibar, Captain William Owen of H.M.S. Leven obtained evidence that the traffic in slaves between Zanzibar and Mozambique was continuing despite the restrictions of the Moresby Treaty. On his return to Bombay, he presented this evidence to the government, which chose not to act on the matter. Owen, a man of deep convictions, followed his own counsel and decided to conduct a personal campaign against the slave trade. As chance would have it, his ship approached Mombasa in February 1824 when the Mazrui were in revolt against Seyyid and the port was under blockade by his war fleet. The Mazrui saw Owen's arrival as an opportunity to lift the blockade and forestall future attempts by the Busaidi ruler to assert his authority over the port. After welcoming Owen, they offered him sovereignty over the town. Although not authorized to do so, he accepted, firm in the belief that a British presence in Mombasa would strike a severe blow against the East African slave trade.

As well could be imagined, Seyyid was outraged by this development and sent a strong protest to India. After an extensive correspondence, Elphinstone, the British governor in Bombay, bowed to Seyyid's remonstrations and the Union Jack was hauled down. He continued to press Seyyid for concessions as there was ample evidence to show that the Moresby Treaty had indeed been flouted. In 1825, Elphinstone sounded out Seyyid on total abolition of the slave trade in exchange for compensation. The matter did not get very far as the Omani put forward conditions he knew would prove unacceptable to the British. Complete abolition would have seriously reduced his revenues, and no offsetting benefits were in the offing. Seyyid, moreover, was not unmindful of the impact such a drastic step would have on the influential territorial and religious chiefs, many of whom were unhappy with his leadership.[60]

Elphinstone's proposal, unusual for the timorous Indian government, demonstrated that support existed in high official circles for a frontal assault on the slave trade in the

Indian Ocean. This view began to crystallize in the 1830s when it became clear that halfway measures were proving ineffectual. Many were prepared to acknowledge that the Moresby Treaty had not lived up to the expectations of its sponsors. In providing a corridor for trading in slaves from East Africa to the Persian Gulf, Arab ships had little difficulty in going beyond these limits and selling slaves in the Indian market. Once in Indian ports, the blacks were easily passed off as passengers or as wives of crew members. For the homebound journey, the ships included in their "cargo" Indian girls who were sold as slaves in the Persian Gulf. The treaty also did not prove to be much of a hindrance in affecting the slave trade between the East Coast and Mauritius. In 1826 the *Anti-Slavery Reporter* carried an article accusing Farquhar of being lax in enforcing the law that banned the importation of slaves into the island.

Each time voices were raised in support of an all-out attack against the slave trade, others responded by calling for a cautious approach. The latter argued that abolition of the slave trade would lead to the collapse of Seyyid's authority and the loss of the only reliable ally Britain could count on in waging its diplomatic attack against the traffic. Britain would then have the unenviable task of enforcing abolition—a task that the British navy was ill-equipped to handle. Some even argued that abolition might tempt unemployed Omani sailors to revert to a life of piracy and again prey on British shipping. Less and less heed was paid to these conservative voices as Britain began stepping up its diplomatic attack on the Indian Ocean slave trade toward the end of the 1830s.

Toward the close of 1835, the chief secretary at Bombay, J. P. Willoughby, submitted a memorandum to the governor showing that an extensive traffic in slaves was being carried on in the whole of western India. The Moresby line, as it stood, terminated in Diu Head, leaving the coasts at Kutch, Kathiawar, and Sind open to the slave trade. It was also pointed out that subjects of other gulf states were under no obligation to respect the Moresby line. In 1839, steps were taken to remedy this situation. Seyyid agreed to move the Moresby line westward so as to bring western Indian within the prohibited zone. The Trucial sheikhs were approached to respect the line, which they readily agreed to do. In addition to these changes, Seyyid agreed to allow ships of the Indian navy to exercise rights of search and seizure, which under the Moresby Treaty were reserved to the Royal Navy.

The purpose of the 1839 agreement was to seal off western India from the slave trade and not to interfere with the workings of the trade elsewhere. This hope was soon dashed when it was realized that the trade to India was as extensive as before. The traffic from the Red Sea and Zanzibar to Arabia and Persia Gulf continued to thrive. Information obtained by Captain Nott of H.C.C. Tigris in September 1840 led him to conclude that as many as 100 vessels sailed from Muscat and Sur for Zanzibar each year, returning with 50 to 200 slaves in each ship, while another 20 or more vessels made their way to Berbera and the Red Sea bringing back 200 to 300 Abyssinians. Of the slaves brought to Muscat and Sur—both *entrepots* for the slave trade—4,000 to 5,000 were sold up and down the Gulf. What was so interesting about this trade, and which helped explain why it was so difficult to eradicate, was that it was fully bound up in regular commerce. Slaves on their way to Basra, it was found, were purchased from the money derived from the annual pearl fishery and profits on the trading with India and Africa. The proceeds derived from their sale at Basra would be used to purchase part of the Basra date crop, which in turn would be sold on the Trucial coast and in India. Slaves had become another commodity which lubricated the transactions of the marketplace.

At the Foreign Office, Palmerston had concluded that nothing short of the abolition of the slave trade could reduce the flow of slaves to the Middle East. On June 8, 1841, the deputy under secretary at the Foreign Office, Lord Leveson, sent a strongly worked letter to the Indian government that Seyyid and the Trucial state sheikhs should be told that henceforth the slave trade would no longer be tolerated. In the letter, which was a landmark in the history of the campaign against the slave trade in the Indian Ocean, Leveson wrote: ". . . So strong a feeling against the Slave trade and so deep a feeling of its criminality have grown up in the minds of the English nation that the British Government cannot avoid using its utmost means to prevent the continuance of such proceedings wherever it may be able to do so."[61]

The letter, which was forwarded to Hamerton in Zanzibar, informed the consul that Seyyid and the Arab chiefs should be asked "to forbid all slave trading by sea and to permit British ships of war to search, seize and confiscate all native vessels found with slaves on board wherever navigating." These were extreme demands, which, when read to Seyyid, caused him to exclaim: ". . . it is the same as the orders of Azrael, the Angel of Death: nothing but to obey." Before he would submit, the wily Arab leader was determined to wring the maximum of concessions from his mentors. He sent a personal envoy to London offering to agree to yield on the slave trade issue but on condition that he be given Bahrein and that the British protect him against France. At the time, France was seeking to gain influence on the coast, which Seyyid viewed as a serious threat because many of his people, enraged at the restrictions imposed on slave trading, were hoping to obtain French support to depose him.

British public opinion toward the trade had changed such that the government refused to bargain on what it considered to be a matter of principle. Under terms of the accord, which took effect on January 1, 1847, Seyyid was duty bound to prohibit the export of slaves from his African dominions and, conversely, to forbid his Asian possessions from importing slaves from many part of Africa. By this sweeping language,

Seyyid could no longer export slaves to Arabia and the Persian Gulf. The British navy would be empowered to enforce these restrictions. However, as a way of showing political support for Seyyid, the British dispatched two warships to Muscat to shore up his position, which was again under threat from domestic foes. There was a certain logic to this move, which made him ever more aware of his need for British protection. As Britain demanded more concessions from Seyyid, it had to be careful that the authority that granted these concessions remain politically viable.

By accepting these terms, Seyyid realized not only that he would incur substantial losses in revenue but that his authority would be deeply compromised in Zanzibar and Oman. Typical of the way he negotiated, Seyyid countered with a last minute proposal that the slave trade carried on within his African dominions be exempt from the ban. He argued with Hamerton that his proposal was consistent with the proposed treaty which was designed to prohibit exports from his African lands to Arabia and the Persian Gulf. Including the African trade in the prohibited zone would, he contended, sound the death knell of slavery in Zanzibar along with its slave-based economy. On the one hand, the British recognized that the practical effect of Seyyid's proposal would be to weaken the treaty. Once slave-laden vessels were allowed to leave east Coast ports, naval patrols would be confronted with the same difficulty in preventing them from reaching the forbidden fields of Asia. On the other, to deny Zanzibar access to African slaves would spell the demise of slavery in Zanzibar, which was not their intention. Mindful of the consequences of banning the slave trade within Seyyid's African domains, the British acquiesced in his request and, in so doing, underwrote the continued existence of slavery in Zanzibar. Thus, it must have been with a great sigh of relief that Seyyid received from Hamerton toward the end of 1844 the Foreign Office communication saying: "Her Majesty's Government claims no right to interfere with the passage of slaves in your ships between the ports and islands on the coast of your African dominions."

In accepting the treaty, Seyyid signed away a great deal and received very little in return. Why he did this is still not clear, although it may have come from a realization that the days of the slave trade were numbered. The simplest explanation, and the one that may be closest to the truth, was his dependence on British power. Understanding that he could not afford to antagonize his protector and only ally, Seyyid drew the obvious conclusion and bowed to the inevitable. In doing this, he managed to wring a last concession whereby British ships would not be allowed to search vessels belonging to his family on the way from the Red Sea or Arabian Sea. He made no secret for his reasons for wanting to protect his ships from such interference. Seyyid, true to the customs of the time, wanted to ensure a continous supply of Abyssinian girl slaves and eunchs for the slave markets of Zanzibar and the other Arab towns on the coast.[62]

## 9.

The moderate hopes engendered by the Hamerton Treaty of driving the slave ships from the Red Sea, Arabian Sea, and the Persian Gulf were quickly dashed. In a gloomy report to Palmerston, who returned to the Foreign Office in 1846, Hamerton expressed fears that the Zanzibaris had failed to comprehend that conveying slaves northward was a criminal offense. The German missionary, John Krapf, noted in 1850 that the same stream of slaves from Lake Nyasa was flowing in full volume to Kilwa and thence shipped to Zanzibar and from there to northward destinations. As old trading routes were interdicted, new ones sprung up. Many slaves, for example, after being transferred to Kilwa were run southward to the Comoros or Madagascar with papers for the northern voyage.[63]

The language of the treaty, moreover, at least as far as Seyyid was concerned, was unclear as to whether Abyssinia was covered. Seyyid clearly had personal reasons for wanting to keep open the slave lanes from Red Sea ports. Far more important was the growing role that these ports, notably Berbera, Zeila, and Tajura, were playing in Persia Gulf slave imports. In 1850, Hamerton reported that the exports of *sidis*, or slaves, from his African dominions were not one-fifth of what they had been a few years earlier. This was offset, however, by the increasing numbers of *habshis*, or Abyssinians, who were being transported to the Persian Gulf. One indication of the size of this commerce can be seen from a caravan made up of seven hundred children of various ages that arrived in Berbera in April 1848 from Harrar in time for the annual trade fair.[64] After a British cruiser weighed anchor and left for Aden, three hundred were bought by dhow owners from Sur and the Persian Gulf.

Unforeseen by the treaty was the aggressive reentry of Réunion (formerly Bourbon) into the East Coast market for *éngagé* labor. This followed the French revolution of 1848 when slavery was abolished in all colonies. The colonists found themselves in the same dire straits for labor as the planters of Mauritius when England took over the island some years earlier. They ingeniously put into effect a system known as the "Free Labor Emigration System" whereby slaves were set free in a sham judicial procedure and then shipped off to Réunion, the Comoros, and Madagascar where they worked under contract for a five-year period. Despite strong objections by the British and Sultan Majid, Seyyid's successor, thousands of men were taken from the Lake Nyasa region by Arab slavers and shipped to the French colonies. The system was finally abolished in 1864 by which time the French could recruit "cooly" labor from British India.[65]

Beginning in the early 1850s, the slave trade from Zanzibar to Arabia and the Persian Gulf picked up considerably notwithstanding genuine efforts by Seyyid to punish offenders. As usual, the complaisant demands of officials in Zanzibar and in the receiving ports made it relatively easy to maintain the illicit traffic. The British government, however, had to share much of the blame. After taking upon itself responsibility for enforcing the Hamerton Treaty, it failed miserably in making available an adequate number of cruisers to apprehend the slave-running dhows. The anti-slavery squadron on duty, usually made up of three or four ships, never succeeded in apprehending but a small fraction of the slaves who were being transported northward in any one year. In the years 1867–69, observers maintained that at least 37,000 slaves slipped pass the naval patrols as against 2,645 who were caught and freed.[66] The complex and lengthy bureaucratic procedure involved in seizing a suspected vessel also had the effect of deterring aggressive patrolling. The offending ship and its crew often had to be brought to a faraway point where the case was adjudicated. Charges could be brought against slave ships only if the slaves were tightly packed together and chained. These conditions did not always exist on board small ships or dhows where there was no need for such guarded confinement.

Events of a political and constitutional order further conspired to weaken the already frail controls over the clandestine shipment of slaves. In 1856, Seyyid died on board his flag vessel on the return voyage from Muscat. Long years of rule and the demands placed on him by an increasingly restive population whose rights to trade in slaves were being eroded sapped much of his strength. There were early signs that Seyyid was becoming disheartened and that the vigor that had once characterized his actions was deserting him. "The Imam is at present fifty-six years old," observed Hamerton in July 1844, "and within the last three years he has become much broken and altered in every way, from the effects of stimulating condiments which he is constantly taking in order to qualify him for the joys of the harem." Twelve years later, when Seyyid was sixty-eight, his spirits and strength had ebbed even more, a decline that was undoubtedly hastened by the death of his second son, Khalid, whom he had directed to succeed him in Zanzibar. A year after Seyyid's death, Hamerton, who had served in Zanzibar since 1841, succumbed to illness. With these two men gone, Zanzibar was in for a long period of political instability.

Before Seyyid died, he had given instructions that Majid succeed to his African dominions and Thuwain, his third son, to his Asiatic dominions.[67] Thanks to Hamerston's precautions, the twenty-one-year-old Majid Ibn Said assumed power without a hitch. The last word, however, had not been heard from Thuwain and from his other brother, Barghash. Thuwain felt cheated that Majid had inherited the more prosperous part of the kingdom while Barghash took deep offense that nothing had been done for him. Following in the long Busaidi tradition, each plotted to remove Majid and become ruler of Zanzibar. Both, however, were foiled by British military power. Thuwain, who had outfitted a fleet in 1859, was intercepted at sea by a British warship and induced to return to Muscat. Some months later, Barghash, with encouragement from foes of his father, attempted to seize the throne but failed and was exiled to Bombay. Again, Majid invoked the aid of the British, whose warships shelled Barghash's supporters, causing them to disperse. The dispute between Majid and Thuwain was finally resolved in 1862 by an arbitration award handed down by Lord Canning, governor general of India. Under this decision, Majid was declared ruler of Zanzibar and the African dominions. As compensation to Thuwain for the inequality between the inheritances, Majid would pay annually to the ruler of Muscat a forty-thousand-crown subsidy. This was to be a permanent arrangement, and henceforth each heritage was to become separate and distinct. In 1862 the British and French governments issued a joint declaration in which they undertook to respect the independence of the two settlements.

Whatever else these developments may have done, they made Majid dependent on Great Britain. The British envoy in Zanzibar was more a magistrate than a consul. British power on the island, once it came ito play, was to be irresistible. Once unreservedly placed in the service of the anti-slave trade cause, it would sweep aside the last obstacles to destroying this trade. The moral climate for the emergence of a firm anti-slavery political stance was developing in England.

Accounts for the horrors of the East Coast slave trade were frequently brought before the public by explorers, missionaries, and government officials. None was more effective than the Scottish minister, David Livingstone.[68] He was of the same humanitarian calling as Wilberforce, Clarkson, and Fowell Buxton, who in their own day galvanized British society and, ultimately, the British government to act against the transatlantic and trans-Saharan slave trades. When Livingstone reached the upper Zambesi River in 1851, he first came face to face with the workings of the Arab slave trade. On his return home, he carried an impassioned plea against the evils of this trade, which, he tirelessly repeated, was cutting a swath of death and destruction across broad expanses of Africa. What he had to say left a deep impression on his many audiences, whose influence radiated into the highest circles of the British government. Livingstone's plea for action carried another message. In attacking the slave trade, it was not enough to sign treaties. This evil, he said, would only give way through the introduction of commerce, Christianity, and Western civilization. To achieve this, the British had the obligation to join other nations in colonizing Africa. Livingstone's thinking reached a large audience in England and did much to condition British society to believe that it was morally right for Britain to seek colonies in Africa. In no small measure, the justification for this supposed *mission civisilatrice* was to root out slavery and the slave trade.

It was against this changing political climate that Britain assumed a more aggressive role in fighting the East Coast slave trade. There was a greater willingness to take a firm hand in resolving the succession crisis in Zanzibar. There were other indications that Britain was prepared to shed its traditional stance in the island's affairs where this involved the slave trade. Once Majid was in power, the British came to his assistance to protect him from what had become an annual depredation of northern Arabs. Many of these Arabs were slave traders, unemployed sailors, and criminals who arrived in Zanzibar with the monsoon and terrorized the population, kidnapped slaves, and clashed with Majid's small Baluchi guard. Majid himself took action against the northern Arabs in 1864 by forbiding dhows from sailing from Zanzibar during the time of the southwest monsoon and imposing heavy punishment upon anyone selling slaves to them. In theory it was impossible to take slaves from the island to northern destinations.

These and other measures, including tightened naval controls, proved ineffectual in stanching the flow of slaves to the north. A new strategy had to be devised in place of the thirty-year-old policy of trying to end the trade by attacking it at sea. A select committee appointed by Parliament to look into the trade came to the only possible conclusion: ". . . All legitimate means should be used to put an end altogether to the East African slave trade." To achieve this objective, it would be necessary to put a stop to all legitimate slave trading within Zanzibar's African dominions. "Any attempt to supply slaves for domestic use in Zanzibar," the committee warned, "will always be a pretext and cloak for a foreign trade."[69] Consistent with this objective, the committee recommended the adoption of a new treaty that would prohibit the East African slave trade completely.

A special mission led by Sir Bartle Frere, a former governor of Bombay, was sent to Zanzibar to gain the sultan's approval to the committee's recommendation. Frere, a committed abolitionist, was not to bargain with Sultan Barghash on the terms of his mandate. When he arrived in Zanzibar, the island was recovering from the effects of a severe hurricane which struck the year before and devastated the island's clove trees. If anything, the immediate need was for more slaves to rehabilitate the clove plantations. Barghash, an able man who understood the need to get along with the British, was not inclined to go along with Frere. The conservative landowners had warned him that implementation of Frere's proposals would ineluctably lead to the end of slavery on the island. Without a continuous flow of slaves from the mainland, they warned him, slavery would wither away. This was the counsel that Barghash followed when Frere came to see him one last time. On February 11 he gave his final answer to Frere: "You request that we signify to you either our acceptance or our refusal. In one word, No."[70]

In giving this reply, Barghash overestimated the nature of his sovereignty and underestimated British resolve to put an end to the slave trade. His father, who enjoyed far greater power and prestige, would never have returned so unequivocal an answer to a representative of the British government. Following this encounter, Frere left Zanzibar. London received the sultan's decision with ill-humor and instructed its consul, Dr. John Kirk, to approach Barghash with a view to reconsider his position. British Foreign Secretary Granville did not give him much time to ponder the matter. On May 15 he sent Kirk a telegram stating that, unless Barghash accepted the treaty, British warships would blockade

Zanzibar. Two weeks later Barghash capitulated. Under terms of the treaty, Barghash agreed to prohibit the export of slaves from the mainland, whatever their destination, close the slave markets in his dominions, protect freed slaves from attempts to reenslave them, and forbid Indians residing in Zanzibar from trading in or owning slaves. Within hours, Barghash closed down the slave markets on Zanzibar and orders went out to his officers on the mainland to comply with the treaty.

With the slave trade by sea abolished, the familiar pattern of temporary dislocation followed by new techniques of evasion was once again repeated. The Arabs could no longer transport slaves by sea, but they could, and did, march them from Kilwa northward along the coast, secretly selling as many as they could in each of the towns along the way. As a result, the traffic in slaves never really ended when the treaty was announced. To remedy this, Kirk, whose great tact and wisdom in handling matters relating to the slave trade had earned him universal respect, pressed Barghash to remedy the situation. The sultan, whose zeal in enforcing the treaty was recognized by the British government, responded by issuing decrees that prohibited caravans with slaves from approaching the coast or transporting slaves from port to port.

There were efforts in the succeeding two decades to keep the traffic going in order to provide slaves to Zanzibar, Pemba, and Kenya, where slavery continued to exist. As supplies thinned out during the 1880s and prices for slaves rose, a brisk trade in slaves developed in places along the coast. There was a recrudescence of the trade in 1884 when famine struck the mainland from Kenya to Tanganyka. People became desperate enough to sell their kinsmen, children, and even themselves in order to survive. This lasted for about five years and then gradually tapered off. By the beginning of the 1880s, the large-scale, centralized slave trade system was at its end. The 1873 treaty sounded the death knell of the East Coast slave trade. It was the continuation of a policy, begun fifty years earlier, which was to reach its final conclusion when slavery itself was abolished in 1897 in Zanzibar and Pemba and in 1907 in Kenya.

# CHAPTER EIGHT

# Slavery in All Its Forms

### 1.

THE RESTRICTIONS IMPOSED BY THE VARIOUS TREATIES and international agreements entered into between Great Britain and the various Muslim states of North Africa and the Middle East gradually achieved their purpose of slowing down the slave trade. The diplomatic history between these countries for the better part of the nineteenth century was a record of continuous retreat by the Muslim states on the slave trade issue. Lamentably, this same record has also shown that by themselves these agreements were only marginally effective in bringing about the demise of the slave trade in the Muslim world in general and in Arab lands in particular. What vastly accelerated this process was the colonization of Africa, which permitted European administrators and soldiers to check the trade at its source.

In some instances, as was the case with Sultan Barghash in Zanzibar, the 1873 agreement that he was forced to sign with Great Britain led to a change of heart on his part; and thereafter he scrupulously enforced its provisions. He was, however, more the exception than the rule among Muslim rulers, who lacked the will or ability to enforce such agreements. As they understood only too well, the slave trade, although bereft of any standing in Islamic law, was indispensable to maintaining slavery, whose roots ran deep in Muslim society and religion. Given this connection, any attack on the slave trade was ipso facto taken to mean an assault against slavery. It was largely for this reason that the boldest of Muslim leaders were loath to enforce anti-slave trade agreements to which they were formally bound.

Until the European powers agreed to join in on the attack against the slave trade, the greatest value of these agreements was that they helped keep alive the slave trade issue in the international community and drive home the point to Muslim and Arab leaders of the illegal nature of the trade. This undoubtedly engendered change in the social and political climate in Muslim countries where, in due time, it became politically respectable to make a case against the slave trade and slavery. Reform-minded Islamic religious leaders who began arguing against slavery toward the turn of the twentieth century undoubtedly drew moral support from the anti-slave trade agreements and from the principled stand of the abolitionists in Western countries.

Muslim countries which gave free rein to the slave trade and slavery became conscious that by doing so they increasingly placed themselves outside the pale of international respectability. Many enlightened political and social leaders in Muslim countries were aware that the image of their society in the Western world was deeply scarred by accounts of missionaries and explorers of the horrors of the slave trade. The wrath of abolitionists was directed against Muslims, particularly Arabs, who were held responsible for the slave traffic. David Livingstone initiated the attack in the 1850s and was soon followed by others. The German Wissman, the

American Stanley, and the Scotsman Cameron emulated one another by proclaiming the vast potential of Africa by contrasting optimistic projections against a picture of the incalculable brutality of the slave trade. In 1874, Cameron would write from Lake Tanganyika, where Arab slavers were deeply entrenched, that "the slave trade is spreading in the interior, and will continue to do so until it is either put down by a strong hand, or dies a natural death from the total destruction of the population. At present events are tending towards depopulation."[1]

These mournful messages reached an ever-widening audience in Europe and the United States and helped set the stage for a concerted diplomatic attack against the slave trade. This noble cause, in reality, was subordinated to the "scramble for Africa" in which a number of European powers, notably, England, France, Germany, Belgium, Portugal, and Italy, competed with one another in slicing up Africa into colonial domains and spheres of influence. Africa beckoned because of its great promise of mineral wealth, its seemingly unlimited potential as a market for Western manufactures, and its strategic value to the geopolitical gamesmen of the day. Somewhere stuck in among these hard-headed reasons for empire-building was a shared willingness to put down, once and for all, the traffic in human beings.

This goal was enshrined in the declaration of the Berlin Conference of 1885 which was convened at the initiative of Germany and France. The chief purpose of the conference was to sort out the conflicting interests of the colonial powers in the western regions of Africa and to make the Congo and Niger river basins free to international commerce. To add weight to its decisions, the conference included not only the European colonial powers but, in addition, Russia, Austria, the Scandinavian states, Turkey, Holland, and the United States. The British, fearful of being upstaged by Bismarck, submitted a far-reaching proposal declaring that the traffic in slaves, as distinct from slavery, should be considered "a crime against the Law of Nations." Few of the countries present were prepared to entertain the proposal, and so it was side-tracked on grounds that it would be impractical to enforce.[2]

In the end, the conference included two relatively mild articles on the slave trade in its final declaration. Article six called upon the signatories ". . . to strive for the suppression of slavery and especially of the Negro slave trade." A comprehensive condemnation was contained in article nine, which held that the maritime slave trade was forbidden by international law and that the operations that sustained it by sea or land "ought likewise to be regarded as forbidden."[3] This extended to the land-based slave trade the same censure and prohibition which until then had applied only to slave trading on the seas. There was no question of abolishing slavery in territories where, in accordance with national customs, it was considered essential.

Five years later, a second international conference was convened in Brussels and was devoted mainly to the suppression of the slave trade. The conference was the most representative of its kind, with invitations being sent to the signatory powers of the Berlin Act as well as to the shah of Persia and the sultan of Zanzibar and to the Congo Free State. The Brussels Act, although it fell far short of the goals of the abolitionists, came close to the expectations of those who championed reform. The provisions of the act, which contained one hundred separate articles divided into seven chapters, reflected the divergent interests of the powers in such matters as the methods to be used in suppressing the slave trade, reciprocal rights of search and seizure of suspected slave ships, and slavery in the slave importing countries *(pays de destination)*.

The first chapter of the act confirmed previous commitments of the participating countries to put down the slave trade. Within a year of the signing of the act, the legislature of each of the contractual parties was to enact laws making all persons involved in manhunting and mutilation of boys liable to punishment for "grave offences against the person" and dealers subject to penalties for infringing on individual liberties. Suspected offenders could be subject to extradition. There were also provisions for assuring the welfare and repatriation of freed and fugitive slaves. Missionaries, who were playing such an important role against the slave trade and hence were vulnerable to reprisals by slave traders, were to be afforded protection. The traffic in arms, which was the main culprit for the escalation of the slave trade, was to be proscribed in defined areas.

The ban on the arms traffic was adopted ostensibly to protect the native population against slave raiders. Its practical effects were somewhat different. While the restriction rarely created difficulties for the Arabs in acquiring weapons, it led to the disarming of the people of the Congo, who were the main victims. Faithfully carried out, the arms agreements strengthened the hands of the colonial nations and were bound to cripple African resistance to European colonization. The conference had given the colonial powers an opportunity to present in a humanitarian guise restrictions that favored their own political and commercial interests.

Chapters two and three were addressed to the transport of slaves. The former, which was concerned with the conveyance of slaves by land, provided for the maintenance of a watch on caravan routes and for the inspection of slave caravans. The rapid colonization of Africa made this provision obsolete even before it could be implemented. Transport of slaves by sea, the concern of chapter three, provided for mutual rights of search and seizure of slave vessels of less than five hundred-ton displacement. This article was a compromise between the bitterly divergent views of England and France over the privileges and immunities of ships suspected of carrying contraband slaves. The British, with their powerful navy, had traditionally favored broad search and seizure powers while France zealously opposed this claim lest England use it as a pretext to become the policeman of the seas. The conference also laid down regulations covering the equally sensitive issue of slave-carrying vessels abusing the use of flags of convenience in order to evade British naval patrols.

An important departure of the Brussels Act was a willingness by the signatories to deal with the slave trade in the *pays de destination*. Under chapter four of the act, the countries bound by this article (Persia, Turkey, and Zanzibar) pledged not only to prohibit the slave trade but to forbid the importation into, the transit through, or departure from their territory of African slaves. Long experience had demonstrated that a strategy directed solely against slave-exporting countries stood little chance of success unless accompanied by similar measures that prohibited the import of slaves into countries where slavery was a way of life.

Having bound themselves to the terms of the act, the powers took the next step to ensure that these measures were carried out. This was to be done by making available information about progress being made toward the implementation of the accord. Under chapter five, international offices were established to collect and disseminate information and statistics on the slave trade carried out in the maritime zone covered by the act. One office was opened in Zanzibar and had the task of assembling information on the slave trade. A second was established in Brussels and was responsible for collecting documentation on the legal and statistical aspects of the slave trade.

The Brussels Act of 1890, despite many shortcomings, has remained the most comprehensive document ever devised by the international community to combat the slave trade. During the twenty-two years the act remained in force, from its ratification in 1892 until the outbreak of World War I in 1914, when it ceased to be operative, it was credited with having done much to suppress the slave trade.[4] At the war's end, it was realized that the dramatically altered political map of the Middle East and the opportunities for international action through the League of Nations required new approaches to suppress slavery and the vestigial remains of the slave trade.

## 2.

The Brussels Act has to be seen as representing a new departure by the European colonial powers to rid Africa for good of the slave trade. While humanitarian motives figured importantly, they were far from being the main factor that prompted the Europeans to mount a sustained attack on the trade. As the European powers came face to face with the difficult problems of administering their newly acquired possessions, they were not long in realizing that the slave trade was inimical to their political, commercial, and economic interests. It was for this reason that the colonial powers moved quickly to liquidate the slave trade. And although they could not stop the demand for slaves in the Middle East, they were in a position to halt the export of slaves from their colonies. The British, once they took up their new colonial role in Egypt, the Sudan, Zanzibar, and Kenya, moved quickly to suppress the slave trade. Germany, which had acquired territories in East Africa, adopted similar measures in 1895 to suppress the traffic in slaves, as did the French, Belgians, and Italians in their colonies.

An innovative feature of the Brussels Act was a willingness, however timid, to suppress the slave trade in the *pays de destination*. Experience had shown that clamping down only on exporting lands stood little chance of success unless accompanied by measures that prohibited the import of slaves where slavery remained legal. In Egypt, such a policy had already been put into effect by prohibiting the importation of slaves from the Sudan, including those disguised as servants and wives. The sultan of Turkey, at the urging of Great Britain, issued a decree on the eve of the convening of the Brussels Conference which declared: "The commerce, entry and passage of black slaves in the Ottoman Empire and its dependencies is prohibited."[5] Those found in violation of this law were subject to a one-year prison offence, and the slaves found in their possession were to be manumitted. Persia, another country represented at the conference where slavery was permitted, had already renounced the slave trade in its 1882 treaty with England.

While these agreements to ban the slave trade in the *pays de destination* represented progress, little in fact, except in Egypt, had changed. There were reports that the slave trade in the Red Sea and Gulf of Aden was actually increasing while the Brussels conference was sitting.[6] In Libya, despite determined efforts by Turkish officials, the trade showed no signs of abating. Slaves were also being shipped across the Mediterranean and the Red Sea disguised as servants or passed off as the wives of the owner. Sometimes they could show fraudulently obtained manumission papers. But even if they could not produce such documents, the owners were spared punishment under the 1889 law by showing they were not slave dealers.

The moral of this story, known to traffickers in drugs, arms, and all illicit commodities which turn a handsome profit, is that as long as there is a demand for these products the supply will somehow find its way to market. Only by abolishing slavery would the slave trade cease to exist. This was something, however, the more important European countries refused to discuss at Brussels. France, Belgium, and England had made it abundantly clear before the conference that they were opposed to any discussion of the slavery issue. As colonial powers, these countries had changed their tune about slavery in Africa once they had to own up to the consequences of abolishing this deep-rooted institution in their own colonial territories. Their vacillating attitude on slavery inclined them to oppose strong action which would raise serious obstacles to the importation of slaves into Muslim countries because of its potential impact on the very institution of slavery. As a result, the Turkish representative in Brussels had no difficulty in fending off proposals for increased surveillance of slave routes to western Arabia. And with the backing of France and Russia, he defeated a British-backed proposal to have an auxiliary slave-trade information office opened in the Red Sea area.

### 3.

As the traffic in slaves slackened off at the turn of the century, more public attention in the West was focused on the institution of slavery, which remained very much alive in many parts of Arabia and the Persian Gulf. What appeared to have accounted for this was a heightened awareness of the dynamics between the demand for slaves and the traffic in this human commodity. As in the trafficking in drugs and arms, the demand factor is crucial in generating a supply of these commodities. The vestiges of the traffic in slaves could be more efficiently dealt with by turning off the demand, which meant nothing less than abolition of slavery.

By the twentieth century realization of this goal was no longer considered to be a utopian dream. The hurdles in arriving there, however, were forbidding. The situation had become vastly complicated by changes in attitudes in official government circles wrought by Africa's rapid transformation into a vast colonial fiefdom. This was best demonstrated by events in Zanzibar starting in 1890 when the island was declared a British protectorate and ending twenty years later when the death knell of slavery was sounded. Initial British attempts to bring about a gradual end to slavery were contained in a decree awarding freedom to all children born after January 1, 1890. A second and more comprehensive edict was issued in August 1890 prohibiting, on threat of penalties, the buying and selling of slaves and allowing all slaves to buy their freedom at a fair price. These moderate measures provoked a storm of protest from the Arab slave owners, who saw in them their ruination. As a result, they were quietly shelved.[7]

When Arthur Hardinge, the new British agent, arrived in Zanzibar in 1894, he cautioned the Foreign Office to follow a gradual and deliberate policy of emancipation. If slavery were abolished by a stroke of the pen, he darkly predicted, slaves would abandon their work, thereby leading to a severe decline in clove production which would push Arab growers, already heavily in debt to Indian creditors, into bankruptcy. According to this gloomy scenario, the economic development of the island would be retarded and revenues of the protectorate would precipitously drop.

Why the freed slaves would not work, in spite of their obvious need for income, Hardinge attributed to the special characteristics of the Negroes. Although convinced that the slaves have no real wish for freedom, Hardinge believed that, once freed, they "would not . . . be able to withstand the temptations of freedom," since, as he later observed, "the Negro in East Africa, at least, is little more than a grown-up child." Hardinge, who served in Egypt under Lord Cromer, had internalized many of the prejudices toward blacks that were commonly held by British civil servants in the colonies. His racist and economic arguments in favor of a slow and distant abolition fell upon attentive ears in the Foreign Office, which was anxious to avoid measures that could lead to social unrest and economic ruin.[8]

Hardinge's views were roundly condemned by abolitionists in England, who organized rallies up and down the country protesting that slavery could be allowed in land over which the Union Jack flew. In Commons, strong support was expressed on both sides of the House in favor of immediate abolition. Faced with this pressure, the government yielded but not without accepting Hardinge's advice to hedge the abolition law with restrictions. On April 5, 1897, a decree abolishing the legal status of slavery was issued and published two days later in the *Zanzibar Gazette*. The law provided compensation to owners whose slaves applied for manumission. Concubines were not to be freed except on grounds of cruelty. The burden of applying for emancipation rested with the slave, who had to apply to a special court administered by Arab *walis* and supervised by British officials. Reflecting the conservative nature of the law, it contained a provision whereby ex-slaves, on pain of being declared vagrants, had to show they had a regular domicile and means of subsistence. The same general manumission law went into effect throughout East Africa. Germany, by contrast, contented itself with introducing legislation to ameliorate the lot of slaves in its East African territories and to make it easier for them to obtain their liberty.

Ten years after emancipation was decreed in Zanzibar, a bare 11,000 slaves were freed with compensation paid to their owners and another 6,200 were emancipated without compensation. There were on the island an estimated 208,700 people, made up of 200 Europeans, 4,000 Arabs, 7,500 Indians, 30,000 free-born Swahili, 27,000 freed slaves, and 140,000 slaves. Those who benefited from the law made up a bare 12 percent of the slave population. Many of the slaves, however, made their own arrangements with their masters and kept their status but continued working for wages. A second anti-slavery law was passed in 1909 allowing two additional years for claims to be made, after which no further compensation would be paid.[9]

In this slow but inexorable manner, slavery in Zanzibar and throughout East Africa declined in importance, although it was many years before it was completely eradicated. It frequently happened that ex-slaves remained in a client relationship with their former owner, a relationship that offered them some degree of social benefits although not without cost to their freedom. The pace of emancipation was henceforth determined by market conditions. As owners discovered that the economic and social costs of slave labor exceeded those of wage labor, they substituted free labor for slaves. The latter, too, realized that working for wages, despite the risks of unstable employment conditions, was far preferable than remaining in bondage. After the First World War, many slaves in Ethiopia fled their masters to seek work in the expanding cotton fields of the Sudan. Compensation offered by the colonial powers to owners also served to accelerate the emancipation process. By contrast, little if any financial support or training were made available to newly freed slaves; and, as a result, they were not prepared to do anything but the most menial forms of work. In this position, they were vulnerable to exploitation by private entrepreneurs and the colonial authorities. Frequently, the latter obliged the local populace to provide unpaid forced labor for railroad construction and public works projects. Herein developed slavelike forms of labor that were less easy to eliminate, particularly as they were usually initiated at the behest of colonial authorities.

The gradualist policy pursued by the British in Zanzibar and in their other colonial possessions was also adopted by the Germans, Belgians, and French in their own spheres of control. A sudden end to slavery, it was feared, would result in a total collapse of the economic system and social order. Such a possibility, which was usually played up by colonial administrators on the spot, sent shivers of fear up the spines of government leaders in the *métropole*. Early application of the gradualist policy in emancipating slaves took place in Egypt and later in the Sudan where Britain's Governor Gen-

eral Kitchener instructed his provincial officers not to interfere with slavery as long as it was based on a slave's willingness to serve his master. Forbearance in applying Egyptian
anti-slavery laws in the Sudan grew out of a belated recognition that previous effort by Baker and Gordon to abolish the
slave trade had kindled flames of discontent and made possible the establishment of a Mahdist state. What distinguished
the British procedure of allowing slavery to fade away
through gradual compensated emancipation was Britain's un-
abashed practice of invoking Muslim law to justify its actions. The architect of this approach was the famous colonial
administrator, Frederick (later Lord) Lugard, who first applied it when laying the foundations of British colonial rule in
the central provinces of the Sokoto caliphate in the western
part of Nigeria, where slavery was deeply entrenched. British
colonial administrators became adept in Islamic law, stressing
those precepts of the law that called for conversion of slaves
to Islam, their emancipation, and eventual integration into
society.

### 4.

With the return of peace, there was a keen desire by the
victorious Allied powers to breathe new life into the international campaign against slavery and the slave trade. The war
had led to setbacks in the struggle against these twin evils. By
the Convention of Saint Germain-en-Laye of 1919, the Allied
powers rescinded the articles of Brussels Act relating to slavery and the slave trade and replaced them with a single phrase
which committed them" . . . to secure the complete suppression of slavery in all its forms and of the slave trade by land
and sea." This was the first time that a pledge for the abolition of slavery, as distinct from the slave trade, had formed
the subject of an international accord.[10]

There was a feeling of optimism which, in part, was

nurtured by the results of the war that slavery and the slave trade would soon become things of the past. Turkey's defeat brought about the dissolution of the Ottoman Empire and the parceling out of most of its Middle East territories to England and France in the form of mandates. Establishment of the League of Nations offered a new but untested approach for concerted international action against slavery. Although the covenant of the League contained no explicit reference to slavery, it did confer on the organization, through the system of mandates, general powers of supervision and inquiry into progress made in the abolition of slavery in these territories. For member states, however, action on slavery depended on the interpretation each one chose to give to article 23 of the covenant. This referred to their obligations to provide fair and humane treatment to their people and to the natives of territories under their jurisdictions.

Those who had pinned high hopes on the willingness of the League of Nations to act resolutely against slavery and the slave trade soon had to scale down their expectations. There was little initial support among member states to deal with the slave question. A request by the secretary general of the League in September 1922 that member states provide him with information on the question elicited responses from only fourteen of the fifty-two countries.[11] It was only in 1924 that the council of the League got around to establishing the Temporary Commission on Slavery. The commission, whose members included Lord Lugard and the Norwegian Dr. Fridtjof Nansen, reknowned for his work on behalf of stateless people, had a broad mandate to make recommendations not only in the area of chattel slavery but in slavelike practices such as serfdom, debt bondage, and servile forms of marriage. The following year it issued a report calling for the adoption of an international convention on involuntary servitude. A draft convention, which was actually drawn up in the British Foreign Office, was submitted that year to the assembly of the League for consideration. The outcome of these deliberations was the Slavery Convention which was signed in Geneva on September 25, 1926, by the representatives of thirty-six states. It was ultimately ratified or acceded to by forty-one states.

Although considered by many the best that could be achieved under existing circumstances, the Slavery Convention was a disappointing document. This short document—it consisted only of twelve articles—dealt with the slave trade, slavery, and other forms of involuntary servitude. The first article defined slavery and the slave trade, something never before done in an international agreement. Article two imposed on the contracting parties the obligation "to bring about progressively and as soon as possible the complete abolition of slavery in all its forms." In the third article the parties pledged to suppress the slave traffic by not allowing "the embarkation, disembarkation and transport of slaves in their territorial waters and upon all vessels flying their respective flags." Under article five, the signatories were bound to prevent forced labor from developing into conditions analagous to slavery. This objective was achieved by the adoption in 1931 of the Forced Labor Convention.

There were many who could not conceal their disappointment over the limited progress that was achieved by the Slavery Convention. In the words of Viscount Cecil, the rapporteur of the Assembly's Sixth Committee, who prepared the draft convention, its definition of slavery and the slave trade were based "on the minimum provisions of existing colonial legislation and on the previous international conventions on the subject."[12] Its definition of slavery was supposed to apply to all forms of involuntary servitude, but it was widely interpreted as applying only to chattel slavery. Even here, there was something to be desired. To an African, the term "right of ownership" might not convey the precise meaning intended, that is, chattel without human rights. A gradualist approach to abolition was very much in evidence in article two, which insisted that slavery be brought to an end "progressively." The provision of the Convention dealing with the slave traffic did not go as far as it could in bringing about an end to this universally condemned traffic. A British proposal that would have considered the trade as piracy was shouldered aside.[13]

The Convention was also flawed by the absence of an appropriate body in the League Secretariat that could collect information, hold hearings, and possibly recommend action for hastening the demise of slavery. Thirty-six years earlier, the framers of the Brussels Act appreciated the need to have a central information bureau which could piece together a clear picture of the changing dimensions of slavery and the slave trade. All that the convention did in this respect was appeal to the goodwill of member states that they communicate to the League and to one another on laws and regulations concerning slavery and the traffic in slaves. Few of them heeded this injunction, and the limited information received could not be put to good use by the League.

In spite of the limitations of the Slavery Convention, progress was recorded during the 1920s and 1930s. Responding to pressure from England and other countries, the League established in 1932 an Advisory Committee of Experts, thereby giving it a central office from which it could prosecute its efforts against slavery. The reports of the committee, which were published in League documents, shed much light on slavery and were helpful in keeping the slave question before world public opinion. Its activities came to an end in 1940, like those of the League itself, following the outbreak of the Second World War.

In 1932, the committee could report that Afghanistan had abolished the legal status of slavery in 1923, as did Iraq in 1924, Nepal in 1926, and Transjordan and Iran in 1929. In Morocco, French authorities had issued a decree in 1922 as a result of which public slave dealing was suppressed and freedom granted to all slaves who requested it. Energetic military action along the country's frontiers about 1930 put an end to the vestigal remains of the traffic into the protectorate. In Ethiopia, where slavery remained commonplace, the government, whose writ did not run far inside the country, decreed an end to the enslavement of free persons and the dealing in slaves, while ordering the emancipation of many household slaves. On becoming a member of the League of Nations in 1923, the government undertook to bring about an end to slavery and to "trading in Negroes on land and sea."[14]

This record of accomplishment, which to some extent reflected gains only on paper, has to be read against a no less substantial record of failure to move ahead in countries where slavery had long been a way of life. Ethiopia, whose estimated population of ten million in 1926 included about two million slaves, showed little progress in abolishing slavery notwithstanding the good-faith promise of Emperor Hailie Selassie. He tacitly acknowledged the widespread and deeprooted nature of the problem when he told a delegation of the Anti-Slavery and Aborigines Protection Society who visited Ethiopia in 1932 that another twenty years would be needed before he could rid the country of slavery.[15] The resistance of slavery to official decrees proclaiming its end can only be explained in the context of the role it played in societies where great numbers of people lived in extreme poverty. For many of them, it offered a tenuous lifeline to survival; freedom, on the other hand, appeared to be an unrealistic option. Without prospects of land, tools, and shelter, many slaves instinctively believed that they and their families would face a bleak future in a life outside of slavery.

A similar situation was found to exist in the southern Sudan, where an extensive traffic in slaves was uncovered in 1929.[16] This form of bondage in the Sudan, often referred to as "voluntary slavery," was defined in a League of Nations report as involving "those born of servile stock who chose for practical reasons to live as their parents lived or as they were brought up, without availing themselves of the full privileges of free citizenship, which they know to be potentially theirs, rather than to take those privileges at the cost of cutting adrift from their moorings."[17] Of the thirteen thousand domestic slaves who were offered freedom papers in 1929 in the White Nile Province, fewer than three thousand accepted. It could have been seen that the solution for eradicating slavery in parts of the Sudan and Ethiopia was not to be found solely in tougher abolition decrees but in accompanying programs of economic development which held out hope for a better life.

Slavery was also a flourishing institution in Arabia when King Ibn Saud in 1925 united by force of arms the Nejd and Hijaz to form the kingdom of Saudi Arabia. The previous year, the League's Temporary Slave Commission reported that ". . . the slave trade is practiced openly in several Mohammedan States in Asia and in particularly in the Arabian Peninsula, especially the Hedjaz."[18] It was also recognized as a legal institution in Yemen in the sultanates of Hadramaut and in the sultanate of Kuwait. Many of these slaves were brought to Arabian slave markets via Yemen from territory belonging to Egypt, the Sudan, Eritrea, the French Somali Coast, and British Somaliland. As the commission pointed out, as long as slave traders could be lured by big profits in Arabia, they were prepared to risk bringing slaves across the Red Sea. Available in the slave markets of Saudi Arabia, Kuwait, and Oman were not only blacks from Africa but whites from the Far East. Many of the latter were young girls smuggled into Arabia by traders or brought there under false pretenses by parents or owners on pilgrimage to Mecca. Once in Saudi Arabia, they would be sold into slavery, usually becoming another concubine in a rich Arab's *harim*. Many unsuspecting free people, as well as slaves, were taken on pilgrimages to the holy cities and, in a manner scarcely ever anticipated by the Prophet, were sold outright or arrested on trumped-up charges and ultimately wound up as slaves. Holland sought to prevent these practices against its Indonesian subjects, as did France and England, by enacting regulations making the head of a family or group of pilgrims accountable for each of its members.

Although Saudi Arabia never signed the League Convention on Slavery, Ibn Saud concluded a treaty with Great Britain in 1927 for the suppression of the slave trade.[19] There is little evidence that it had much impact. Many European residents in the country who were understanding of the life of the inhabitants have testified in their writings to that fact. One of the most prominent, Eldon Rutter, who spent a great part of his life in Saudi Arabia and wrote sympathetically about the country in his book *The Holy Cities of Arabia,* said in a lecture delivered to the Royal Asian Society in London in 1933: "Slavery exists in every part of Arabia, except Aden, as a normal social institution, but I have only seen one slave market where slaves are displayed in a public place like merchandise. This was in Mecca in a narrow street called *Suk el Abid* (slave market). In all other towns and villages, including the Persian Gulf towns, the slaves are sold privately. In some places there are dealers who keep a definite stock of slaves; in others there are merely agents who dispose of any slave whom a person may wish to sell."[20] Dr. Paul Harrison, an American medical missionary who spent many years in Muscat and in other parts of the Gulf, revealed in his writings the widespread existence of slavery.[21] He pointed out that while many slaves were treated decently, particularly those who worked in the date plantations around Muscat, others, notably those who worked as pearl divers along the coast of Oman, were dealt with harshly. Another long-standing residence of the Middle East and extensive traveler in Arabia who gave evidence about the prevalence of slavery was H. St. John Philby.[22]

Any lingering doubts there may have been about the existence of slavery and the slave trade in the Saudi kingdom were dispelled with the issuance in October 1936 of a royal decree carrying the title "Instructions Concerning Traffic in Slaves."[23] Its purpose was to curtail slave imports, regulate the sale of slaves, and ensure proper standards of treatment for them. In so doing, it gave formal recognition to the existence of slavery. Importing slaves into the kingdom was henceforth forbidden, and only individuals recognized recognized as slaves in the country from which they were imported could be lawfully brought in by land routes. The law, which contained penalties for noncompliance, imposed on owners the obligation that slaves be properly fed, clothed, and sheltered and be provided with free medical care. Under article seven of the decree, any slave had a right to apply and receive a *mukataba,* or agreement enabling him to purchase his freedom. It was also stipulated that only licensed agents could engage in the slave traffic. To oversee the implementation of these regulations, an office of Inspector of Slave Affairs was created in the Ministry of Interior.

That an office of Inspector of Slave Affairs was created, the baldest possible admission of the existence of slavery, might have been taken as an earnest indication of the government's intention to bring about a drastic reduction in the import of slaves. Such a conclusion would be warranted only if the new decree constituted a step toward the abolition of slavery. No one in authority need have been reminded that only by a constant infusion of fresh supplies of raw slaves from abroad could the slave population in the country, variously estimated at between 500,000 and 700,000,[24] maintain itself. Without such imports, the numbers would begin dwindling almost immediately. In fact, this was the last thing that anyone wanted. In adopting the decree, the government served notice that its objective was to reform the slave system and not abolish it.

As long as slavery was legally recognized in Saudi Arabia and allowed to operate in the open, it was bound to serve as a magnetic field for the attraction of slaves from external sources. Slaves continued to be imported legally across land routes and smuggled in by sea. Although no figures have ever been provided by Saudi authorities on the extent of this traffic or, for that matter, the total number of slaves registered under the 1936 decree, there are unofficial accounts suggesting that illicit slave imports did not stop. In a memorandum submitted to the United Nations ad hoc Committee on Slavery in 1955, C. W. W. Greenidge, secretary of the British Anti-Slavery Society, drew attention to reports indicating "an ineffective application of the Saudi Arabian law and that slave markets . . . in the country were still fed by slaves smuggled across the frontiers."[25] According to these same reports, a slave market was operating in Mecca as late as 1941. That there was an upswing in the sea-borne slave trade was acknowledged by the British foreign secretary in a statement to Parliament on September 22, 1943. This he attributed to a relaxation of surveillance measures by British ships which had to be redeployed elsewhere.

Unofficial accounts by travelers and reports by special investigators also pointed to the continued existence of the slave traffic into Saudi Arabia customarily by way of Yemen. Colonel Gerald de Gaury, a longtime resident of the kingdom who had been honored by King Ibn Saud, wrote in his book *Arabian Journey,* published in 1950, that slaves were imported into Saudi Arabia. They were brought to Mecca by way of Yemen, to which they were transported by small sailing boats from the African side of the Red Sea. De Gaury reported that he had heard on good authority that shipments of boys were arriving in Oman in 1947 from the Mokran coast of Baluchistan. He also drew attention to reports that girls were transported from Aleppo in Syria to Saudi Arabia, where they were sold as slaves.[26]

## 5.

The last official pronouncement by the League of Nations Advisory Committee on Slavery in 1938 concerning the legal status of slavery throughout the world pointed to the continued existence of slavery in a number of Arab countries. Except in Bahrein, where slavery was abolished in 1937, it continued to exist in Saudi Arabia, Yemen, Aden, the Hadramaut (under British protection), Oman, Muscat, Qatar, and Kuwait. As was demonstrated in Bahrein, the initiative for reform had to come from within these states. No outside state had the power to impose abolition on an unwilling ruler. Great Britain, the leading power in the Persian Gulf region during the interwar period, had special treaty rights with Bahrein, Qatar, and the seven Trucial states that were limited to defense and foreign policy. While the British government pursued its anti-slave trade activities in the Persian Gulf, it consistently refrained from interfering with domestic slavery in these lands. To have done so would have been incompatible with Great Britain's treaty rights and could have undermined its strategic position in the Persian Gulf.[27] To the extent that the British used their influence, it took the form of quiet persuasion and gentle prodding, an approach that yielded few visible results.

In the post-World War II period, the situation began to show improvement. Slavery was abolished in Kuwait in 1949, and three years later its legal status was outlawed in Qatar. Not many slaves were freed as a result of these actions since slavery never amounted to much in either country. In May 1950, Dr. Paul Harrison, the American medical missionary, wrote to the United Nations ad hoc Committee on

Slavery that the slave population in Oman had declined. A fall in demand for dates reduced the need for slave labor in the plantations. Here, economic forces succeeded in accomplishing something that reformers would not even dare whisper doing. Twenty years were to elapse, however, before slavery was abolished in Oman following a palace revolution in which the despotic Sultan Said Ibn Taimur was deposed by his son.

Despite progress in these sheikhdoms, the bulwark of slavery in the region remained firm in its commitment to slavery. Slavery was unchallenged in Saudi Arabia, whose ban on the import of slaves by sea was pretty much a dead letter. Slaves continued to be brought into the kingdom from different parts of Africa, the Makran coast of Persia and Pakistan.[28] A continuous stream of blacks from West Africa, as well as people from Ethiopia and the southern Sudan, was filtered across the porous boundaries of these countries by enterprising slave merchants from Saudi Arabia who brought them back home and sold them as slaves.

One particular incident that came to light involving the sale in 1949 of a sixteen-year-old boy from the French Sudan (Mali) shed light on the nature of this traffic. The boy, Awd el Joud by name, who was probably a slave at home, was taken by his master to the holy cities in Saudi Arabia. There he was told that he would have to work for the son of the governor of Jedda to earn money for the trip home. When the boy realized that he had been sold as a slave and not hired out for wages, Awd el Joud succeeded after several years in escaping from his master's household and making his way back to Mali. There he related his story to a priest of the White Fathers order, Fr. David Traoré. This young man, who spent more than five years in slavery, also told of slave markets in different towns in Saudi Arabia.

The matter was brought before the Assemblée l'Union Française by M. La Gravière during a debate on slavery that was held in February 1956. La Gravière told the Assemblée, a consultative body that dealt with French empire affairs, of the case of Awd el Joud, who was an example of many French African citizens who were sold into slavery in Saudi Arabia. Little credence was placed in the story by the Assemblée and it allowed the matter to drop. During the debate, La Gravière placed before the Assemblée a letter from none other than the French ambassador to Saudi Arabia, who was responsible for the welfare of the numerous French citizens who made the pilgrimage. In the letter, dated November 7, 1953, the ambassador, M. Morillon, wrote: "Some merchants settled in Jeddah or Mecca send naturalised Saudi emissaries, but mostly Senegalese by birth, charged with bringing back a certain number of persons whom they enticed from villages in the Sudan, Upper Volta or Niger; Timbuktu, in particular, is said to be a center often visited by these shady characters who pretend to be 'missionaries' with the delicate mission of leading their countrymen to the holy places of Islam so that they may make the pilgrimage and teach them the Koran in Arabic.[29] After being transported across the Red Sea in "sambooks," they are taken to Jedda, where they are handed over to the police. The ambassador estimated the number of those taken each year from France's African territories at around several hundred. Blacks from French Africa, he noted, made up the largest contingent of slaves brought to Saudi Arabia because the traffic from Ethiopia had become more difficult.

By the end of the 1950s, African colonies began achieving their long-cherished goal of independence. They were in a stronger position to protect the interests of their citizens against the predatory tactics of domestic and foreign slave merchants. Comforting as this was, it would not be sufficient since their people could still be taken across unmarked boundaries and fall victim to the wiles of the slave merchant. The Nigerian *Morning Post* carried on November 4, 1961, an article dealing with destitute Nigerian children in Saudi Arabia and, alluding to Anti-Slavery Society reports, asked whether they were simply stranded or had become slaves.[30] The sole solution for dealing with these vestigal remains of the slave trade was to abolish slavery in Saudi Arabia.

There were compelling reasons why the Saudi government just might cross that threshold and end the centuries-old institution of slavery. Its continued existence made the country and its leaders vulnerable to criticism in the United Nations and among progressive Arab leaders. Slavery was incompatible with rapid economic development and was totally at odds with the image it was trying to project in the Western world. Perpetuation of slavery would almost certainly lead to unpleasant situations with the newly emerging African nations which would regard the enslavement of their people as an affront to their dignity. The Saudi government could also feel safe in opting for abolition from a religious point of view since the Muslim World Conference had long ago met in Mecca and adopted a resolution calling for the abolition of slavery.

Indications that the Saudi authorities might be planning to abolish or severely curtail slavery were in evidence by 1960, by which time the slave markets in the country had been suppressed. On November 6, 1962, Prince Faisal, who was appointed prime minister by his brother King Saud, issued a Ten-Point Program that called for the total abolition of slavery. Article ten stated, in part: "The Government now finds a favorable opportunity to announce the absolute abolition of slavery and the manumission of all slaves. The Government will compensate those who prove to be deserving of compensation."

Within the social and religious context of the Saudi Arabian context, this was a revolutionary move. Faithfully implemented, it would dramatically alter Saudi society, in which, from the time of the Prophet and before, slave owning was an integral part of community and family life. How effectively was the cautiously worded law implemented? The Saudi Arabian government passed up an opportunity to clarify the matter when it ignored the questionnaire sent to it in 1965 by Mohamed Awad, the United Nations special rapporteur on slavery.[31] The Awad report contained information supplied by the Anti-Slavery Society, whose sources were newspaper article and accounts of "a traveler in Arabia." If the society's information was close to the mark, then the picture that emerged in the Awad report was not very encouraging. The government, according to an article in the London *Sunday Express,* paid £1,785,000 in compensation for the freeing of 1,682 slaves. This was a miniscule number considering there were anywhere from 100,000 to 250,000 slaves in 1962. Prime Minister Faisal, who had become the real power in the country, is reported to have revealed in an interview with the English journalist, John Osman, that "the slave population numbered many thousands."[32] A semi-official estimate placed the figure at a quarter of a million, of whom about 60 percent were foreigners. In response to the Anti-Slavery Society's allegations, the representative of Saudi Arabia to the Economic and Social Council dismissed them as "tendentious" and based on "hearsay and rumors." He also accused the society of abusing its consultative status by making such remarks. To be sure, the difficulties could have been avoided had the government of Saudi Arabia submitted its own progress report on slavery.

Two French writers, Soulié and Champenois, presented a wildly optimistic picture, claiming that slavery had ceased to exist as a result of the decree. A far more realistic view of the situation was offered by the journalist Eric Rouleau.[33] He argued that, while Faisal freed several tens of thousands of slaves in 1963, the law had little apparent effect. Lack of opportunities and a fear of dealing with the uncertainties of the real world prevented the majority of the freed slaves from adapting to their new-found freedom. This should not have been surprising since the majority of slaves, especially the concubines, were foreigners and had no one to turn to once having left their masters. Nor should it have been surprising if many slaves, upon gaining the status of freed persons, stayed on in the homes of their masters and continued to perform the same services that had been expected of them in return for wages. The Saudi emancipation law indirectly encouraged this by offering compensation to the master and not to the slave. For the slave, his compensation was winning his freedom.

Slavery was on its way out as well in Yemen and Oman. In Yemen, republican forces overthrew the imamate in September 1962 and, in a subsequent civil war that dragged on until 1970, jolted this medieval polity across the revolutionary divide and brought into being the Yemen Arab Republic. As part of their efforts to transform the country, which had been untouched by modernization, the new leaders quickly moved to abolish slavery. This may have hastened abolition in neighboring Saudi Arabia, which issued its abolition program a few weeks later. Slavery was also abolished five years later in Marxist South Yemen, officially known as the People's Democratic Republic of Yemen, which gained its independence in 1967 following a guerrilla war against British forces in Aden. In both countries slavery appeared to have lingered on for a while. The Friends World Committee for Consultation, a nongovernmental organization, submitted a report to the United Nations rapporteur on slavery in which it was stated a certain "black market" in the buying and selling of slaves still went on in 1964 in the Yemen Arab Republic.[34]

The coup de grace was administered to slavery in Arabia in 1970 when Qabus Ibn Said overthrew his xenophobic father and became ruler of Oman.[35] Among the personal effects found by the new sultan in the palace were some five hundred slaves. Some had been forced, under pain of beating, never to speak and as a result had become mute. Others suffered from paralysis of the neck because they had been forbidden to raise their eyes from the ground. This maltreatment, which had to have gone on for a number of years, was exceptional, although it is sobering to think that the sultan's British advisers must have turned a blind eye to what was going on in his palace.

Abolition of slavery in Arab lands was largely a consequence of internal political and economic forces at work at both the national and regional levels. To be fully appreciated, however, the movement in the post-World War II period towards the abolition of slavery and the suppression of the slave trade have to be placed within the framework of United Nations activities. In important respects, the efforts of the United Nations in this field bears some similarity to the work done by its predecessor. Like that of the League, the detailed work of the United Nations on slavery did not begin until the appointment of a temporary body of experts. On July 20, 1949, the Economic and Social Council adopted a resolution creating an ad hoc Committee of Experts on Slavery. The committee, made up of five experts, circulated a questionnaire on slavery and received replies from sixty-four countries. Based on these responses, the committee concluded that slavery continued to exist in the world and steps ought to be taken by the international community to bring it to an end.

The committee made three important recommendations to achieve this objective. One was that the United Nations should assume, by means of a protocol, the powers of the League of Nations under the Slavery Convention of 1926. In addition, it recommended that a Supplementary Convention on Slavery be adopted declaring debt bondage, the sale of women into marriage without their consent, and the sham adoption of children be considered forms of slavery and should be prohibited. A third recommendation, which bore all the markings of the League of Nations discussions, was that the United Nations should establish a standing committee of Experts on Slavery.[36]

Favorable action was soon taken on the first two recommendations. The Economic and Social Convention approved the preparation of a protocol on the 1926 Slavery Convention and member states were invited to adhere to it. The recommended protocol was soon approved. After much discussion, the Economic Council approved a draft supplementary convention on slavery, based on a British proposal, and circulated this to all member states. The views derived from the responses formed the basis of the Supplementary Convention on the Abolition of Slavery, the Slave Trade, and Institutions and Practices Similar to Slavery, which was adopted at an international conference that convened in Geneva in September 1956.

The Convention, which has been ratified by most of the members of the United Nations, is a long stride forward in the abolition of slavery through international action. Its definition of slavery, contained in article one, includes practices analogous to slavery. Article two binds the signatories to set suitable minimum ages of marriage and to encourage consent by both partners. Conveyance of slaves by whatever means from one country to another is a criminal offense, and each nation is to take effective measures to ensure that its ports, airfields, and coasts are not used for the transport of slaves. The original draft called for search and seizure of any ship suspected of carrying slaves. This was opposed on grounds that it infringed on national sovereignty, the very ground on which a similar provision was attacked at the Congress of Vienna in 1815 and at other international conferences which dealt with the slave trade.

A glaring omission, however, was the absence of machinery to supervise the application of these two conventions. Responsibility for executing them became the task of the Economic and Social Council, aided by the United

Nations Secretariat. Such an approach ran counter to the practice established under the Brussels Act and followed by the League of Nations of creating a body of experts to oversee the application of these conventions. In fact, opposition to the establishment of a committee of experts came mainly from the colonial powers which feared that it would become yet another forum for attacks on them by anticolonial states.

This shortcoming was corrected in 1974 when the United Nations established a working group on slavery which meets three days a year in Geneva to study reports of slavery and to make recommendations. Reflecting the changing face of slavery, most of its deliberations are given over to reviewing institutions and practices similar to slavery. Like its League of Nations predecessor, it possesses no money or authority. It depends for its information on nongovernmental organizations, particularly the Anti-Slavery Society. Its deliberations have done much to focus public attention on the issue of slavery. Its expert services were made available in investigating the question of slavery and the slave trade in Mauritania at the invitation of the government.[37]

The United Nations has given yeoman service to the struggle against slavery, slavelike practices, and the traffic in slaves. It has done this by the moral authority it commands on an issue on which it represents the collective conscience of all humanity. The Supplementary Convention followed in the tradition of the Berlin and Brussel Acts and the 1926 Slavery Convention of the League of Nations. The United Nations information-gathering activities also have done much to report on the existence of slavery in parts of the Middle East, Africa, and Asia and, in doing so, to shed much valuable light on a problem which for many people had ceased to exist. Countries that allowed slavery to exist gradually recognized the incompatibility between this practice and membership in the world organization. Those countries which did practice slavery could be more readily called to account to world public opinion in the United Nations forums. With the abolition of slavery in the Arab world, the slave trade has been reduced to a police problem. If slaves are shipped across the Red Sea, more efforts are required by the police of the concerned nations to bring a halt to what is now a criminal act. The abolition of the vestiges of slavery, particularly in the desperately impoverished nations of Africa and Asia, can only be brought about through economic development programs which would raise living standards and thereby eliminate the basic cause for involuntary servitude. It is in this domain that the United Nations can ultimately prove most effective in extinguishing the last dying embers of chattel slavery.

# Notes

## Chapter 1

[1] Esmond B. Martin and T. C. I. Ryan, "A Quantitative Assessment of the Arab Slave Trade of East Africa, 1770–1896," *Kenya Historical Review*, vol. 5, No. 1 (1977), p. 86.

[2] Mbaye Gueye, "The slave trade within the African continent," *The African slave trade from the Fifteenth to the Nineteenth Century*, UNESCO (Paris, 1979), p. 150.

[3] Joseph Ki-Zerbo, *Histoire de l'Afrique Noire, D'Hier à Demain*, (Paris: Hatier, 1978), pp. 208–10.

[4] Edrisi, *Description de l'Afrique et de l'Espagne*, trans. by Dozy and Golje (Leyden, 1866), p. 90.

[5] Walter Rodney, "African slavery and other forms of social oppression on the Upper Guinea Coast in the context of the Atlantic slave trade," *Journal of African History*, vol. 7, no. 3 (1966), pp. 431–33; Paul E. Lovejoy, *Transformations in Slavery: A History of Slavery in Africa* (Cambridge: Cambridge University Press, 1983).

[6] Joseph E. Harris, "A commentary on the slave trade", *The African Slave Trade from the Fifteenth to the Nineteenth Century*, UNESCO, pp. 289–95.

[7] Hubert Gubeau, "The slave trade in the Indian Ocean: Problems

*239*

facing the historian and research to the undertaken", *The African Slave Trade from the Fifteenth to the Nineteenth Century,* UNESCO, p. 185.

[8] Reginald Coupland, *East Africa and Its Invaders. From the Earliest Times to the Death of Seyid Said in 1856* (Oxford: Clarendon Press, 1938); *The Exploitation of East Africa, 1856–1890: The Slave Trade and the Scramble,* (London: Faber and Faber, 1939).

[9] Raymond Mauny, *Les Siècles Obscurs de l'Afrique Noire* (Paris: Fayard, 1970).

[10] G. S. P. Freeman-Grenville, *"The Coast, 1498–1840," History of East Africa,* ed. R. Oliver and Gervase Mathew, vol. I (Oxford: Clarendon Press, 1963), p. 162.

[11] Edward A. Alpers, *The East African Slave Trade,* Historical Association of Tanzania, paper no. 3 (Nairobi: East African Publishing House, 1967), p. 4.

[12] Joseph E. Harris, *The African Presence in Asia: Consequences of the East African Slave Trade* (Evanston, Ill.: Northwestern University Press, 1971), chap. 9.

[13] Quoted in R. W. Beachey, *A Collection of Documents on the Slave Trade of Eastern Africa* (London: Rex Collings, 1976), p. 77.

## Chapter 2

[1] J. H. Breasted, *Ancient Records of Egypt* (New York, 1906), vol. 2, p. 204.

[2] C. W. W. Greenidge, *Slavery* (London: George Allen and Unwin Ltd., 1958), p. 60.

[3] *Ibid.,* p. 59.

[4] Terence Brady and Evan Jones, *The Fight Against Slavery* (New York: W. W. Norton & Company, Inc., 1975), p. 37.

[5] M. I. Finley, "Slavery," *International Encyclopaedia of Social Sciences,* David L. Sills (ed.), The Macmillan Company and the Free Press, 1968), vol. 14, p. 309.

[6] Edward Gibbon, *The Decline and Fall of the Roman Empire,* (Abridged with an introduction by Frank C. Bourne) (New York: Dell Publishing Co., Inc., 1963), p. 52.

[7] Majid Khadduri, "Harb," *The Encyclopaedia of Islam,* (2nd edition) London: Luzac and Co., 1971), vol. 3 p. 180.

[8] Allan G. B. Fisher and Humphrey J. Fisher, *Slavery and Muslim Society in Africa* (London: C. Hurst & Co., 1970), pp. 18–19.

[9] Majid Khadduri, *War and Peace in the Law of Islam* (Baltimore: The Johns Hopkins Press, 1955), p. 132.

[10] C. E. Bosworth in *The Legacy of Islam,* edited by Joseph Schacht with C. E. Bosworth, (Oxford: Oxford University Press, 1979, 2nd edition), pp. 119–20.

[11] Fisher and Fisher, *op. cit,* pp. 17–18.

[12] N. R. Bennet, "Christian and negro slavery in eighteenth century North Africa," *Journal of African Studies,* 1980, vol. 1, pp. 64–82.

[13] Fisher and Fisher, *op. cit.,* p. 23.

[14] J. C. Froelich, "Essai sur les causes et méthodes de l'Islamisation de l'Afrique de l'Ouest du XIe siècle au XXe siècle," in I. M. Lewis (ed.) *Islam in Tropical Africa* (London, 1966), pp. 168–69.

[15] J. Rouch, "Contribution à l'histoire des Songhay", *Mémoirs de l'Institut français de l'Afrique noire,* 1953, no. 29, p. 193.

[16] Benjamin L. Kedar, *Crusade and Mission: European Approaches Toward Muslims* (New Jersey: Princeton University Press), p. 48.

[17] H. Barth, *Travels and Discoveries in North and Central Africa* (London, 1957–58), vol. 2, p. 189n.

[18] H. A. R. Gibb and Harold Bowen, *Islamic Society and the West. A Study of the Impact of Western Civilization on Moslem Culture in the Near East* (London: Oxford University Press, 1957), vol. I, part ii, p. 114.

[19] Fisher and Fisher, *op. cit.,* p. 24.

[20] D. Denham and H. Clapperton, *Narrative of travels and discoveries in northern and central Africa in the years, 1822, 1823, and 1824,* (A. Major Denham's narrative, B. Captain Clapperton's narrative) (London, 1826), A. p. 149.

[21] Khadduri, *War and Peace in the Law of Islam op. cit.,* p. 131. 'Umar, who was inspired by the spirit of Arabism, and considered the Arabs to be, in his own words, "the essence of Islam", laid down the rule that they could not be made into slaves even if taken as a prisoner of war or purchased for money.

[22] I. B. Kaka, "The Slave Trade and the Population Drain from Black Africa to North Africa and the Middle East," *The African Slave Trade from the Fifteenth to the Nineteenth century, UNESCO op. cit.,* pp. 164–65.

[23] Quoted in Fisher and Fisher, *op. cit.,* p. 30.

[24] *Ibid*

[25] Bernard Lewis, *Race and Color in Islam* (New York and London: Harper Torchbooks, 1971), pp. 67–68.

[26] I. Mendelsohn, *Slavery in the Ancient Near East* (New York, 1949), pp. 57–58.

[27] H. R. P. Dickson, *The Arab of the Desert. A Glimpse into Badawin Life in Kuwait and Saudi Arabia* (London: George Allen & Unwin Ltd., 1959), p. 498.

[28] Joseph Schacht, *The Origins of the Muhammadan Jurisprudence* (Oxford: Clarendon University Press, 1979, paperback), p. 281.

[29] Quoted in Greenidge, *op. cit.*, p. 60.

[30] Mendelsohn, *op. cit* p. 54.

[31] Khadduri, *War and Peace in the Law of Islam, op. cit.*, p. 130.

[32] Edward William Lane, *An Account of the Manners and Customs of the Modern Egyptians* (London: Ward, Sock & Co., 1890, reprinted from the third edition, 1842), p. 89.

[33] Schacht, *op. cit.*, pp. 279–80.

[34] J. Spencer Trimingham, *Islam in West Africa* (Oxford: Clarendon Press, 1978), p. 133.

[35] William G. Palgrave, *A Narrative of a Year's Journey Through Central and Eastern Arabia (1862–1863)* (London: Macmillan, 1865), vol. 2, p. 272.

[36] Schacht, *op. cit.*, pp. 264–65.

[37] Robert Capot Rey, *Géographie de L'Union Française, Le Sahara Français* (Paris: Presse Universitaire De France, 1953), p. 216.

[38] H.A.R. Gibb, *Mohammedanism: A Historical Survey,* London, Oxford University Press, 1949, p. 182.

[39] Ahmed Shefiq, *L'esclavage au point de vue musulman,* Cairo, 1891.

[40] Norman Anderson, *Law Reform in the Muslim World,* London, The Athlone Press, 1976, p. 186.

# Chapter 3

[1] Andrew M. Watson, *Agricultural Innovation in the Early Islamic World: The Diffusion of Crops and Farming Techniques* (Cambridge: Cambridge University Press, 1983), p. 166.

[2] A. B. Wylde, *'87 in the Soudan*, vol. 2 (London, 1888), cited in R. W. Beachey, *A Collection of Documents on the Slave Trade of Eastern Africa* (London: Rex Collins, 1976), pp. 64–5.

[3] G. E. Von Grunebaum, *Classical Islam: A History 600–1258*, trans. Katherine Watson (London: George Allen and Unwin, Ltd., 1970) p. 105–6.

[4] Ibid.; A. Papovic, *"Les facteurs economiques et la révolte des Zanj,"* paper presented at Princeton University Conference on Economic and Social History of the Middle East, 1974.

[5] Gabriel Baer, "Slavery in Nineteenth Century Egypt," *Journal of African History*, vol. 8, no. 3 (1967), p. 26.

[6] Ibid.

[7] G. E. Tidbury, "Agriculture in Zanzibar: The Clove Industry", *East African Agriculture*, ed. J. K. Matheson and E. W. Bovill (London: Oxford University Press, 1950), p. 268.

[8] Fred Cooper, *"Plantation Slavery in East Africa in the 19th Century"* (New Haven: Yale University Press, 1977).

[9] Abdulaziz Y. Lodhi, *The Institution of Slavery in Zanzibar and Pemba*, The Scandanavian Institute of African Studies (Uppsala, 1973), p. 6.

[10] Philip D. Curtin, *The Atlantic Slave Trade: A Census*, (Madison, Wis.: University of Wisconsin Press, 1969), p. 266.

[11] Bethwell A. Ogot, "Population movements between East Africa, the Horn of Africa and the neighboring countries", *The African Slave Trade from the Fifteenth to the Nineteenth Century*, UNESCO, (Paris, 1979), p. 179.

[12] Jonathan Derrick, *Africa's Slaves Today* (London: George Allen and Unwin, Ltd., 1975), chap. 1; Bruno Hadji, "J'ai vu les derniers Esclaves," *Africa International*, No. 201, pp 39–41.

[13] Dickson, *op. cit.*, p. 502.

[14] Terence Walz, "Trade Between Egypt and Bilad As-Sudan," *Institut Francais d'Archeology Orientale du Caire* (Cairo, 1978), p. 208.

[15] Baer, "Slavery in Nineteenth Century Egypt," *op. cit.*, p. 423

[16] Bertram Thomas, *The Arabs*, (London: Thornton Butterworth, Ltd., 1937), p. 266.

[17] Maila Minai, *Women in Islam Tradition and Transition in the Middle East* (New York: Seaview Books, 1978), p. 20.

[18] Adam Mez, *The Renaissance of Islam*, first ed., Eng. trans. by

Salahudden Khuda Bukhsh and D. S. Margoliouth (London: Luzac and Co., 1937), p. 156.

[19] Germain Mouette, *Histoire des Conquestes de Mouley Archy, Connu sous le Nom de Roy de Talifet; et de Mouley Ismael ou Sméin son Frère et son Successeur à Présant Régnant, tous Deux Rois de Frez* (Paris: E. Couterot, 1683), p. 407.

[20] L. Valensi, *"Esclaves Chrétiens et Esclaves Noirs à Tunis,"* XVIIIe Siècle Annales-Economies-Sociétés, November–December, 1967, pp. 1273–76.

[21] R. Brunschwig, "Abd," *Encyclopaedia of Islam*, rev. ed. vol. I, p. 33.

[22] H. A. R. Gibb and H. Bowen, *Islamic Society and the West*, vol. I (London: Oxford University Press, 1950), p. 43.

[23] B. G. Musallam, *Sex and Society in Islam* (Cambridge: Cambridge University Press, 1983), p. 107.

[24] Mez, *The Renaissance of Islam*, chap. 11.

[25] Paul E. Lovejoy, *Transformations in Slavery. A History of Slavery in Africa* (Cambridge: Cambridge University Press, 1983), pp. 28–9. Daniel Pipes, *Slave Soldiers and Islam*, The Genesis of a Military System, Ch. 3 (New Haven: Yale University Press).

[26] Gernot Rotter, "Die Stellung Des Negers In Der Islamisch—Arabischen Gesellschaft Bis Zum XVI Jahrhundert" (Ph.D. diss. Bonn, 1967), pp. 64–74.

[27] Yusuf Fqdl Hasan, *The Arabs and the Sudan from the Seventh to the Early Sixteenth Century* (Edinburgh: The University Press, 1967), p. 44.

[28] Quoted in Lewis, *Race and Color in Islam*, pp. 78–9.

[29] Michael Brett, "Ifriqiya as a Market for Saharan Trade from the Tenth to the Twelfth Century A.D.," *Journal of African History*. vol. 10 (1969), p 354.

[30] M. Canard, "Fatimids," *Encyclopaedia of Islam*, rev. edition vol. 2, p. 858.

[31] Magali Morsy, "Moulay Ismail et l'Armée de Métier", *Revue d'Histoire Contemporaine*, April–June, 1967.

[32] Ibid., p. 117.

[33] Louis Frank, *Mémoire sur le Commerce des Négres au Kaire* (Strasbourg: A. Koenig, 1802), pp. 37–8.

[34] Alan Moorehead, *The Blue Nile* (London: Hamish Hamilton, Ltd., 1962), chap. 12.

[35] Gabriel Abir, "Slavery in Nineteenth Century Egypt," *Journal of African History,* vol. 8, no. 3 (1967), p. 420.

## Chapter 4

[1] Fisher and Fisher, *op. cit.,* p. 101.

[2] E. W. Bovill, *The Golden Trade of the Moors,* 2nd ed. (London: Oxford University Press, 1968), p. 96.

[3] Dr. Georg Schweinfurth, *The Heart of Africa. Three Years of Travels and Adventures in the Unexplored Regions of Central Africa,* trans. from German by Ellen E. Frewer (New York: Harper and Brothers, 1874), vol. 1, pp. 346–47.

[4] Lane, *op. cit.,* p. 168.

[5] Adam Mez, *The Renaissance of Islam,* first ed., Eng. trans. by Salahudden Khuda Bukhsh and D. S. Margoliouth (London: Luzac and Co., 1937), p. 156.

[6] Ibid.

[7] Gerald J. Bender, *Angola under the Portuguese* (London: Heinemann, 1978), p. 202.

[8] Fisher and Fisher, *op. cit.,* p. 99.

[9] William H. McNeill and Marilyn Robinson Waldman, *The Islamic World* (New York: Oxford University Press, 1973).

[10] Quoted in Bovill, *The Golden Trade of the Moors,* p. 96.

[11] N. M. Penzer, *The Harem* (London: Spring Books, 1936), pp. 139–40.

[12] E. W. Bovill, *Caravans of the Old Sahara* (London: Oxford University Press, 1933).

[13] Frank, *op. cit.,* p. 14.

[14] J. L. Burckhardt, *Travels in Nubia,* 2nd ed. (London, 1822), p. 295.

[15] Bovill, *Caravans of the Old Sahara,* p. 257.

[16] L. Marc, *Le Pays Mossi* (Paris, 1909), p. 171.

[17] Henry Barth, *Travels in North and Central Africa,* vol. 2 (London, 1857–58), p. 290.

[18] Penzer, *op. cit.*, p. 141; Brunschvig, *op. cit.*, p. 33.

[19] Frank, *op. cit.*, p. 16.

[20] Lewis, *op. cit.*, p. 64.

[21] Gernot Rotter, "Die Stellung Des Negers," (Ph.D. diss., Bonn, 1967), pp. 94–131.

[22] Lewis, *op. cit.*, pp. 33–4

[23] Ibid, p. 36.

[24] Ibid. p. 38.

[25] Eric Williams, *Capitalism and Slavery* (New York: Russell and Russell, 1961), p. 7.

[26] Lewis, *op. cit.*, p. 97.

[27] Ibid., pp. 96–7.

[28] Rotter, "Die Stellung Des Negers," pp. 173–4.

[29] Lewis, *op. cit.*, pp. 99–100.

[30] Pruen S. Tristram, *The Arab and the African* (London: Seeley and Co., Ltd., 1891), 251.

## Chapter 5

[1] R. Brunschvig, *Encyclopaedia of Islam*, rev. ed, p. 31.

[2] Tamara Talbot Rice, *The Seljuks in Asia Minor* (London: Thames and Hudson, 1961), p. 100.

[3] L. Kropàcek, "Nubia from the late 12th century to the Funj conquest in the early 15th century," *Africa from the Twelfth to the Sixteenth Century*, ed. D. T. Niane UNESCO General History of Africa, vol. 4 (California: Heninemann, 1984), chap. 16.

[4] R. Mauny, "Notes on the Protohistoric Period in West Africa", *Journal of the West African Science Association*, vol. 11, no. 2 (August 1952). "Une route préhistoriqué à travers le Sahara occidental," *Bulletin de l'Islam* (1950), pp. 341–60.

[5] D. Lange, "The kingdoms and the people of Chad," UNESCO General History of Africa, p. 250.

[6] Ki-Zerbo, *op. cit.*, p. 104.

[7] E. W. Bovill, *Caravans of the Old Sahara.* p. 119.

[8] Michael Brett, "Ifriqiya as a Market for Saharan Trade from the Tenth to the Twelfth Century," *Journal of African History.*

[9] Leo Africanus, *The History and Description of Africa*, trans. En-

glish by John Pory, ed. Robert Brown, 3 vols, The Hakluyt Society (London, 1896).

[10] Ibid., pp. ii, 309.

[11] A. Adu Boahen, "The Caravan Trade in the Nineteenth Century," *Journal of African History*, vol. 3, no. 2 (1962), p. 351.

[12] J. L. Miege, "La Libye et le Commerce Transsaharien," *Revue de l'Occident Musulman et de la Mediterranée*, no. 19, 1975, pp. 50–63, 136–37; 144–45.

[13] Boahen, "The Caravan Trade," p. 358.

[14] Gervase Mathew, "The East African Coast Until the Coming of the Portugese," *History of East Africa*, ed. Roland Oliver and Gervase Mathew (London: Oxford University Press, 1976), vol. 1, p. 107.

[15] Maçoudi, *Le Livre de l'avertissement et de la révision*, trans. B. C. de Vaux (Paris, 1897), pp. 471–72.

[16] T. Lewicki, "External Arabic Sources for the History of Africa to the South of the Sahara," in T. O. Ranger, *Emerging Themes of African History: Proceedings of the International Congress of African Historians* (Nairobi, 1968) pp. 14–21.

[17] Cited in Bovill, *Caravans of the Old Sahara, op. cit.*, p. 34.

[18] This is a late nineteenth century edition of an earlier compendium which was probably put together in the Shungwaya area in Somalia.

[19] Basil Davidson, *The African Slave Trade*, rev. ed. (Boston: Little Brown and Company, 1980), pp. 178–88.

[20] M. Guillain, *Documents sur l'histoire, la géographie et le commerce de l'Afrique orientale*, vol. 1 (Paris, 1856), p. 189.

[21] "Ya'qubi, Kitab al-Buldan," *Bibliotheca geographorum arabicarum*, 2nd ed., ed. M. J. de Golje, vol. 7 (Leiden, 1892), p. 345. French translation by G. Wiet, *Les pays* (Cairo, 1937), p. 205.

[22] R. Coupland, *East Africa and Its Invaders*. p. 32.

[23] Michel Mollat "Les Relations de l'Afrique de l'Est avec l'Asie: Essai de Position de Quelques Problèmes Historiques," *Cahiers d'Histoire Mondiale*, vol. 13, no., 2 (1971), pp. 294–5.

[24] Joseph E. Harris, *The African Presence in Asia: Consequences of the East African Slave Trade*, (Evanston, Ill.: Northwestern University Press, 1971), p. 5.

[25] P.A. van der Lith, *Kitab al-Ajaib al-Hind* (Leiden, 1883–96), p. 22.

26 V. Faurec, *L'Archipel aux Sultans batailleurs*, 2nd ed. (Morononi, *Promo Al Camar*, n.d.; first ed., 1941); quoted in Gubeau, "The Slave trade in the Indian Ocean."

27 Gervase Mathew, "The Land of Zanj," *The Dawn of African History*, ed. Roland Oliver (London: Oxford University Press, 1961).

28 Bethwell A. Ogot, "Population movements between East Africa, the Horn of Africa and the neighboring countries", *The African Slave Trade from the Fifteenth to the Nineteenth Century*, UNESCO, p. 176.

29 D. G. Keswani, *Indian Cultural and Commercial Influences in the Indian Ocean, from Africa and Madagascar to South-East Asia* (Port Louis, 1974).

30 Gervase Mathew, "The Land of Zanj," pp. 107–8.

31 J. L. L. Duvenydak, *China's Discovery of Africa* (London, 1949), pp. 13–4, 22.

## Chapter 6

1 Paul E. Lovejoy, *Transformations in Slavery: A History of Slavery in Africa* (Cambridge: Cambridge University Press, 1983), p. 23.

2 Mbaye Gueye, "The slave trade within the African continent", *The African Slave Trade from the Fifteenth to the Nineteenth Century*, UNESCO, p. 150.

3 J. Spencer Trimingham, *The Influence of Islam upon Africa*, 2nd ed. (London: Longman, 1980), pp. 10–1.

4 Mbaye Gueye, "The Slave trade within the African continent," p. 158; E. W. Bovill, *Caravans of the Old Sahara*, p. 258.

5 George A. Lipsky, *Ethiopia: Its People, Its society, Its culture* (New Haven: Hraf Press, 1962), p. 12.

6 Fisher and Fisher, *op. cit.*, chap. 1.

7 A. McPhee, *The Economic Revolution in British West Africa* (London, 1926), pp. 126–7, 249–50.

8 Bovill, *Caravans of the Old Sahara*, p. 71.

9 John A. Works, Jr., *Pilgrims in a Strange Land* (New York: Columbia University Press, 1976), p. 23.

10 Fisher and Fisher, *op. cit.*, p. 123.

[11] Walter Rodney, "African Slavery and Other Forms of Social Oppression on the Upper Guinea Coast in the Context of the Atlantic Slave-Trade," *Journal of African History,* vol. 7, no. 3 (1966), pp. 431–43.

[12] J. D. Fage, "Slavery and the Slave Trade in the Context of West African History," *Journal of African History,* vol. 10, no. 3 (1969), p. 400.

[13] Reginald Coupland, *East Africa and Its Invaders,* p. 35.

[14] G. S. P. Freeman-Glenville, "The Coast, 1498–1840," *History of East Africa,* ed. Roland Oliver and Gervase Mathew (Oxford: Clarendon Press, 1963), p. 152.

[15] Ibid. p. 152

[16] Gervase Mathew, "The East African Coast Until the Coming of the Portuguese," p. 106.

[17] R. B. Serjeant, *The Portuguese off the South Arabian Coast, Hadrami Chronicles* (London, 1963), pp. 10, 34.

[18] Coupland, *East Africa and Its Invaders, Chap. 3.*

[19] Malyn Newitt, "The Comoro Islands in Indian Ocean Trade before the 19th century," *Cahiers D'Etudes Africaines,* vol. 23 (1–2) (1983), p. 150.

[20] G. S. P. Freeman-Grenville, *The East African Coast. Select Documents from the First to the Nineteenth Century* (London: Oxford University Press, 1966), p. 162

[21] Cited in Newitt, "The Comoro Islands," p. 150.

[22] Ralph A. Austen, "The Trans-Saharan Slave Trade: A Tentative Census," *The Uncommon Market: Essays in the Economic History of the Atlantic Slave Trade,* ed. H. A. Gemery and J. S. Hogendorn (New York, 1979), pp. 23–76.

[23] Edward A. Alpers, *Ivory and Slaves in East Central Africa* (London: Heinemann, 1975), pp. 70–6.

[24] G. S. P. Freeman-Grenville, *The French at Kilwa Island—An Episode in Eighteenth-Century East African History* (London: Oxford University Press: 1965), p. 82.

[25] Edward A. Alpers, *The East African Slave Trade* (Nairobi: East African Publishing House, 1967), p. 6.

[26] Philip D. Curtin, *op. cit.*

[27] Lovejoy, *Transformations in Slavery,* pp. 24–25, 45–46.

[28] Joseph C. Miller, "Mortality in the Atlantic Slave Trade: Statis-

tical Evidence on Causality," *Journal of Interdisciplinary History*, vol. 11, pp. 385–423.

## Chapter 7

[1] A. Adu Boahen, "The Caravan Trade in the Nineteenth Century," *Journal of African History*, vol. 3, no. 2, (1962), p. 350.

[2] E. W. Bovill, *The Golden Trade of the Moors*, 2nd ed. p. 238.

[3] C. W. Newbury, "North African and West Sudan Trade in the Nineteenth Century: A Re-Evaluation," *Journal of African History*, vol. 7, no. 2 (1966), p. 244.

[4]. Bovill, *The Golden Trade of the Moors*, p. 245.

[5] Lucette Valensi, "Escalves chretiens et esclaves noirs a Tunis au XVIIIe siecle," *Annales, Economies Societes Civilisations*, no. 6 (Novembre-Decembre, 1967), pp. 1273–6.

[6] Dennis D. Cordell, "Eastern Libya, Wadai and the Sanusiya: A Tariqa and a Trade Route," *Journal of African History*, vol. 18, no. 1 (1977), pp. 21–36.

[7] Cited in Lisa Anderson, "Nineteenth Century Reform in Ottoman Libay," *International Journal of Middle East Studies*, no. 16 (1984), p. 334.

[8] E. F Gautier and R. Chudeau, *Missions au Sahara*, vol. 2 (Paris, 1908–9), pp. 294–95.

[9] Cordell, *op. cit.*, p. 34.

[10] Henry Barth, *Travels and Discoveries in North and Central Africa*, vol. 2 (London, 1857–8), p. 339.

[11] Boahen, "The Caravan Trade in the Nineteenth Century," p. 358.

[12] Thomas Fowell Buxton, *The African Slave Trade and Its Remedy*, (London: Frank Cass, Ltd., 1967), p. 69. This is a reissue of the 2nd edition, first published in 1840.

[13] R. Mauny, *Tableau geographique de l'ouest africain au moyen age* (Dakar, 1961), p. 379.

[14] A. Adu Boahen, "Britain, the Sahara and the Western Sudan, 1788–1861," *Journal of African History* (Oxford: Clarendon Press), 1964, p. 128.

[15] Austen, *op. cit.*, "The Trans-Saharan Slave Trade: A Tentative Census," p. 66.

[16] Bovill, *The Golden Trade of the Moors,* p. 239.

[17] Fisher and Fisher, *op. cit.,* p. 79.

[18] Boahen, "Britain, the Sahara and the Western Sudan," *op. cit.,* p. 134.

[19] Francis Renault, *Lavigerie, l'Esclavage Africain et l'Europe,* vol. 2 *1868–1892* (Paris: E. De Boccard), p. 13.

[20] Dwight L. Ling, *Tunisia, From Protectorate to Republic,* (Bloomington, Ind.: Bloomington University Press, 1967), p. 61.

[21] Boahen, "Britain, the Sudan and the Western Sahara," *op. cit.,* p. 142.

[22] Quoted in Suzanne Miers, *Britain and the Ending of the Slave Trade* (London: Longman), 1975, p. 64.

[23] Ibid., p. 65

[24] Boahen "Britain, the Sahara and the Western Sudan," *op. cit.,* p. 144.

[25] Miers, *op. cit.,* p. 70.

[26] Cited in Boahen, "Britain, the Sahara and the Western Sudan," *op. cit.,* p. 149.

[27] John Wright, *Libya* (New York: Frederick A. Praeger), pp. 113–4.

[28] Lovejoy, *op. cit.,* pp. 147–9.

[29] Terence Walz, "Trading into the Sudan in the Sixteenth Century," *Extrait des Annales Islamologique,* t. XV, 1979, p. 213.

[30] R. S. O'Fahey, "Slavery and the Slave Trade in Dar Fur," *Journal of African History,* vol. 14 (1973), p. 31.

[31] Katharine Sim, *Jean Louis Burckhardt. A Biography* (London: Quartet Books, 1981), p. 254.

[32] Terence Walz, "The Trade Between Egypt and the Bilad As-Sudan, 1700–1820" (Ph.D diss., Boston University, 1975), pp. 177–78.

[33] Gabriel Baer, "Slavery in Nineteenth Century Egypt," *Journal of African History,* vol. 8, no. 3 (1967), p. 422.

[34] Richard Hill, *Egypt in the Sudan, 1820–1881* (London: Oxford University Press, 1959), p. 13.

[35] P. M. Holt, *A Modern History of the Sudan* (London: Weidenfeld and Nicholson, 1961), p. 65.

[36] Hill, *op. cit.,* Chap. 11.

[37] Pierre Crabitès, *Gordon, the Sudan and Slavery* (London: George Routledges and Sons, Ltd., 1933), p. 30.

[38] Baer, *op. cit.*, pp. 433–4.

[39] R. W. Beachey *The Slave Trade of Eastern Africa* (London: Rex Collins, 1976), p. 140.

[40] Ibid., p. 144.

[41] G. S. P. Freeman-Grenville, "The Coast, 1498–1840," *History of East Africa* (Oxford: Clarendon Press, 1938), p. 161.

[42] C. S. Nicholls, *The Swahili Coast: Politics, Diplomacy and Trade on the East African Littoral, 1798–1856* (New York: Africana Publishing Corporation, 1971), chap. 8.

[43] Ibid., p. 199; Robert Louis Stein, *The French Slave Trade in the Eighteenth Century, An Old Regime Business,* (Madison, Wisc.: University of Wisconsin Press, 1979), p. 123.

[44] Nicholls, *op. cit.*, p. 202

[45] Freeman-Grenville, "The Coast, 1498–1840," pp. 157–8.

[46] Coupland, *East Africa and Its Invaders.*

[47] Michael F. Lofchie, *Zanzibar: Background to Revolution* (Princeton: Princeton University Press, 1965), pp. 32–3.

[48] Martin and Ryan, *op. cit.*, p. 76.

[49] Nicholls, *op. cit.*, p. 204.

[50] Ibid., p. 205.

[51] Cooper, *op. cit.*, p. 51.

[52] E. A. Alpers, *The East African Slave Trade.* p. 18.

[53] Margery Perham, *Lugard: The Years of Adventure, 1858–1898* (London: Collins St. James Place, 1960), p. 79.

[54] Norman R. Bennett, "The East African Slave Trade," *Emerging Themes of African History,* p. 145.

[55] Alison Smith, "The Southern Section of the Interior," *History of East Africa* (Oxford: Clarendon Press, 1938), pp. 288–98.

[56] Zoë Marsh and G. W. Kingsworth, *An Introduction to the History of East Africa* (Cambridge: Cambridge University Press, 1957), pp. 47–8.

[57] J. B. Kelly, *Britain and the Persian Gulf, 1795–1880* (Oxford: Clarendon Press, 1968), p. 424.

[58] Marsh and Kingsworth, *op. cit.*, p. 49.

[59] Nicholls, *op. cit.*, p. 224.

[60] Ibid., p. 225.

[61] Ibid., p. 231.

[62] Coupland, *East Africa and Its Invaders,* pp. 515–6.

[63] Gill Shepherd, "The Comorians and the East African Slave Trade, *Asian and African Systems of Slavery,* ed. James L. Watson (Berkeley: University of California Press, 1980), p. 78.

[64] Kelly, *Britain and the Persian Gulf,* p. 602.

[65] Hubert Gubeau, "The slave trade in the Indian Ocean," *The African Slave Trade from the Fifteenth to the Nineteenth Century,* UNESCO, p. 196.

[66] Kelly, *op. cit.,* p. 622.

[67] J. M. Gray, "Zanzibar and the Coastal Belt, 1840–1884," *History of East Africa,* ed. Oliver and Mathew (London: Oxford University Press, 1976), pp. 230–3.

[68] R. Coupland, *The British Anti-Slavery Movement* (London: Thornton Butterworth, Ltd., 1933), pp. 206–13.

[69] Quoted in Kelly, *Britain and the Persian Gulf,* p. 630.

[70] Ibid., p. 633.

## Chapter 8

[1] V. L. Cameron, "Slavery in Africa: The Disease and the Remedy," *National Review,* 10 (1888), p. 265.

[2] Miers, *Britain and the Ending of the Slave Trade,* pp. 170–73.

[3] C. W. W. Greenidge, *Slavery* (London: George Allen and Unwin, Ltd., 1958), pp. 174–6.

[4] Ibid., p. 178.

[5] R. W. Beachey, *A Collection of Documents on the Slave Trade of East Africa* (London: Ref Collins, 1976), p. 120.

[6] Miers, *Britain and the Ending of the Slave Trade,* p. 249.

[7] Frederick D. Lugard, *The Rise of Our East African Empire* (London: Frank Cass and Co., Ltd., 1968; first ed., 1893), pp. 186–7.

[8] L. W. Hollingsworth, *Zanzibar Under the Foreign Office, 1890–1913* (London, Macmillan and Co., Ltd.), chap. 9.

[9] Michael F. Lofchie, *Zanzibar: Background to Revolution* (Princeton: Princeton University Press, 1965), p. 61.

[10] Frederick D. Lugard, "Slavery in All Its Forms," *Africa,* vol. 6, no. 1, pp. 2–3.

[11] United Nations Economic and Social Council, Ad Hoc Commit-

tee on Slavery, Memorandum by the Secretary-General, "The Work of the League of Nations for the Suppression of Slavery," E/AC.33/2. January 23, 1950, p. 4.

[12] John Harris, *A Century of Emancipation* (London: J. M. Dent and Sons, Ltd., 1933), p. 226.

[13] Ibid.

[14] Greenidge, *Slavery*, p. 46.

[15] Richard Greenfield, *Ethiopia, A New Political History* (London: Pall Mall Press, 1965), p. 172.

[16] K. D. D. Henderson, *Sudan Republic* (London: Ernest Benn, Ltd., 1965), p. 172.

[17] League of Nations, *Official Journal,* January–June, 1937, p. 410.

[18] League of Nations Document A. 19. 1925, VI. p. 6.

[19] Simon, *Slavery*, p. 51.

[20] C. W. W. Greenidge, *Memorandum on Slavery* (London: The Anti-Slavery Society), p. 7.

[21] Paul W. Harrison, *The Arab at Home,* pp. 257–258.

[22] H. St. John Philby, *Sa'udi Arabia* (London: Ernest Benn, Ltd., 1955), p. 337.

[23] Derrick, *Africa's Slaves Today* (London: George Allen and Unwin, Ltd., 1975), p. 136.

[24] Simon, *Slavery*, p. 50.

[25] C. W. W. Greenidge, *Memorandum on Slavery*

[26] Gerald de Gaury, *An Arabian Journey and Other Desert Travels* (London: George G. Harrap and Co., Ltd.), 1950, p. 89; André Falk, *Visa pour l'Arabie* (Paris: Gallimard), chap. 11.

[27] Sir Arnold Wilson, *The Persian Gulf,* p. 230.

[28] Phillips, *Unknown Oman,* pp. 87–8.

[29] Cited in Assemblée de l'Union Franccaise, session de 1955–1956, no. 75, Annexe au procés-verbal de la séance du 17 novembre 1955, pp. 23–4.

[30] Quoted in *Anti-Slavery Reporter,* January, 1966, pp. 29–30.

[31] Mohamed Awad, *1966 Report on Slavery,* United Nations publications, Sales No. 67, XIV, 2.

[32] John Osman, "Slavery Lives on," *Sunday Telegraph,* March 17 and 24, 1963.

[33] *Le Monde,* June 24, 1966.

[34] Awad, *1966 Report on Slavery,* p. 175.

[35] Kurt Glaser and Stefan T. Possony, *Victims of Politics: The State of Human Rights* (New York: Columbia University Press, 1979), p. 457.

[36] Greenidge, *Slavery,* p. 194.

[37] United Nations Document E/CN.4/Sub. 2/1983/23; and resolution 1985/11 entitled Slavery and Slavery-like practices: Mission to Mauritania, adopted by the Sub-Commission on Prevention of Discrimination and Protection of Minorities on 29 August 1985.

# Index